YOUR LOVE IS ALL I NEED

CJ ANDREWS

ISBN: 978-0-9979087-2-5 (eBook)

ISBN: 978-0-9979087-3-2 (Paperback)

Library of Congress Control Number: 2016956444

Edited by Joy Editing

Published by Daydreamer Press, PO Box 291, Temple, PA 19560 USA

CONTENTS

CHAPTER 1

COUNTDOWN

I pushed away from the marble pillar I'd been clinging to for the past fifteen minutes and paced by the lobby doors, searching for Will between glances at the text message I didn't want to answer.

Kendra: *So, how's the party?*

The question looked innocent enough to someone who couldn't read between her lines. But I could, and ignoring my best friend wouldn't be an option.

Me: *Kinda fun, I guess. Better than I expected.*

My phone buzzed within seconds of sending my reply, and Kendra's face lit up the screen.

I turned my back to the band and pressed the phone tight to my ear. "Happy new—"

"You guess?" Her voice boomed through the line. "I sure as hell hope that doesn't mean you're standing around, looking pathetic, while your husband's off . . . doing whatever he does."

I could always count on Kendra to tell me exactly what she thought, especially when it came to Will.

"He's socializing. And I don't mind." Not a total lie since

standing around, away from the other guests, spared me the embarrassment of trying to make small talk and pretending to fit in.

The truth was I hated to be alone, which Will knew, but he continued to wander off anyway. I stretched on my toes, craning my neck to see over the crowd gathering in Elevations' grand ballroom. "It's just—I don't know where he is." And if he didn't come back soon, I'd be welcoming the new year alone.

"Look, Danni, if you're serious about fixing things with Will, you need to hunt his ass down and have your way with him. Now."

"Okay. Fine. You're right." I let out a frustrated groan. "And I *am* serious."

The large double doors behind me flew open. An enraged woman in a green dress stormed through, mumbling under her breath. She barreled straight into me, and her drink sloshed over the top of the glass.

"What the—" I checked the front of my expensive new dress, amazed that nothing had spilled on it. "Kendra, I gotta go." I powered off my phone and waited for an apology.

The woman stopped. She pivoted toward me on spiky heels. Her eyes raked over me, a look of disgust on her face. "Why are you even here?" She waited as though expecting me to answer. Or vanish. When neither happened, she swiped a loose tendril of hair from her face, turned with a huff, and continued on her way.

She was right though. I didn't belong here.

I sagged against the cool marble pillar. *Shake it off, Danni.* My head fell back. I gazed at the vaulted glass ceiling where hundreds of delicate lights were suspended, twinkling like distant stars. The tension in my shoulders gradually slid away as I got lost in the soothing beauty.

"Hey, babe. Miss me?" Will's smooth voice floated by my ear.

I turned to lean against his solid chest. "More than you could imagine." My confidence returned now that I was back in his arms. Safe. "I was beginning to think you ditched me."

Will gave me one of the champagne flutes he'd brought with him. I sniffed the top of the glass and gave him a puzzled look.

"Prosecco. You can't toast with club soda, Danielle."

I shook my head, biting back a grin. "You know I decided to stay sober tonight."

"And I also know you're overreacting. Come on." He grabbed my hand and led me toward the dance floor where everyone else had gathered.

Wide stone archways lined two sides of the grand ballroom, separating the spacious area from several bars and intimate alcoves. We found a spot along the far side of the room, near the wall of folding glass doors with a breathtaking view of the snow-covered Kuwayoke Mountains. During the warmer seasons, the wall opened onto a massive patio that overlooked the lake.

I caught a glimpse of our reflection in the glass and barely recognized myself. There I stood, wrapped in the arms of my sweet husband, wearing the most gorgeous dress I'd ever owned. Shimmering black fabric hung off my shoulders and clung to my body in all the right places.

I'd starved myself for weeks to fit into it. I'd even bought one of those exercise videos . . . and used it. It was torture, but it sure did pay off.

I smiled, thinking about the sexy black lingerie hiding underneath that dress—a special treat for Will later. But I had to admit I'd been enjoying the way it made me feel all evening, just knowing it was there.

Will rocked our bodies to the rhythm of the music. He swept my hair to one side and skimmed his nose along the length of my neck.

"What are you up to?" I laughed.

"You smell really good tonight." He nibbled a trail from my ear to my shoulder.

A chill ran down my arms. He was a bit drunk, but I loved that he was being playful.

"Just how much have you had to drink tonight?" I teased. Not that it really mattered since he'd arranged for us to spend the night in one of the prestigious resort's luxurious suites.

"Don't know. Don't care either." He rested his chin on my shoulder, still nuzzling my neck. "Pretty much, I guess, but . . . who's counting?" He splayed his hand across my stomach, his thumb grazing my breast. "Now . . . tell me that you're glad we're here, or I may be forced to find more places to nibble." He traced his thumb upward.

I jumped and grabbed his wrist, pulling his hand lower on my stomach. "Will! There are people around us." I glanced to each side, wondering if any of them had noticed, then turned my head to kiss him. "Behave yourself, mister. I'm glad . . ." I paused, taunting him, "to be with you."

Will's chest shook with laughter. "Always so stubborn." He squeezed me tighter.

The music stopped, and a buzz of excitement filled the space. Everyone cheered as Dr. VanBergen crossed the stage and took the microphone from the lead singer. He cleared his throat then began his speech, most of which I tuned out.

My mind wandered as I looked at the faces around me—celebrities, professional athletes, wealthy entrepreneurs. I didn't know any of them, but some were easy to recognize. They were all here to celebrate the start of a new year.

Not me. Despite my resolution and my plans to see it through, tonight I would say good-bye to the life I'd dreamed of and a decade I'd have rather held on to. I shuddered just thinking about it.

Will pulled away to look at me, his brows pressed together. "You okay?"

I nodded and rested my head against his shoulder, enjoying the way he continued to trace circles on my stomach. "Dr. VanBergen's a lot younger than I expected. How do you know him?"

"Hm? Oh, that's VanBergen's son—Logan. Weren't you paying attention?" Will rolled his eyes. "Anyway, I don't know either of them. I met Logan earlier tonight though, and he seems nice. Why?"

I shrugged one shoulder. "I was just looking around and thinking it's a little . . . surreal, I guess. Being here. I still can't figure out how you managed to get us on the guest list."

He kissed my temple. "Don't worry about it. I wanted tonight to be special for you. Turning forty doesn't have to be a bad thing, babe."

Ugh, that "F" word again. From my point of view, there wasn't anything *good* about forty. That made it *bad* by default.

"Thank you." I snuggled tighter against him.

The large screen behind the stage came to life with a view of the massive crowd gathered at New York's Times Square.

VanBergen rambled on. "All right, folks. It's show time, so let me hear you!"

He barely finished his sentence before the whoops and hollers drowned him out. The countdown flashed across the screen as the ball dropped: Ten . . . nine . . . eight . . .

It was coming, and there wasn't a damn thing I could do to stop it.

"No worries, babe. Everything's gonna be just fine."

The countdown continued, three . . . two . . . one.

"Happy new year," everyone shouted in unison.

Cannons fired, and multicolored confetti fell all around us. We raised our glasses then downed their contents in one giant gulp. The band played "Auld Lang Syne," and the drunken partygoers attempted to sing along.

Will turned me to face him. "Happy new year, Danielle." Before I could respond, he pulled me in for a long kiss.

He released me and gave our empty glasses to a waiter passing by. Wearing a mischievous grin, Will made a show of checking the time. His eyes flashed between my face and the face of his watch, waiting as the seconds ticked by.

I bit back a smile and shoved my fists on my hips. "You're enjoying this way too much, you know."

At exactly two minutes past twelve, he turned his full attention to me and cradled my face in his hands. "And happy birthday too," he said in a tender voice and kissed me again.

My head began to spin from the love I felt for this man. I let out a groan of disappointment when his jacket vibrated.

He stepped back to retrieve his cell phone and paused to look at the screen with a confused expression. "I have a feeling this is for you." He passed it to me.

"Sorry, I forgot I turned mine off earlier."

My sister's picture smiled at me. She probably thought I was avoiding her, which I may have been. A little.

Might as well get this over with. I pressed the phone tight against one ear and covered the other with my free hand. "Hey, Jen. Happy new year!"

"Danni!" she shouted in a singsong voice. "Hap-happy birthday, old lady! The big four-oooh. Haha!" It took a while, but she finally managed to get out the words.

"Yeah, thanks for that reminder. Your day will come soon enough, you know." She probably couldn't even hear me with all the noise around her.

"Nah, I've got five more years to be young. You, on the other hand . . ." She paused for another fit of laughter. "Look on the bright side—maybe they'll give you a senior discount on your drinks the rest of the night."

"Thanks—"

"Or maybe you'll get lucky and some young hottie will take your arm to help you cross the ballroom." Again she was laughing excessively, definitely drunk.

I didn't respond. Figured it was best to let her get it out of her system.

She eventually pulled herself together and asked, in what was probably her best attempt at a sober voice, "Seriously though, you doin' okay? I know what this birthday means to you, but it's just a number. You know? Don't stress over it."

Easy for her to say.

I blew out a heavy breath. "How 'bout we don't talk about it right now, okay? I just want to enjoy tonight." Actually, I didn't want to talk about it any other time either, but that was an argument for another day. "Sounds like quite a party going on there, so I'll let you get back to it. See you tomorrow. Love you, Jen."

My head knew she was right, but my heart . . . well, that was a different story.

Will tugged the phone with a dramatic flair and slipped it back into his pocket. He placed a soft kiss on my bare shoulder and took my hand, leading me toward the dance floor. "Well, my dear, you may be getting old"—he winked—"but the night is still young. And I want to dance."

He laughed and dodged the playful swat he'd earned.

Our bodies molded together perfectly from so many years of practice, and we began swaying to the music. I nuzzled his neck and inhaled the familiar woodsy scent of his cologne. With a deep sigh of contentment, I relaxed into his chest, my fingers idly caressing his neck as they slid along the top of his collar.

The song ended, morphing into another slow song, and we continued to dance.

"Listen. They're playing our song." I nudged his shoulder. "The one that was playing when you proposed to me. Remember?"

"Um huh." His head bobbed slightly, but his response was unenthusiastic.

I wasn't sure he was even paying attention to me, and that needed to change.

I trailed kisses up his neck to his jaw then continued to the corner of his mouth while raking my fingers through his hair and grabbing the silky gold strands to pull his face closer. A small sigh slipped out when I skimmed my tongue along his lips, tasting the Prosecco from our midnight toast.

Maybe it was the lingerie or my plans for after we returned to our room, but right now, I didn't care about the hundred or so people around us. It was a new year, and my resolution was to spice things up in the bedroom . . . or whatever room we happened to be in.

Will seemed uncertain at first but soon opened to welcome my kiss, his lips gentle against mine.

I got lost in the moment, and one hand slipped from his hair. It glided down the side of his body.

My breath quivered. I imagined him peeling away my dress and his reaction when he revealed the black lace, aching for him to explore every inch of my body. It fueled a hunger that spread through me, a desperate need to be closer to him. My hips moved of their own volition, pressing into his and grinding against him.

Will's step faltered. His body tensed.

I opened my eyes to look at him. Instead of seeing desire in his ice blue eyes, I was greeted by his startled gaze. "What's wrong?" I said.

"Um, sorry, babe. We just bumped into the couple next to us. That's all." He cupped the nape of my neck and guided my head toward his chest then smoothed his hand down my back. "No worries."

Will's shoulders shifted. He glanced back at the other couple, so I stretched my neck to catch a glimpse of them too.

Unbelievable. The same woman who'd nearly run me down earlier. She gave Will a sly smile before hitting me with an icy glare.

What the hell is her problem?

Will continued dancing as though nothing had happened. Nothing. Our kiss, the interruption . . . none of it.

I sighed, feeling foolish, and settled my head on his shoulder. But my thoughts kept wandering to that other couple, and I couldn't resist the urge to sneak another peek.

The woman was stunning. Her upswept chestnut hair shimmered under the ballroom lights, as did her tiny emerald dress. She looked young—late twenties, I'd guess. And she had an amazing body, which we all could get a glimpse of if she were to move a bit too far in any direction.

Then I saw her partner, and she became a distant memory.

I'd noticed him earlier. Dinner was already being served when he'd arrived, late and alone. He'd crossed the ballroom in long, easy strides, looking confident and sexy in a black tailored tux. All the women had turned to watch him, including me. He'd disappeared into a section of tables, and I hadn't seen him for the rest of the evening . . . until now.

Checking out this guy was wrong, especially while I was in

my husband's arms, but something about him intrigued me. I couldn't resist.

No harm in just looking, right?

He was tall, about six foot three, with jet-black hair that stopped just short of touching his collar. His fitted white shirt tapered to a narrow waist. The sleeves were turned up at the cuffs, revealing just a hint of his toned forearms and an expensive looking black-and-silver watch. My gaze drifted toward his face, pausing to notice that his tie and top button were undone.

My eyes continued their journey to his jaw, admiring the dark stubble that covered his olive skin, then moved on to his warm chocolate eyes that were staring right at mine. I sucked in a sharp breath.

He winked then smiled at me, igniting a fire in my cheeks.

I buried my face in Will's chest, trying to hide and wanting him to keep me safe like he always did. I needed to get out of here, now, and placed a single kiss on Will's neck. "Let's go back to our room and finish what we started."

One hand tightened on my waist while his other tipped my chin toward him. "It's still early, babe. I thought you were having fun."

I shrugged and tried to look away. His dismissal stung, but I didn't want him to see that. "I was, but—"

Will placed a finger over my lips. "How about we relax and have a drink or two. You look so beautiful tonight. I want to show you off a little longer." He caressed the side of my face and gave me a tender kiss. "Then you can have me all to yourself for the rest of the night."

I didn't want to stay, but maybe a drink and a little flirting would restore my mood. "Sure. Whatever." My response sounded as deflated as I felt.

When the song ended, Will led me to a small table in one of

the alcoves. He gave me a peck on the cheek, pulled out a chair, and motioned for me to sit down.

"The usual?" he asked over his shoulder as he walked away.

Sure, why not? I nodded in response.

"I'll be right back." He disappeared into the crowd of people gathered around the bar.

Will returned a few minutes later with our drinks: a whiskey on the rocks for him and an absolutely huge strawberry margarita for me.

"Are you trying to get me drunk?" I teased, attempting to get us back on track. I swirled my straw in my drink and took a tentative sip. It was sweet and refreshing. "Mmmm, this is really good." I took another sip, this one longer.

Will tossed back half of his drink then laughed as he sat down across from me. "Better take it easy, lightweight. You *will* get drunk at that pace." He reached across the table and took my hand. "And then I just might be forced to take advantage of you."

I wiggled my eyebrows and took another long sip of my drink, daring him to bring it on.

Will glanced at his watch then let his eyes wander slowly around the room before settling on me. We sat there silently, enjoying each other's company. He caressed my hand and watched while I sipped away at my drink.

Before I realized it, I'd sucked down the entire thing. My head felt a little woozy, but my mood had definitely improved.

"You really do look very beautiful tonight, Danielle."

It wasn't something I heard often. Will's compliment, a few simple words, was more perfect than any gift he could have given me. Except for one, maybe, but the night wasn't over yet.

"Why thank you, Mr. DeLaney, and you're looking quite handsome yourself." I continued in a less playful voice. "Thanks for bringing me here tonight. I know I gave you a really hard time about going out, but I'm glad we're here . . . and"—I motioned for him to come closer—"if you come upstairs with me, I'll show you just how glad I am."

Will leaned back in his chair. He picked up his glass and swirled its contents then downed the last of his drink. When he returned the glass to the table, he kept his fingers wrapped around it, mindlessly wiping at the condensation.

Clearly, he was stalling.

"I was thinking we could hit the dance floor one more time before we call it a night," he finally said, his eyes fixed on his glass.

Well, that wasn't the response I was looking for. I didn't say anything—I couldn't. My efforts to rekindle our sex life couldn't be so ambiguous as to go unnoticed, which meant he was ignoring my attempts to seduce him. But why? I waited for him to look at me, hoping he was teasing.

Instead he stood and leaned across the table to give me a chaste kiss. "I just need to use the restroom first. Wait here."

That quickly, he was gone, walking across the room toward the lobby.

I had no idea what had just happened. What man wouldn't jump at the opportunity to take his wife to bed?

I needed a distraction, something to keep me entertained until Will returned. I pulled out my phone to check my messages. A long list of birthday wishes and New Year's greetings waited for me when I signed into my social network. I scrolled through, reading and acknowledging each one. When I reached the end of the list, I checked the time—twenty minutes had gone by. Will should have been back by now.

I motioned to a nearby waitress and asked her to bring me another giant margarita—*so much for staying sober tonight*—then went back to surfing the web.

Still no sign of Will. I was beginning to get worried and, I had to admit, a bit annoyed. He'd better have a good reason for leaving me alone for so long.

I called his cell. No answer. I typed a quick text—*Where are you? I'm lonely*—and hit the send button just as my drink arrived . . . in the hands of the hot-as-hell stranger from the dance floor.

CHAPTER 2

PERFECT STRANGER

I closed my eyes, waited a beat, then opened them again . . . *nope, not hallucinating.* The most gorgeous man I had ever seen stood there, waiting for me to acknowledge him. My skin tingled from the magnetic energy flowing from him as he towered over me.

Every inch of him was pure perfection, as though he could have fallen from the pages of *GQ*. His unruly dark hair, a total contrast to his refined style, somehow made him even more attractive. It hinted at a rebellious side.

Earlier I'd thought the view of the mountains was breathtaking, but this view . . . wow, I could look at this one all night long.

Mister Tall-Dark-and-Sexy cleared his throat, pulling me from my reverie. My dreamy gaze settled on his magnificent face.

He was biting his lip, clearly struggling to hold back a smirk.

The blood rushed from my brain to my cheeks. Okay, so I was caught checking him out. Again. In my defense, he was standing right in front of me looking more delicious than the sweet drink in his hands—it had to be done.

"Hi." My voice squeaked, shooting up a full octave. I lifted one shoulder and grinned. No point trying to deny it. I was guilty, and we both knew it.

"I believe you ordered the obscenely large pink margarita." He managed to keep his expression serious, but the sparkle in his eyes suggested he was here to play.

"Are you—you don't—" Jeeze, I used to know how to talk. *Way to make a memorable first impression, Danni.*

I swallowed hard, took a deep breath, and tried again. "Sorry. I guess I was expecting the waitress to bring my drink, not—I could have picked it up at the bar myself. I mean, you don't look like a waiter, but—uh, I'll just shut up now." The fire in my cheeks grew to an inferno.

He shrugged, his suppressed smirk breaking into a lopsided grin that revealed a dimple in his left cheek. "I couldn't pull off wearing the uniform, but they were nice enough to let me jump in anyway so I had an excuse to come over here." He placed the glass on the table, leaning closer as he slid it toward me. His eyes never left mine. "Hope you don't mind."

I expected him to deliver my drink then make a quick exit, especially after my brilliant display of communication skills. Instead, he lingered, leaning on the table while he studied my face. The length and intensity of his gaze unsettled me, stirring unfamiliar emotions.

"You know, if I were a cop, I'd have to arrest you." His warm breath brushed my cheek when he spoke.

The smooth tone of his deep voice pulsed through me with a soothing rhythm that would put most people at ease, which made it difficult to explain the jumble of nerves bouncing around in my chest.

I didn't usually get flustered around men, no matter how gorgeous they were. I couldn't even remember feeling that way around Will when we first met. So what was it about this man that had me in knots? His dynamic presence intimidated me, yet I felt drawn to him in a way I couldn't explain.

Will should be back soon. I glanced around the small alcove, looking for him. A few people lingered at the bar. One couple stood in a dark corner, groping each other. No one seemed to pay attention to us.

And no sign of Will.

I hated to admit it, even if only to myself, but I was relieved—eager for the opportunity to spend a few minutes with this Adonis. I reached for my drink and took a much needed sip, anxious for the alcohol's calming effects to kick in, then I struggled to find my voice again. "E-excuse me?"

"See, it's a crime for a beautiful woman to sit alone, drowning her sorrows in fishbowl margaritas."

That had to be the cheesiest pick-up line I'd ever heard, but it managed to break the ice and make me laugh.

He grabbed a chair and turned it around to straddle the seat. "Why don't I join you." He sat and crossed his arms on the backrest. A carefree smile spread across his face as he extended his hand. "I'm Nico."

A fresh wave of adrenaline rushed through me. I wanted to take his hand and introduce myself, but I resisted. Instead, I rested my elbows on the table and looped my fingers together under my chin.

He was sexy and charming. And younger—early thirties at best, if I had to guess. I didn't understand why he was sitting with me instead of spending time with that miserable tiny-green-dress chick, but I wasn't about to ask. Or complain.

"So, Nico, I'm curious."

He tipped his head and arched one eyebrow.

"Does that line ever work for you?" I watched him closely, or tried to, hoping to shake his confidence and level the playing field. My plan might have worked better if I wasn't the one who kept looking away.

He laughed and drummed his fingers on the back of the chair. The movement drew my attention to a platinum signet ring on his right hand. The onyx face contained the initials DG and a diamond accent.

None of the men I knew wore jewelry—other than the wedding rings their wives insisted they wear. It reminded me I was mingling with a different social class tonight, one that Nico seemed to fit into very comfortably. My mind wandered, thinking about the letters—what they stood for.

"Well . . ." He waited until my attention returned to him. "I guess that depends on whether or not it works on you."

My impaired brain cells screamed, *It totally worked on me—* good thing he couldn't hear them. A married woman shouldn't feel so attracted to a man who isn't her husband, and I definitely felt . . . something . . . after only a few minutes with Nico.

That was when I realized we were playing a dangerous game.

I leaned back in my seat and let my hands slip into my lap. My fingers twisted in the fabric of my dress. "Thanks for delivering my drink, Nico, but I'm not alone." I struggled to find the confidence to look into his warm eyes. "My husband will be back soon."

Nico's smile faded, and he nodded as though he'd expected that response. "Sorry. I just wanted to make sure you were okay. You've been alone for a while and seemed upset."

He'd been watching me? The possibility shouldn't excite me, but I'd be lying if I said it didn't.

My head felt fuzzy from too much alcohol. Or too much Nico. I couldn't decide which.

"Well, if you need anything, just let one of the staff

members know. They'll take good care of you." He stood to leave but hesitated, his eyes still locked on mine.

His intense gaze reached deep into my soul, holding me. I imagined he could see everything I was feeling about him, but this time I couldn't look away.

Nico closed his eyes, breaking our connection, and took a deep breath before he opened them again. "Your husband's a lucky man. Happy new year." He returned the chair to its original position and walked away.

My heart sank the instant he was gone, but sending him away was the right thing to do. As I turned to watch him leave, my gaze drifted toward the doorway. Will stood there, adjusting his jacket and tie. His shoulders were slightly hunched, his gaze cast downward.

An uneasy feeling twisted in the pit of my stomach. How long had he been there?

Will tucked his hands in his pockets and entered the room, closing the distance between us at a leisurely pace.

Nothing happened with Nico beyond a little harmless flirting, so there was no reason I should feel guilty. Okay, maybe those few exhilarating minutes with him made me—but I'd never let myself explore any of the emotions he sparked. Not even if I wanted to.

Which I don't. I love my husband.

The two men politely acknowledged each other as their paths crossed. Nico stopped. He turned and watched as Will made his way back to me.

I forced myself to focus on Will and tried to control the tension building inside me. Nico wouldn't have had a reason to check on me if Will hadn't left me sitting alone for so long. He only had himself to blame for . . . whatever he thought happened. I angled my chair toward him and tried to be patient. Jeeze, could he move any slower?

"I was starting to wonder if you were coming back." My voice was more harsh than I intended. "Do you even know how long you left me sitting here? Alone?"

Will stood silently, staring at me, hands still in his pockets. He gave a noncommittal shrug and acted as though my tone had no effect on him, but I could see a shadow of pain in his beautiful blue eyes.

Desperate to prevent myself from saying something I might regret, I grabbed my drink and tightly clamped my lips around the straw. I didn't want to start an argument with Will and needed a moment to compose myself. It wasn't going to be easy.

Tonight was supposed to be a special night, a celebration, and it all seemed to be falling apart.

My eyes drifted to a couple seated by the bar, their bodies turned toward each other, their legs intertwined. They talked and laughed, always touching and leaning in so their faces brushed together. His undivided attention focused intently on her. The way it should be.

Maybe Will and I had been like that. Long ago.

I sucked harder on my straw, cheeks hollowing, but the cool liquid stopped flowing. The distraction pulled me from my trance. Will had pinched the straw and continued holding it between his thumb and forefinger. I lifted my eyes to find him watching me.

"Take it easy, babe." He eased the half-empty glass from my hands and pushed it toward the center of the table. "I'm sorry I was gone so long."

He reached for my hands, gently lifted me from my seat, then wrapped me in a tight embrace. Several moments passed without a word. I snuggled against him, eager for that familiar sense of security I always felt in his arms. It didn't come.

A shiver ran through me. I tried to pull away from him.

There had to be a reason he was gone so long, and he was obviously trying to avoid discussing it.

I'll be damned if I'm going to let it go.

He'd ditched me for half an hour . . . on my birthday . . . in a room full of strangers . . . and I deserved to know why. I broke free from his tight hold and stepped back enough to glare at him. "Where were you?"

Seconds ticked by. No response.

"Will?"

"I forgot how feisty you get when you drink." His mumbled comment was barely audible. He skimmed his knuckles down the side of my face. "Babe, I'm sorry. Okay? I didn't realize how much time had passed."

Music filtered in from the ballroom where the band resumed playing.

Will reached for my hands, laced our fingers together, and pulled them to his lips. "Come here. Let's go dance." He attempted to tug me toward him.

I took a step back, pulled my hands free, and held them up to stop him. "I'm glad you're sorry, but I'm not going anywhere until you tell me what's going on. It doesn't take that long to use the restroom. So what are you hiding?" I crossed my arms and waited.

"Shhh . . . calm down." He reached for my arms again, but I took another step back and continued glaring at him.

"Okay. Fine." Will retracted his hands and held them up in surrender, his frustration evident. "There was a fight in the hall outside the men's restroom."

That's it? Did he think that was enough of an explanation to satisfy me? After fifteen years, you'd think he would have known better.

Most of the other guests who were in the alcove with us had returned to the ballroom. A quick glance around reassured me we weren't drawing the attention of the few who remained.

I struggled to keep my voice down. "And what does that have to do with you? Do you expect me to believe that had you trapped in the men's room for half an hour? You could have called me. Or even answered your damn phone when I called you!"

My vision blurred as I fought back tears. He knew how much I hated to argue. How could he do this to me? Especially tonight.

Will reached for me, hesitating before fully extending his hand to touch me. He moved as though approaching a stray dog, testing to see if it would attack.

I didn't step back this time.

He brushed my hair away from my face and stroked my ear. When I began to relax, he eased me closer and wrapped his other arm around me. "I wasn't going to tell you because I didn't want to upset you on your birthday."

The calm tone of his voice soothed my raw nerves.

He paused to look at me, as though gauging my reaction, then skimmed his nose along mine. "There was another guy there. The two of us were able to break apart the men who were fighting, but then we had to wait for security to show up." He placed a gentle kiss on my temple. "Security made us wait so they could talk to us. I came straight back to you as soon as I could get away. I swear." He framed my face and looked into my eyes.

My brows pressed together as I studied him, considering his explanation. The sincerity in his expression melted my anger. How could I have doubted him? I wished I could take back my words, erase the pain they'd surely caused him.

The best I could do was try to make it up to him. "I was worried about you." I turned to kiss his palm then reached up to caress his face. "And I missed you." I locked my hands behind his head and stretched on my toes to kiss him. After a few seconds, I brushed my lips across his face to whisper in his ear, "Come dance with me, and then I want you to take me to bed."

Will wrapped me in his arms, crushing me to his chest. He drew in a ragged breath and pressed a long kiss against my head.

"Let's skip the dance." He took my hand and led me toward the exit.

CHAPTER 3

LOVE ME TONIGHT

I t was a good thing Will had cut me off when he did. If I'd finished that second drink, he would probably be carrying me right now. He unlocked the door then caught me around the waist as I stumbled into our suite. I braced my hands against his chest, struggling to find my balance.

A broad smile spread across my face as I gazed up at him. "Hey, handsome. It's about time you brought me here."

He looked awfully sexy in his tux, but I was more interested in getting him out of it. I slid my hands up his shirt as I stretched to kiss him and pushed the jacket off his shoulders.

Will's chest shook as he chuckled. "I could've sworn you told me you were staying sober tonight. Come here." He took my hands in his and walked backward, leading me toward the large four-poster bed.

"I like the way you think." I wanted to touch him, finish pulling off that jacket—and more—but I couldn't wiggle my hands free.

Will wrapped my fingers around one of the tall bedposts, making sure I had a good grip on it. He lowered his eyes to mine. "You all right there?"

I couldn't wait to see what he had planned. I nodded eagerly but regretted the sudden movement as the room swayed.

"Give me a minute." He pressed his lips to mine. "Don't let go, okay?"

Having learned my lesson, I gave just a single nod this time.

Will crossed the spacious room, pausing to drop his jacket on a plush chair. He paired his phone with the Bluetooth speaker on the dresser then pushed a few buttons. A sultry soft jazz melody filled the suite.

He sauntered toward me, humming along with the music. In one swift move, he scooped me up and spun around, making me shriek with laughter.

I grabbed hold of his arms as he put me back down, clinging while I waited for the room to stop moving.

Will tapped his finger on the tip of my nose. "I'm going to grab a quick shower, and then we have a birthday to celebrate."

"Not so fast, mister." I caught his shirt as he tried to step away and pulled him to me. "You promised you would be all mine when we came back to the room. It's my birthday, and I want to open my present."

I watched his face closely as I undid his bow tie and eased the silky fabric from under his collar. "Hmm . . . We could have some fun with this later." I wrapped the tie around my wrist and let it slip through my fingers.

He arched a brow and looked at me but didn't say a word.

I tossed the tie on the bed then slowly went to work on his shirt buttons. "You know . . ." I kissed the warm skin exposed at the top of his chest. "I could join you in the shower."

Another button, but this time Will hooked his fingers under my chin before I could place another kiss. He tipped my face toward his, and his eyes locked on mine. Without saying a word, he gently shook his head.

My face sagged forward, pressing the weight of my disappointment into his fingers. I didn't want to wait. This was what I'd been working toward all evening. All week . . . or nearly three weeks, to be more accurate.

I rolled my hips against him and bit back a victorious grin. "Seems you've been outvoted."

His body's reaction empowered me. I resumed my endeavor on his buttons, fingers fumbling with alcohol-induced clumsiness. "Almost there."

I slid my hands inside his unbuttoned shirt, caressing his warm skin, and worked to pull his shirttail free.

Will grabbed my hands and trapped them behind my back. "Patience, babe." He nuzzled my neck. "I'll only be a few minutes, and then I have plans for you."

"I've been patient long enough." I pouted and tried pleading with my eyes, but he didn't give in.

Will nipped my extended lip then smoothed over the spot with his tongue. "Why don't you pour us a drink while you wait. I had some wine delivered." He motioned toward the counter where an open bottle was chilling in a bucket of ice then chuckled. "I'm not sure it's the best idea anymore though. You've already had a lot more than you usually drink when we go out. Sex will be more fun if you're conscious."

He released me and turned to make his way to the bathroom, removing his shirt as he walked. The door closed behind him.

"You are such a tease, Will DeLaney." I laughed and followed after him. "I know you're just standing there. Waiting for—"

The lock clicked. I froze in place.

"Or . . . maybe not." Another small stab of pain to my heart. It was beginning to feel like a pincushion tonight.

Will emerged from the steamy bathroom a few minutes later with a towel wrapped around his waist. He walked toward me, his casual strut back in place.

It wasn't easy in my intoxicated state, but I'd managed to pour our wine and waited for him on a stool by the bar. I wrapped my arms around his waist when he reached me, needing the physical contact.

I leaned into his bare chest and breathed in the scent of his soap, wiggling my nose as the light smattering of hair tickled me. "I'm sorry for overreacting earlier. I didn't mean to hurt you."

"Shhhh, let's forget about that, okay?" He placed a kiss on top of my head and stroked my hair, winding the curls around his fingers. "But we do have a problem."

Every muscle in my body tensed. One thought ran through my head. The same fear that had hit me when I'd seen him standing in the entrance to the bar—he saw me flirting with Nico. It all made sense now . . . suddenly leaving the party, wanting some time alone, making me wait for sex.

I pulled back to look at him, prepared to explain the innocence of our chat. Instead, I was greeted by a teasing smile plastered across his handsome face.

Talk about a guilty conscience, phew.

But if he wasn't upset about finding me with another man, what could our problem be? I pushed aside thoughts of Nico and grinned at my husband, trying to play along. "And what might that be?"

"You're still dressed." He picked up his glass and drained its contents. "And I want you naked."

My smile grew without being forced. Whatever had Will

upset earlier had faded, and we were back on track for a romantic evening. The first of many.

Other than a few odd moments tonight, Will had been very attentive. Loving. That had to mean he wanted to change our relationship too.

So why am I suddenly nervous?

I stroked the stem of my wine glass, waiting for the queasy feeling to pass. "I-I thought maybe you could help me."

I'd felt good about my brazen lingerie decision when I got dressed this evening, but after seeing all the fit, glamorous younger women at the party—what if Will just didn't find my forty-year-old semi-in-shape body sexy anymore?

"Oh, really?" Will rubbed his freshly shaved chin, his smile still in place. "Well, I think that can be arranged." He took my hand to help me stand and guided me toward the bed. "So where shall I begin?"

He dipped me in a movie-style dramatic kiss then rained kisses down my neck and across my collarbone, knowing all the right places to nip. I squirmed and giggled under his assault, trying to keep a tight grip on his shoulders for support. Alcohol and stilettos did not make a good combination, something I should probably keep in mind in the future.

"Will, stop! I need to take off my shoes before—" Too late. We were already tumbling toward the floor.

Will caught hold of the bedpost and prevented our fall. His other arm tightened around my waist, holding me to him. "No worries, babe. I've got you."

"Oh my God, Will!" I could barely get the words out through my laughter. "You're going to put us in the emergency room if you don't take it easy!"

He laughed and snagged the top of my dress with his teeth, giving a playful growl as he tugged at the fabric. He pouted after a moment, apparently not getting the result he'd hoped for, and settled for placing a lush kiss on my partially exposed breast.

I pulled my fingers through his hair, still damp from his recent shower. "I've missed this."

He tilted his head at me, a crease between his brows. "What's that?"

"The playing. It's been a really long time—before tonight, I mean. It-it's nice. The way I want us to be." I rubbed my cheek against his chest.

He didn't respond. Instead, he reached behind me and slowly tugged on my zipper, leaning against my chest to hold my dress in place. When the zipper was down, he pressed his lips to my ear. "Bomb's away." Stepping back, he allowed my dress to fall to the floor.

This was it. The moment of truth. I exhaled, pulling my stomach muscles as flat as I could get them, and closed my eyes. I heard his sharp intake of breath when he saw my lingerie.

"Well, this is a nice surprise." He ran his fingers along the top of the black satin bustier then traced the laces along the front of it.

My skin tingled as his touch revived its dormant senses. I opened my eyes and saw a look of approval on Will's face, his relaxed grin and heavy eyes easing my anxiety.

"Mmm . . . very nice. I feel like it's my birthday instead of yours."

My muscles contracted as his hands brushed across my stomach then around to cup my bottom. He lowered himself, kneeling to get a closer look at the wide lace garter belt covering my hips.

Will's head snapped toward me, his brows raised. "No panties? The whole time?"

I shook my head, nervously biting the inside of my lip. A tiny black thong had come with the set, but I'd tossed it aside and decided to be daring. It was a desperate move, but it looked as though my decision was paying off.

"Christ, it's no wonder you were so horny on the dance floor. I would've been sporting wood all night if I'd known this was under your dress."

His hands slid down my silky black stockings as he sat back on his heels, the front of his towel jutting forward from his erection. He seemed to get lost in his thoughts as he watched me for what felt like an eternity.

I couldn't tell what he was thinking. A crease formed between his brows, and his lips pressed into a tight line. His expression looked conflicted, and it was making me nervous.

"Are you going to sit there all night, or are you going to take me to bed?"

My words seemed to draw his mind back from wherever it had wandered. "Definitely taking you to bed." He stood and took my hands to help me step out of my dress, which lay pooled around my ankles. As he guided me to the bed, he leaned in and brushed his lips across my ear. "Keep the shoes on."

CHAPTER 4

TWO STEPS BACK

I awoke to the morning sun on my face. As I lay there basking in its warmth, my mind drifted to the heated moments Will and I'd shared just a few hours earlier. I skimmed my hands over my body, remembering each touch. He'd even woken me during the night to make love a second time—that never happened.

A satisfied hum escaped me as I stretched my aching body and turned to face him, planning to return the favor. I opened my eyes. The bed was empty.

"Will?" I sat up and squinted into the room. He wasn't here.

Reaching for my cell, I discovered a glass of orange juice next to a bottle of aspirin on the nightstand. The simple gesture said so much. I brushed my fingers over the tepid glass before grabbing my phone and pressing the button to call him.

Something vibrated against the empty wine bottle still on the counter from last night—Will's phone.

Waking up alone sucked, especially after last night. I hugged my knees to my chest, fighting the empty feeling gnawing at me.

My head snapped up at the sound of the door opening. I

hopped from the bed and rushed to greet Will, a huge smile on my face. We'd gotten off to a rough start, but last night had turned out to be pretty amazing. I couldn't wait to be back in his arms.

He stepped inside, a takeout mug of coffee and a small white bag in one hand.

I didn't care. I crashed into him, knocking him off balance, and squeezed him in a huge hug. "Good morning!" I barely recognized the bubbly voice as my own. "I was just about to go search for you."

He reached behind me to set the coffee and bag on the table by the door. "I was up early. I didn't want to wake you, so I decided to take a walk."

I grabbed his face and covered his mouth with mine, skimming my tongue along his lower lip.

He was slow to respond but gradually wrapped his arms around me and returned the kiss.

"Well, I'm awake now . . ." My stomach made a loud growling noise that made us laugh. "And starving, it seems. Guess we should probably get some breakfast."

I snuggled against Will then stretched up to nibble on his earlobe. He shivered and tried to pull away, but I didn't release him.

"Or I could just eat you," I whispered.

"Okay then, breakfast it is." He picked up the bag he'd carried in and handed it to me.

I hesitated, waiting for him to crack a smile then sweep me up in his arms.

He extended the bag a second time.

No arguments, Danni. Just go with it.

The sweet aroma of fresh-baked cookies greeted me when I opened the bag. "Smells delicious. Chocolate chip?"

He nodded. "With pecans. They're from the bake shop we saw when we checked in yesterday."

I put them aside, deciding they'd be better as dessert, and traced my fingers down Will's chest. "Actually, I was thinking—we have an hour until we have to check out." I took a step closer so my breasts brushed against him. "And I have a few ideas on how we can fill it."

He kissed the top of my head. "Hate to break it to you, babe, but we need to hit the road. It's a long drive to your sister's, and you promised we'd be there by two."

I tugged at the button on his jeans. "I'm sure she wouldn't mind if—"

He pressed a finger to my lips and shook his head. "Go get dressed, and I'll finish packing our things."

I smiled under his finger, determined not to give up.

Will grabbed my hand to stop me before his zipper was halfway down. "Babe, last night was a lot of fun." A crease formed between his brows, and he paused briefly before shaking it off to continue. "But we can't play all the time."

All the time? I pulled back to stare at him. "You're joking, right?"

He turned me toward the bathroom and gave my bottom a gentle swat to send me on my way.

"And we're back to boring," I grumbled as I crossed the room and shoved the door closed behind me.

After a quick shower, I threw on a sweater and jeans, brushed my teeth, then pulled my hair into a messy ponytail. Will had apparently packed most of our bathroom items earlier this morning. The only thing left was my makeup bag. I pulled out my mascara and leaned toward the mirror, pausing to scrutinize myself, tugging at the small lines visible around my eyes.

"Why bother." I dropped the tube back into the bag and zipped it shut.

Tears threatened to spill down my cheeks. I grabbed a tissue from the counter to wipe them away, but it was futile. A new supply quickly took their place. I sucked in a ragged breath, my earlier joy extinguished, and dragged myself from the room.

A few minutes later we were in the elevator, headed for the walkway to the parking garage. I stood next to Will, my arms crossed, and maintained enough distance between us to show I wasn't happy with his mood swing. What happened to the fun, wonderful man he was last night?

"Stop it."

I raised my eyes to him, my only response.

"You're sulking." He wrapped his arm around my shoulder and pulled me against him.

When I opened my mouth to protest, the elevator dinged, warning that we wouldn't be alone much longer. Rather than argue in public, I closed my mouth and settled for turning my head away from him.

The doors opened. Nico entered the elevator, engrossed in something on his phone screen. With barely a glance up, he slipped a key into the panel and pressed the button for the top floor.

The air became thick as soon as the doors closed. His fresh clean scent wrapped around me like an ocean breeze. Intoxicated me. I tried not to look at him but couldn't resist the strong pull. I shifted my eyes. *Just one tiny peek.*

He was watching me, casually leaning against the far wall. A faint smile played on his lips. Mischief sparkled in his warm brown eyes when they locked on mine.

My pulse raced, his effect on me magnified in this small space.

Will draped his other arm across my chest, pulling me into a tight embrace. His possessive hold suggested even he was able to feel the energy between Nico and me. He reminded me of a boy on the playground, clutching his favorite toy so the other kids couldn't take it away.

The elevator stopped at our floor. Will ushered me out as soon as the doors opened, without saying a word.

I risked a glance at Nico as I passed, wondering if I would ever see him again.

He simply winked and flashed that sexy smile.

CHAPTER 5

SEEDS OF DOUBT

We pulled up in front of Jen's house a full thirty minutes ahead of schedule.

"Told you we had plenty of time." I glanced at Will as I reached behind my seat to grab my bag. No doubt he knew exactly what I was referring to, but his stoic expression concealed whatever thoughts he had on the subject.

As I climbed out of the passenger side of Will's car, my sister's front door flew open, releasing a three-foot-eight blur of energy named Caden. I stooped and braced for impact.

"Aunt Danni!" He ran across the snow-covered lawn and crashed into me with the full force of his forty-pound body. His little arms wrapped tightly around my neck as he planted a sloppy kiss on my face.

It was perfect.

"Hey, little man. Happy new year!" I ruffled his mop of blonde hair and wrapped my open jacket around him. "You must be freezing. Where's your coat?"

"Mom said I didn't havta wear it, but I couldn't go out without my boots. See?" He squeezed my shoulders as he lifted one leg, providing the evidence that he'd followed orders. He returned his foot to the ground and continued his excited chatter without missing a beat. "Mom said we havta be extra nice to you 'cause you're old today."

I heard the low rumble of Will's laughter as he came around the back of the car. Caden's hand flew up, ready for their customary high-five greeting.

"You're the only one who could get away with saying that, buddy." Will tapped his palm against Caden's. "What your mom meant is that today is Aunt Danielle's birthday." He leaned down to whisper in Caden's ear, which happened to be right next to mine. "But you don't want to ask her how old she is." Will laughed and backed away.

I released Caden and walked up the shoveled path to the house. Will and Caden tromped through the snow, stopping occasionally to make snowballs and toss them at each other.

Boys.

My sister waited inside the door to greet us, her pale face and bloodshot eyes proof that she'd partied hard last night.

"Happy new year! You look like hell," I said as I walked into her open arms and squeezed her tight, "but it's good to see you."

Jen laughed, returning the hug. "At least I don't feel like hell. Happy new year, and happy birthday!"

I closed my eyes, taking a deep breath through my nose. "Mmm . . . it smells great in here." The aromas of fresh-baked apple pie and roast pork filled the house, making my mouth water. The cookies I'd eaten on the ride here hadn't done much to satisfy my hunger.

"Hey, Danni, happy birthday!" Jen's husband, Ryan, entered from the kitchen carrying a large bowl of pretzels. "You look as young and beautiful as the first day I met you." He leaned forward to give me a one-armed hug and kissed my cheek.

"Now I see why you keep him around." I winked at Jen and nudged Ryan with my elbow as he released me.

"Yeah, he has a few redeeming qualities." Jen brushed the side of her husband's face with her fingertips. Her sparkling eyes fixed on his, conveying an unspoken message. It was easy to feel the love between them.

Ryan hooked his arm behind Jen to pull her close then pressed his lips to her ear as he spoke, his volume unaltered. "One of which is making you scream wildly."

"Shhh . . ." Jen clamped his lips between her fingers. "You're awful!" A hint of laughter seasoned her voice, and a rosy glow covered her pale cheeks. She dropped her hand to Ryan's chest, forcing him to take a step back as she glanced down the hall toward the entrance and the murmur of Will's voice.

"That's not what you said this morn—"

"Don't you have a football game to watch or something?" She swept her fingers forward, motioning for him to be on his way.

Ryan wiggled his eyebrows at Jen and stole a quick kiss before calling to the foyer. "Hey, Will. When you're ready, there's a frosted mug with your name on it in the den."

"I think I hear it calling. I'll be right in. Just gotta get this little monkey to sit still long enough to pull off his boots."

Jen waited until Ryan neared the den, his chuckling fading as he went, then turned toward me. "I didn't expect you to get here for at least another hour." Jen slid her hands in mine as she looked at me then shifted her gaze past my shoulder to glance at Will, studying him for a brief moment. She leaned forward and lowered her voice. "So? How'd it go last night?"

Good question. "You know, I'm not really sure." I shook my head, remembering the roller coaster of emotions from last night and this morning.

Jen tilted her head and gave me a questioning stare. "How

can you not know? Either—never mind. We'll talk in a few minutes."

Caden raced toward us, offering a welcome interruption. I wasn't ready to delve into everything that had happened. Hell, I wasn't even sure what had happened.

"Mommy, I'm gonna take Uncle Will to the man cave so he can watch football with me and Dad." Caden tugged on Will's sleeve. "Come on, Uncle Will."

Will gave Jen a quick hug and wished her a happy new year then scooped up his nephew. He draped the giggling four-year-old over his shoulder. "Anybody see where Caden went? He was here a minute ago."

Caden's giggles turned to squeals of laughter. "Uncle Will, I'm back here." He kicked his legs and pounded his small fists against Will's back.

"Well, what the heck are you doing back there?" Will returned Caden to his feet and smoothed the boy's hair before grabbing his hand. "Come on. Let's go find your daddy. We've got man stuff to do."

The two of them disappeared through the family room toward the den.

Jen took my arm and pulled me into the kitchen. She dropped her cell on the table as she motioned for me to sit then grabbed a pitcher of iced tea from the fridge and two glasses from the cabinet before joining me. She leaned forward, hands folded in front of her, and pinned me with a determined stare. "All right, spill. What's going on with you two?"

For a younger sister, she could be rather bossy at times. I sighed and poured some tea, stalling as I tried to figure out where to start and how much information I wanted to share. Once I got going, everything flowed until I had spilled every detail about the party itself, Will's attentive behavior, his disappearances, my encounters with Nico, making love with Will, and his shift back to indifference this morning.

When I finally finished, I looked at Jen, who had been quiet the whole time. Her jaw was hanging down, and her eyes were opened wide.

"Wow! That has got to be some sort of record." She pressed the button on her phone to show the time. Fifteen minutes had passed. "You really needed to get that off your chest, didn't you?"

I shrugged, not quite sure what I needed. "I think I'm just confused. Aside from a few bumps in the road, last night was great. Amazing, even." I paused, remembering how great the sex had been last night. My smile faded as I shook off the memory. "But this morning—I don't know what happened." I took a giant gulp of my iced tea to wash down the lump that had formed in my throat.

Jen hesitated, poking at an ice cube in her glass. "Maybe . . . I don't know. Are you sure last night wasn't just an act or something?" She paused to look at me then reached across the table and took my hand. "You said yourself that he was being more affectionate and playful than he'd been in months."

"So you think he just *pretended* to care last night? That's pretty insulting, don't you think?" I could hear the pain in my voice but couldn't decide if it was there because her question hurt or because a small part of me was afraid it could be true. I tried to pull my hand away, but she tightened her grip.

"Don't get defensive. Just hear me out, okay?" She waited until I nodded to confirm my willingness to listen. "I know Will cares about you, loves you. He understood how stressed you were about turning forty—"

"Still am."

Jen narrowed her eyes then continued. "All right, how stressed you *are* about turning forty. Maybe he was trying his best to give you a happy memory of that night." A timer went off, but Jen continued talking as she got up to remove her pie from the oven. "I think what I keep getting stuck on is that you described his behavior as being more than just that, almost like he was trying *too* hard. You know, overcompensating for something?"

"I don't know what you're getting at." I grabbed our empty glasses and carried them to the sink then washed the peppers that were sitting out.

Jen was piling the pork into a bowl. She paused with the ladle in the pot and faced me. Her mouth opened and closed several times before she spoke, her voice gentle. "Do you really buy that story about a fight?" She held up her index finger to ward off an interruption. "Think about it, Danni. Wouldn't other people have heard or seen it? Stuff like that usually causes a big commotion."

I paused to let her think I was considering the possibility. "Of course I believe it. Will wouldn't lie to me about something like that." I crossed my arms, tensing as a sudden chill ran through me.

"Maybe you just *want* to believe him. You know it would be easy to confirm his story. Prove me wrong." Jen raised her brows as she looked at me then looked at her phone on the table. "All you have to do is call Elevations and ask."

"I'm not calling." My sister moved toward the phone herself, as I'd expected, but I reached the table first. I stood facing her, my arms still crossed. "And neither are you. If it were Ryan, would you trust him, or would you call to check his story?"

"If I thought he was lying and feeding me some ridiculous bullshit line to cover what he was really doing? Yes. I'd call in a heartbeat." She reached around me and picked up her phone then held it out to me. "You taught me to be tough, Danni. So when are you going to learn to stand up for yourself?"

I drew in a shaky breath before answering, my voice quiet and laced with despondence. "Will always says that a good marriage is built on trust." I took the phone, turned it over in my hand, and placed it back on the table. Squaring my shoulders, I stared into Jen's eyes and hoped I looked more confident than I actually felt. "I trust my husband."

"Mommy!" Caden's voice echoed through the family room as he ran to the kitchen, allowing me to escape my sister's inquisition. "Daddy and Uncle Will wants to know when the food's gonna be ready." He stretched on his toes to get a better view of the pie cooling on the counter. "Mmmm, can I have some of that?"

I loved this little guy as if he were my own and couldn't resist the chance for another hug, especially after that emotionally draining conversation. Kneeling down to wrap my arms around him, I placed a kiss on his soft, warm cheek. "You bet you can. And I bet Mommy has vanilla ice cream to go with it."

"Yum! So we can eat now?"

"As soon as Daddy and Uncle Will are ready. Can you tell them?"

Caden started calling out his message for Will and Ryan as he ran back through the house.

When I turned to face my sister, she stood watching me with her hands on her hips.

"We're not finished with this conversation, just so you know." She picked up the bowl of pork and walked toward the dining room.

I groaned, wondering when and how our roles got reversed.

Will bounced into the kitchen a few minutes later with Caden riding piggyback. They were singing "The Wonderful

Thing About Tiggers," and I couldn't tell which one of them was having more fun.

"Hey, monkey," I said, prying Caden off Will. "You want to help set the table?"

"Sure!"

I handed him a basket of utensils and a stack of napkins, and he took off for the dining room, almost crashing into his mom as they passed in the doorway.

"Dinner smells great, Jen." Will leaned against the counter, next to where I was working, and reached in front of me to grab a strip of red bell pepper. He held it up for me to take a bite before popping the rest of it in his mouth.

"That's because my wife is an amazing cook," Ryan said as he entered the room. He hugged Jen from behind and nuzzled into the crook of her neck. "Among other things."

She turned in his arms, clasped her hands around his neck, and pulled him down for a kiss.

A sense of pride swelled inside me as I watched them, seeing her so happy. Even after eight years of marriage, they always needed some sort of physical contact whenever they were together, almost as if they were magnetically drawn to each other. Maybe Will and I were that way in the beginning, but I couldn't remember it.

"All right. You two are sickening." Will grabbed Ryan by the shoulders and guided him toward the dining room. "Get moving before I lose my appetite." Will collected the tray of veggies from the counter with one hand and took my hand in his other, then he placed a soft kiss on my lips. "Let's go eat."

CHAPTER 6

BLIND DEVOTION

Will brushed his hand along my arm as we pulled into the garage around ten that evening. "Wake up, babe. We're home."

I collected my things and got out of the car, my movements automated. Thoughts of a long, hot shower and a good night's sleep served as my only motivation. Jen's words ran through my head the whole ride home, accompanied by the pounding bass of Will's head-banging playlist of eighties rock bands. *Better add aspirin to that list of things I'm looking forward to.*

After dinner, Jen had upheld her threat to resume interrogating me on Will's behavior, telling me she admired my devotion to my marriage but worried about my blind trust. "Just promise me you'll think about everything I've said . . . and keep your eyes open," she'd said.

When that topic ran dry, she moved on to Nico, though I didn't know why. She seemed entertained by my juvenile reaction to him, gushing as she recounted a similar encounter with Ryan when they first met and babbling something about chemical attraction. I was half-afraid she was going to suggest braiding each other's hair and swapping first-kiss stories at any minute.

I followed Will into the house, lost in my thoughts. If he realized I hadn't spoken, he didn't mention it. He tossed his wallet and keys on the kitchen table, kicked off his shoes beside one of the kitchen chairs, and slung his jacket over the back of it. His usual routine. I paused for a moment then decided I could wait until morning to straighten up.

I SLIPPED on my nightgown after a nice, long shower and crawled into bed, anxious for sleep to take away the uneasy feeling I'd had all evening. I clung to the edge of the king-sized mattress, my back toward Will's half of the bed.

The covers lifted as he climbed in and slid over to spoon me, not taking the hint that I wanted to be left alone. My body tensed as his hand caressed my waist then skimmed over my hip to my thigh. He pushed my nightgown up as he retraced the path and pulled me against him.

"I get that you're upset about this morning." His lips grazed my jaw when he spoke. "It's still your birthday, you know. Just in case you feel like opening your present one more time." He rocked his hips, pressing his semi-hard erection against my backside.

I raised my hand to rub the arm he'd draped across me. "I'm really tired. It's been a long two days."

Will rolled to his back without a word and tucked his hands behind his head. Several minutes of awkward silence passed as the tension hanging between us grew.

"Have you ever lied to me?" My eyes flew open wide, and I held my breath. The thought had been gnawing at me for hours, but I'd never intended to just blurt it out.

He remained quiet, making me wonder if he was already asleep. I hoped he was.

"That's a loaded question," he finally said. "Everyone tells lies . . . sometimes they're a good thing if they prevent hurting the other person."

"Is that what happened last night?" I cringed and bit the inside of my lip.

Will's voice was calm when he answered. "What exactly are you asking me, Danielle?" His arm moved, and I imagined him rubbing his forehead the way he did when he didn't want to talk about something. As he continued speaking, I could hear his struggle to maintain a placid tone. "What do you think I lied about? Because I put in a lot of work to make your birthday special. For you."

The mattress shifted. Will got out of bed and grabbed his phone off the night table.

I propped myself on one elbow and watched as he walked toward the door. "Where you going?"

Will turned to face me, illuminated by the glow of the nightlight in the hallway. He leaned into the door frame with an exaggerated sigh. "Kitchen. I'm thirsty . . . you want something?"

"No." I dropped my head back to the pillow and pulled the covers up to my chin. "Nothing."

When he walked away, I glanced over my shoulder at the bottle of water on his nightstand. My eyes fell closed, but I couldn't escape Jen's words as they echoed through my throbbing head.

CHAPTER 7

FIT FOR LOVE

"It's a gym, Will. People go there to exercise."

He could be so unreasonable sometimes, and I was not in the mood to deal with his attitude this morning. If he'd taken a different approach—been reasonable—or just shown some kind of interest in me over the past few days, I would have agreed to cancel on Kendra.

I pushed past him and slipped into the bathroom. "You're acting like I'm going to singles' night at some sleazy bar."

I flicked aside the open tube of toothpaste lying by the sink instead of cleaning up after him like I usually did. Every. Single. Day.

He followed and leaned against the counter, crowding me. The resulting lack of elbow room made it difficult to brush my hair and pull it into a ponytail.

"They're practically the same thing." Will bit out the words as he snatched up the toothpaste, closed the cap, and tossed it into the cabinet.

"Wow, you do know how to do that."

He moved behind me, arms crossed over his chest, and scowled at my reflection. "Don't try to change the subject."

"Fine. Guys go to the grocery store to pick up women, but it doesn't seem to bother you when I go there to get your food every week." I traded my brush for the can of hairspray to glue down any loose ends.

"Dammit, Danielle, take it easy with that shit!" He choked out the words, fanning the air with both hands.

Whoever invented this stuff was a genius in my book. I bit back a grin and gave another long, unnecessary spray.

Instead of taking the hint and leaving me alone, Will stepped closer. He caught my wrist and confiscated the can, holding it at bay. His jaw tensed as he stared into my eyes. "I doubt you're bending over and sticking your ass in the air at the grocery store."

"I don't plan on sticking it in the air at the gym either. Kendra said—" I shook my head. "Never mind." Her ambiguous explanation about how a few trips to the gym would improve my sex life was hard enough for me to believe. There was no way Will would buy it. "She's just trying to help."

"Yeah. I just bet she is." His voice oozed sarcasm.

I yanked free and ducked under his outstretched arm, escaping to the other side of the bathroom. *One. . . . two. . . . three . . . screw it.*

"You know, I'm not even going to ask what that's supposed to mean." I scooped up his wet towel from the floor, rolled it in a ball, and tossed it at him on my way out of the room. "This gets folded in half and draped over the bar on the wall. It's pretty simple. I'm sure you can figure it out."

It was one thing for Will not to trust Kendra's motives, but he sure as hell should trust me.

"You should be thanking her." I gathered a change of clothes and shoved them into my gym bag. "Who do you think convinced me to get the lingerie and wax job you enjoyed so much on New Year's Eve?"

She'd joked that her New Year's resolution would be to get me fixed up.

Maybe Will didn't hear my mumbled comment when he sulked back into the bedroom. More likely he just chose to ignore it. He glanced at the bag then glared at me. "So you're still going?" His voice mirrored his incredulous expression.

I pressed my fingers to my temples, a futile effort to release the tension building there. Arguing with Will over something stupid wasn't fixing anything or moving our relationship in the right direction. Eyes closed, I took a few calming breaths. "Look, I'm sure I'll hate it and never want to go back. Okay?" I opened my eyes and waited.

He stood stock-still with his arms folded and a stern look on his face.

After zipping my bag shut, I walked to where Will stood and rubbed his arms. "I don't have time to argue with you. Kendra will be here soon. And I'm going with her." I pried his arms open and wiggled closer, clinging to him. "I'll be fine. You know you can trust me."

Will pressed his lips against my hair. His body relaxed slightly as he let out a heavy sigh and wrapped me in his embrace. Neither of us moved for what felt like minutes.

"I know, babe," he said, his words a whispered conviction.

"So." I backed away and turned in a circle. "How do I look?"

He smacked my bottom when I stuck it in the air. "Adorable."

I grabbed the collar of Will's polo and pulled him to me. "Since you're clearly hitting on me, mister, maybe you'd like to take me out tonight. Or, even better"—I traced my fingers down his chest—"we could have a romantic evening in?" My pulse skipped in anticipation, hoping for an encore of my birthday celebration.

He caught my hands and lifted one palm to his lips. "Sorry, babe, I brought home some files that I need to work on tonight."

"On a Saturday night." I leaned back to glare at him, making no effort to hide my skepticism. "Really? You never work weekends."

The doorbell rang as if signaling the end of round one. I turned and headed for my corner—the walk-in closet. "I'll be ready in a minute. Can you get the door?"

I pulled on my sneakers then hurried down the stairs. Will hovered in the foyer, avoiding the door and my friend on the other side.

"Will . . . the door?" I shouted out my reminder and raced toward the mud room to grab my coat.

By the time he finally turned the latch, I was coming back down the hall. I let out a frustrated groan. *Could have done it myself by now.*

"Hey, Wet Willie. Sorry, I would have invited you to join us, but . . ." Kendra slapped her hand on Will's chest and laughed. "Oh hell, who am I kidding? I didn't invite you 'cause I don't want you to come." She pushed past him and moved into the family room. "Danni? Where you hiding, girl?"

Will shook his head. "Always a pleasure to see you too, Kendra."

"Play nice, you two." I entered the room, carrying my coat and gym bag.

Kendra held up her hands, frantically waving as I approached her. "Stop. Right. There. What the hell are you wearing?"

I skimmed a hand down my outfit and bent forward to examine myself. It looked fine to me. I shrugged. "A T-shirt and a pair of gym shorts . . . we are going to your gym, right?"

"Not with you dressed like that. Jeeze, Danni, it looks like you're wearing Will's clothes." She dropped her bag on the couch and rooted through it. "Lucky for both of us, I came prepared." Kendra pulled out a small piece of rolled up black fabric and pushed it into my hands. "Here. Go put this on. And hurry, or we'll miss the ten o'clock Zumba class."

I set my coat and bag next to hers on the couch. "I really don't see the point—"

"You can thank me later, sweetie." She turned me around and nudged me toward the stairs.

I kind of liked the idea of wearing something more feminine to the gym and didn't bother arguing. Not that Kendra would give in anyway. And Will would get over it. Eventually.

I hustled up the stairs to my room and tossed the outfit on the bed—a bright pink-and-white tie-dyed sports bra, black spandex crop pants with a pink stripe down each side, and a white racer-back tank. My eyes grew wide. *She can't be serious.* I picked up the tiny scraps and closely examined them, stretching the fabric that couldn't possibly fit me.

"Kendra?" I shouted. "I think you grabbed Callie's clothes by mistake." I poked my head out of the room to listen for her to answer. Honestly, these had to be even too small for Kendra's teenage daughter. *Maybe they got into the dryer by mistake.*

"Danni, they're fine. Just get moving and put them on."

"Okay?" I drew out the word and gave the waistband another tug. "I'll . . . um . . . give it a shot." *Even though you've clearly lost your mind.*

"I can't believe you told her it was okay to wear your clothes in public." Kendra's voice dripped with disdain as she reprimanded Will.

Their muffled conversation continued to drift up the stairs, but I couldn't make out Will's response. Leaving those two without a referee for more than a few minutes was never a good idea. I moved closer to the door and strained to listen while attempting to squeeze into my new exercise outfit.

"Did you give her a pair of your boxers too?"

By now, Will would be standing with his arms crossed, drilling Kendra with a condescending stare. Which would only irritate her further.

I stumbled, catching my feet in the tight pant legs as I tried to hurry.

"I don't like the idea of your slimy gym rats drooling all over my wife. She was safer wearing that."

"Danni is going to draw attention no matter what you put on her, which you *should* already know. Besides, that outfit would have scared those sexy gym rats away from me. My divorce is final next week, so I'm officially back on the market."

I needed to get downstairs before those two wound up in a full-out brawl. One deep breath for courage, then I forced myself to take a quick glance in the mirror.

"Wow." The word slipped out. I turned, taking in every angle and sliding my hands over my body. I never imagined getting dressed for the gym could make me look or feel so good.

"Okay, let's go," I called as I ran down the stairs, surprised that I was actually excited about going now.

Will's eyes looked like they were about to pop when he saw me, and his reaction made my smile grow even wider.

"Damn, babe, you—"

"Gotta run." Kendra stepped in front of him and shoved my bag and coat at me.

Struggling to get past her, I stretched up to give Will a quick kiss. "I promise I'll be fine."

He looped an arm around my waist and pulled me tight. His other hand held my head in place while he prolonged the kiss. I wasn't sure what his point was, but I wasn't complaining.

"You're not supposed to break a sweat before you get to the gym, sweetie." Kendra grabbed my arm and tugged me toward the door. "Keep it in your pants, Will." She paused to glare at him, her icy expression delivering an unspoken challenge.

The cold January air cut through me the moment we stepped outside. I pulled my coat tighter around my neck then tucked my hands in my pockets. The door closed behind us.

"What was that about?" I said when we were far enough from the house to avoid being overheard.

"Hm? Oh, just screwing with him." She waved it off and gave a small shake of her head. "I don't know why you put up with that asshole."

I bumped my shoulder against hers. "It's easy. We love each other."

KENDRA and I entered The Next Level, a state-of-the-art gym filled with far more intimidating machines than I had any intention of using. Ever. Large windows covered most of the wall space, letting in an ample amount of natural light. Small clusters of scantily clothed men and women scattered throughout appeared to be socializing more than exercising.

To the left of the entrance, wide metal stairs led to classrooms on the second floor. The glass front wall of each room put the participants inside on clear display—would put *me* on clear display in a few minutes.

What was I thinking?

"Un-huh. I know that look." Kendra grabbed my wrist and pulled me toward a door just beyond the stairs. "We're not leaving."

After depositing our coats and bags in the locker room, she towed me up the dreaded steps. We slipped into a classroom right as the music started. I broke free and worked my way to the back corner where I hoped no one—in here or out there— would see me. Coordination was not one of my strong points.

A grueling hour later, I dragged myself from the room and collapsed on the floor, the cool tile a refreshing contrast to my overheated body. A weak groan escaped me. "I'm dead. And it's your fault." I lifted my fifty-pound head to look at her. "I hope you're happy."

Kendra stepped over me to reach the vending machine, pushed money into the slot, and collected the two bottles that dropped out. She laughed and dripped cold water on my face before settling beside me. "Sit up, drama queen. You're not dead. Yet. We still need to hit the weights."

"You're evil." I pulled myself up to sit against the wall and grabbed a water bottle from her lap. "I hate you," I said, bumping my arm against hers before chugging half of my water.

"You love me." She returned my bump. "And you're going to love me even more when you see the incredible display of hot male bodies downstairs."

I rolled my eyes and chuckled. Kendra was always horny, especially since Nate cut her off after she told him "the whole marriage thing" wasn't working for her anymore.

"Don't laugh," Kendra said. "I've got some shopping to do." She stood and pulled me to my feet.

My legs were like rubber when I tried to stand. I stumbled, struggling to regain control of them.

"Holy hell, Danni. I thought you said you've been exercising with your video." She grabbed my shoulders and helped me to stabilize. "You're moving like you just lost your virginity in an all-nighter with some well-hung sex god!"

Typical Kendra. I shook off the mental image of Sex-God Nico as quickly as it appeared. "At home I have enough common sense to press Pause so I can stop and take a break when I get tired, but that instructor . . . he's a sadist!"

"There was a time when *you* were the sadist pushing me to run faster, run farther."

"Yeah, well, I stopped running a long time ago." I took another long drink before collecting my towel from the floor. "I'm, um . . . I'm gonna go check out the equipment downstairs."

Kendra reached for me as I started to walk away. "Danni, wait."

I turned and held up my hand. "It's all right. I just need a few minutes alone." My voice faded as I spoke.

I eased my way down the steps, keeping a tight grip on the handrail, and ducked into the locker room. Anxious to hide from my memories, I retrieved my iPod from my bag and curled up on a bench. The door opened as I fumbled with my earbuds.

Kendra approached. "You okay, sweetie?" She sat next to me and pushed back the hair that had worked free from my ponytail.

I nodded. Kendra knew what I'd been through. She didn't need me to explain anything.

"He was forty, wasn't he? So, coming up on twenty-five years this spring?"

"Yeah." I stared at my hands in my lap and mindlessly twisted the cord to my earbuds.

Kendra hooked one finger under my chin, tugging until I looked at her. "You're not him. You know that."

She was right—I did know that. But sometimes it was hard to be rational.

Dad had always been perfectly healthy and fit. Right up until the moment he'd collapsed in the park during our Satur-day-morning run. The doctors had said it was an anomaly, some heart condition he'd had his whole life and never known about.

All I knew was that one moment we were joking and having fun, and the next he was gone. Forever.

"Just because you're forty, it doesn't mean the same thing's gonna happen to you. They tested you?"

"Yes. You know that."

Kendra smiled. "Yeah, I just wanted you to remember. Sweetie, you can't be afraid to live, or life's just gonna pass you by."

We sat in silence for a few minutes. Dad's life had ended at forty. For me, forty marked the death of a dream. It meant giving up on the life and family I'd always imagined. I couldn't explain—or didn't want to explain—that I wasn't afraid to live; I just didn't feel vibrant. Full of life. And I was afraid I never would. *Which is why saving my marriage is my last hope.*

"So you ready to go out there?"

What I really wanted to do was go home to Will.

"Yeah, I think I am." I pulled her in for a hug. "Thank you," I whispered, squeezing tighter. "Now what about that promise you made earlier about hot male bodies? You may need a second opinion. And I could use a little distraction."

Kendra's eyes sparkled. "You are gonna love it!" She took my hand and led me toward the door.

Something about the tone of her voice gave me the impression she was enjoying a joke, and I had missed the punch line.

We wandered past rows of cardio equipment. When we finally reached the weights, my feet stopped moving. The finest examples of masculine perfection I'd ever seen were all gathered in one place, ripped muscles bulging. No wonder Kendra put herself through the torture of exercising so often.

"You've got a sappy, dreamy look on your face." Kendra laughed, poking me in the ribs. She leaned close to my ear.

"And you ain't seen nothin' yet." Her voice had the same devious tone it had in the locker room. She rubbed her hands together as she scanned the room. "Now, let's find you a good machine."

Kendra gave a quick briefing on what muscles the different machines worked then headed toward one that she said would give her a sexier butt.

I turned on my iPod and tucked it in my waistband. "Happy," my favorite song to lift my spirits, soon filled my ears making me feel . . . well, happy. I picked a machine in the area she'd suggested, relieved to find instructions printed on it. It was one Kendra had said would work on my chest.

After adjusting the seat to a comfortable height, I set the weight pin to forty pounds. *One for each year?* It sounded good to me. I rolled my shoulders and shook out my arms. *Okay, I can do this.*

Head bopping to the music, I sat down and grabbed the bars, pushing forward as shown in the picture.

The weights didn't budge. I took a quick peek around to make sure no one was watching, got up and moved the pin to thirty pounds, then settled back into position. "Okay. Take two."

This time the bars moved forward, and the weight stack—all two bricks of it—lifted. *Woohoo!* I finished a set of fifteen reps, guessing at how many to do, then dropped my heavy arms to take a break. *This is a lot harder than it looks.*

My head pressed into the padded backrest. My eyes fell closed, allowing me to escape into my own little world where nothing existed but my music and me. I tapped my hands against my legs, silently clapping along with Pharell, and fought the urge to dance in my seat.

A sudden rush of electricity charged the air, reminding me of the feeling I got when a storm approached. It made my skin tingle and created a burst of energy that motivated me to take on the next round.

I blew out a breath, grabbed hold of the bars, and adjusted my grip. Ready to begin, I opened my eyes as I sucked in a sharp breath—followed by intense coughing and sputtering.

Adonis himself leaned toward me, hands resting on his knees. His face was directly in front of mine. It couldn't be . . . but it was. Nico.

God, he was even more gorgeous than I remembered. And that was without taking into account the impressive display of well-defined muscular arms and shoulders revealed by his tank this time.

He tugged my earbuds free. "Hey, you all right?" His expression held a mixture of concern and humor.

I nodded, trying to regain control of my body.

"You remember me?" He flashed his adorable, lopsided grin with that damn single dimple.

Was he kidding? How could I have possibly forgotten him? I bit my lower lip and squinted at him while tapping against the bar I gripped. "Wait a sec." I held up my finger. "New Year's Eve, right? You're, um . . . Nicky, was it?"

His head dipped, and his grin stretched to a sly smile. "Well, I see I made a lasting impression." He drew a hand to his chest, a wounded look on his face.

Male egos were such fragile things. I bit back an amused smile.

"I'm Nico, but I don't think I ever got your name."

"Nico!" I froze when Kendra's voice blasted from behind me. "I see you met my good friend, Danni!"

His eyes flashed to Kendra then back to me, a stunned look on his face. His expression shifted, replaced by a playful one with a familiar spark of mischief as his grin grew wider.

"Well, Danni, it seems we have a friend in common." He

took a step closer, his eyes locked on mine. When he spoke, he leaned toward me and lowered his voice, as if sharing a deep, dark secret. "And I have a feeling we're gonna see a lot more of each other."

The jumble of nerves bouncing in my chest threatened to consume me. I swallowed hard and glanced over my shoulder, looking for Kendra. Looking to escape. She was a good fifteen feet away, pretending to be busy, and seemed in no hurry to join us.

I'd handled a few minutes of harmless flirting, enjoyed them even, when I thought he was some random drop-dead gorgeous guy I'd never see again. But this changed everything. The idea of spending time with Nico terrified me, because I couldn't remember the last time I'd wanted anything more.

CHAPTER 8
SINFULLY SEXY

My soon-to-be-ex-best friend inched her way toward me, casually smoothing the top that clung to her flat stomach.

Kendra was going to die. Plain and simple. As soon as I could feel my arms again, I was going to kill her. Nothing she could say would make me believe running into Nico was a coincidence.

Tired of waiting, I stood and took three large steps, closing the distance to meet her. "Well, I guess I figured out the punch line to your little joke in the locker room."

Kendra's smile beamed triumphant, almost to the point of being contagious. If I wasn't so furious with her.

I admonished her through gritted teeth, attempting to keep my voice low—which was not an easy feat. "You. Set. Me. Up! How the hell did you even know—"

"I didn't." She shrugged. "Not exactly. But from the detailed description you gave, I had a pretty good hunch." She looked at her nails and buffed them against her chest, acting as though this was no big deal.

"You mean the details you pulled out of me with your little

game of twenty questions? What about all that talk about 'getting me fixed up' and how going to the gym would improve my sex life?"

She clung to my shoulder, shaking with a wicked chuckle. "Sweetie, have you taken a good look at Nico?"

"Oh my God!" I sucked in a sharp breath and tried to control my conflicting emotions. "I'm in love with Will. You remember him? My husband?" Although intended for Kendra, my declaration served as a reminder to me as well.

Kendra shuddered. "Oh, please. You mean the husband who ditched you on your birthday without a believable explanation?" She folded her arms, a smug look on her face. "I'm curious, were you thinking of him when you told me about the sinfully sexy man you met that night? The man who damn near melted your panties off you and left you feeling voraciously horny for days?"

"What—I wasn't even—ugh. That was *not* my description."

"So I paraphrased." She waved, dismissing any possible misconception of remorse. "You practically gushed when you talked about him. And I have never, in thirty years, seen you act that way about any guy. Definitely not Will. I had to see your reaction for myself. And let me tell you, the sparks? They are flying." She motioned between Nico and me, driving her point home.

Dammit, she was right. I bit the inside of my lip and averted my eyes, hoping to hide the truth from her. There was no way I could deny it to myself, but just because I felt something for Nico—whatever this feeling was—didn't mean I would act on it.

Despite that fact, the mere thought of acting on it made my skin tingle. I turned to sneak a peek at Nico and found him standing directly behind me, casually leaning against a machine as he shamelessly eavesdropped on our conversation.

He wore the same mischievous expression I remembered him wearing that morning in the elevator, the same one I'd seen in my dreams every night since.

"Do you mind?" I crossed my arms to wait for his response, hating the nervous edge in my voice.

"Not at all. I'm kind of enjoying myself." His smile didn't fade. Without releasing his grip on the equipment, he leaned toward me and lowered his voice. "So, I'm sinfully sexy, huh? Looks like you do remember me after all. Danni."

His warm breath brushed against my neck when he spoke, sending a chill through me. I closed my eyes, ordered my body to get a grip, and tried to ignore the heat building . . . everywhere. *What the hell is going on with me?*

"This is Danni's first visit to a gym, Nico. She should probably have a personal trainer to make sure she knows how to use the equipment correctly. Don't you think?"

I glared at Kendra through wide eyes, screaming all sorts of obscenities at her in my mind while I clenched my jaw shut.

She smiled and flipped her honey-blonde hair away from her face, clearly daring me to stop her. After taking a step closer to Nico, she continued with a suggestive purr in her voice. "Think *you* can take care of her?" She traced the intricate black lines that wrapped around Nico's left bicep. "I mean, we wouldn't want her to get hurt, wou—"

"Enough, Kendra. Are you even sure you're still talking about the gym equipment?" My eyes followed her French-tipped nails still gliding along their path, taunting me until my blood simmered. I swatted them away from his arm. "I'm going to grab a cab home. To my husband. I'll call you later to talk about . . . this." I made a wide sweeping motion to make it clear we'd be covering everything that had happened today.

Kendra drew one side of her mouth into a victorious grin, and her eyes lit up like neon signs flashing the words *I was right.*

Unfortunately, she knew me well enough to recognize my pattern of running from the truth when I didn't want to face it.

I shook my head and moved toward the machine I'd abandoned, needing to collect my things and get the hell out of there.

"Danni, wait. Don't run." Nico's fingers brushed against my arm, branding me.

My chest clenched. The heat of his gentle touch kept me frozen in place. Despite my best efforts to resist temptation, I turned back, pulled in by the sultry tone of his deep voice. I lifted my eyes to meet his, skimming every glorious inch of him in the process.

Big mistake. I'd heard the saying that our eyes were windows to our souls, but I'd never understood what that meant. Until now.

Nico visibly tensed. His eyes closed, and I wondered if he felt it too. That sense of familiarity, both invigorating and terrifying at the same time. He ran a hand through his already messy hair and clasped the back of his neck, pausing to take a few deep breaths.

He spoke in a subdued tone. "Danni, I'm really sorry." He opened his eyes but didn't look directly at me. "I know you're married, and I-I don't—it won't happen again." He rocked back on his heels. "I do think Kendra's right about having someone show you the ropes though, but I can't do it today. Logan is still in town and hangin' out here. I'm sure he'll take good care of you."

Logan. He said the name so casually, as though it should mean something to me, but it wasn't registering. Kendra gave me a nudge, and her excited expression told me she clearly knew who this Logan guy was.

"Logan VanBergen?" Nico said. "I assumed you knew him since you were at his party New Year's Eve."

"Oh. Um, no. Will—that's my husband—he got us on the guest list. I don't know how, but . . . anyway, neither of us knows him."

He shrugged. "No time like the present to thank your host for a wonderful party." He shook his head and chuckled. "Besides, he'll just get into trouble around here if I don't—"

"Nico, baby. I've been looking all over for you." The sickeningly sweet voice came from a petite blonde in tiny spandex shorts. She sashayed up behind Nico and latched onto his thick bicep with her bright pink talons. Her periwinkle crop top perfectly matched her eyes but barely contained her breasts, now pressed into the side of Nico's chest. "You didn't forget about me, did you?" She looked up at him, batting her lashes.

Kendra leaned into me. "Holy shit, I'm gonna puke."

Her muffled complaint echoed my thoughts, eliciting a smile.

She straightened and spoke up in her normal brash tone. "So Nico, who's your little toy *du jour*?"

I stifled a laugh, wondering if blondie even knew what that meant.

The woman slinked her other arm around Nico, giggling. "You can play with me any time you like." She snuggled against him, pinning me with a catty sneer.

"Ladies, this is Trina. A client." He peeled her off his bicep and grasped her shoulders, holding her in place as he took a step away. The gesture created a slight distance that she immediately shifted to fill. "Trina, why don't you head over to the mats and start stretching. I need to take care of something for my friend Danni before I join you." He kept his eyes on me the whole time he spoke to his pouting little groupie.

"Oh, come on, Nico. Is she even legal?" Kendra asked, watching Trina walk away.

"She's twenty-three, which is well above the legal age . . . for hiring a personal trainer." He cut a quick glance to Kendra at the end of his response, making it clear that follow-up questions were not welcome, then returned his attention to me.

"All right, let's get you set up with Logan." Nico extended his hand to me as he spoke but slowly lowered it when I didn't move. "You are staying, aren't you?" A trace of despondence hung in his voice.

I hesitated for what felt like minutes, torn between staying and leaving. The slight nod I eventually gave earned a warm smile from Nico.

He seemed more relaxed. "You can tag along if you want, Kendra. I'm sure Logan can give you some advice to step up your workout and make it more challenging for you."

"Sounds fair to me since you dragged me here," I said with a forced smile. Grabbing Kendra's arm, I leaned closer and growled through that smile. "Besides, I have a feeling you'll just get into more trouble if someone doesn't keep a close eye on you." I motioned for Nico to lead the way. "Let's go see if I can survive the rest of your torture. Then I can go home and tell Will that he was right. I shouldn't have come."

Thoughts of Will's concern this morning lingered in my mind as we crossed the room. My pace slowed until Kendra was practically pulling me along.

"You know . . . on second thought, I'm going to go take my shower. You go ahead. I'll wait for you in the locker room." Without giving either of them a chance to protest, I released my hold on Kendra's arm and made a hasty retreat in the opposite direction.

I HAD SURVIVED both the Zumba class and Kendra's meddling. My time alone in the locker room—complete with a long, relaxing shower—had allowed me to cool off before she'd finished her lengthy session with Logan. We were finally in Kendra's car, heading for home.

Or so I thought.

"Where are you going?" I asked as she blew past the highway entrance.

"Lunch. Did I forget to tell you?" She gave a quick glance in my direction then returned her attention to the road. "Logan said a few people were going to Pepper's Deli and invited us to join them."

"And let me guess, Nico just happens to be among those people? Dammit! You need to stop—"

"Okay. I get it! You still think you can fix things with Will." Seconds ticked by in silence, her knuckles turning white from clenching the wheel. She eventually reached across the center console to squeeze my hand. "It's just . . . I had a lot of fun with Logan. Can we do this for me? Please?"

I let out a heavy sigh, unsure of whether I could handle spending time with Nico. "Fine," I said, squeezing back, "but we eat, and we leave. No hanging around. No going somewhere else. And no trying to stir things up with Nico. Deal?"

"Thanks, sweetie." She gave me a grateful smile as we pulled into the parking lot.

"I'm going to give Will a quick call to let him know why I'm late. I'll meet you inside." I grabbed my phone from my bag and pressed the button without waiting for her response.

"Don't be long." She blew me a kiss and walked toward the entrance.

Will's phone went straight to voicemail.

"Hey, babe. Just want to let you know I went to lunch with Kendra. I'll be home soon."

As I ended the call, a sporty blue Ferrari zipped into the space next to me. I dropped my phone into my bag and closed my eyes, letting my head fall back against the seat. *How on earth am I going to get through this?* Every minute I spent with Nico made it harder to ignore the feelings he stirred in me.

A loud knock on my window made me jump.

Nico pulled open my car door and leaned inside. "Hey, beautiful. You know you have to go inside to get service, right?" His nervous laugh accompanied a stiff-looking grin. After reaching across to unclasp my seat belt, he held out his hand for me. "Come on. I promised to behave. Remember?"

"I'm sorry, miss, is this degenerate harassing you?" A rugged face pushed past Nico's in the open doorway. The man wrapped Nico in a headlock and thrust his right hand toward me. "You must be Danni. It's nice to finally meet—umph—you." He laughed, undeterred by the elbow Nico had delivered to his ribs. "I'm Logan."

Of course, I recognized him from his party without an introduction. I took his hand.

In one swift move, he tugged me from the car, shoved Nico aside, and caught me against his chest. I squealed with laughter, smiling broader than I had in days.

Nico shook his head, an amused sparkle in his eyes. "Let's go eat, shall we?" He grabbed my bag from the seat and closed the door, then the two men escorted me inside.

The little deli was packed. Kendra waved to us from her place in line and pointed toward a group of people preparing to leave. "Danni, grab that table for us, and I'll get your food—Caesar salad?"

"As always." I reached for a chair as soon as the other customers moved away, but Nico grabbed it first and motioned for me to sit. "This is a pretty small table—I don't know how many more people are coming." I scanned the room, but nothing else was available. "Do we need more chairs?"

Nico tilted his head, a confused expression on his face. He

sat directly across from me. "It's just the four of us. Well, maybe one more."

Our legs brushed under the table, and the aftereffects of the brief contact rippled through me. "It's just—"

I swept a crumb from the table and fumbled with my bag, all the while searching for Kendra. *What is taking her so damn long?* Instead of hurrying right over, rushing to my rescue, she lingered by the deli counter. Her hand rested on Logan's arm as she laughed at whatever he was saying, the tray with our lunch carelessly balanced on one hip.

"Kendra said—well, I thought—" I propped my elbows on the table and let my forehead crash against my palms. *Set up again.* There was no holding back the frustrated groan building inside me. "Could I really be that gullible?"

"Don't blame me."

I split my fingers apart to peek at Nico.

He held up his hands in surrender. "I had nothing to do with this. Not that I'm complaining."

And there it was, that damn irresistible grin again.

Focus, Danni. You can get through this. Taking a deep breath, I leaned back in my seat and let my hands drop to my lap. "So, you're a personal trainer?"

"I'm certified, but—"

"It's worse than that." Logan returned with a tray full of food and settled into the seat next to Nico. "He owns that joint." He took a bite of his wrap and let out a satisfied groan.

"Really?" I didn't know why, but that surprised me.

Kendra slipped into the seat beside me without a word.

"Nice of you to join us . . . finally," I whispered and grabbed my salad from her tray.

"Yeah. Scrawny as he is, it was the only way he could get hired." Logan drew back, apparently expecting some sort of retaliation from Nico, but it never came.

I loaded my fork and paused. "How long have you two known each other?" They clearly had a close relationship, acting the way brothers would.

"Freshman year in college. Our rooms were on the same floor," Nico said.

"I was impressed that anyone could have such a steady stream of sexy co-eds flowing in and out of his room. I had to introduce myself." Logan had a very animated way of talking with hand gestures and facial expressions that drew me in.

Nico shrugged. "He worshiped me. I took pity on him. And we eventually became best friends."

I couldn't help but join in with Logan's infectious laughter.

His eyes locked on Kendra. "And that's still working in my favor." He reached across the table and brushed his fingers over her wrist.

I squinted at Kendra's face, certain I must have imagined the rosy glow on her cheeks. *Probably just the lighting.* I picked at my lunch and glanced around the room—anything to avoid looking at Nico.

The door opened. A dark and formidable-looking man entered the deli—black hair, black sunglasses, black jeans, black boots, and black leather jacket. He approached our table, staring at me with an unreadable expression.

"What can I say? Women love me." Nico's voice recaptured my attention. His smile was smug.

Logan leaned on his forearms with a knowing grin. "All women, Nico? What about New Year's Eve?"

Nico's eyes flashed to me.

"Uh-oh, care to dish about what happened with your *charming* date that night?" I shoved another bite of salad in my mouth and watched him squirm.

Nico's mouth pressed in a hard, straight line. "Nothing to tell—"

The man in black walked up behind Nico and slapped his hands on Nico's shoulders, leaning past him to talk to me. "Ahh, now that's a touchy subject. See, Nico here's not used to getting shot down."

The man squeezed Nico's shoulders and gave them a shake. He dragged a chair from a nearby table and plopped down next to Nico, grabbed his veggie wrap, and took a huge bite.

"Oh, that's disgusting!" He washed it down with a giant gulp of Nico's water, making exaggerated faces the whole time. "Why do you insist on eating that healthy shit? An occasional burger isn't going to kill you."

Nico hooked his arm around the man's neck, pulling him close. "Glad you could finally make it. Danni, this barbarian is my little brother, Ben."

Ben struggled in Nico's hold while scanning our trays.

"What happened to your plan for the gym this morning?" Nico asked, tightening his hold.

"Plans change. I had an incredibly hot date last night . . ." Ben grabbed an unused plastic fork from the center of the table and poked Nico's forearm. A satisfied grin spread across his face when Nico let go. Ben pulled off his sunglasses and winked at me with exotic jade eyes. "And it didn't end until noon today."

Logan reached across Nico to deliver a high five.

What was it with guys needing to announce their conquests? My eyes rolled, an involuntary reflex. I looked at Kendra, needing someone to commiserate with. She'd been quiet since joining us, presumably enjoying the interaction between these three men as much as I was, but the lecherous look on her face told a different story. Logan had better watch out.

"Hey, there are ladies present," Nico said in a dignified tone, but I wasn't buying the act.

"So I guess that means we can't talk about the way Trina

was hanging all over you last night either?" Logan landed a slap on Nico's stiff back as he teased his friend. "I was worried you two weren't even going to make it the four blocks to her apart—" The table shook, and Logan let out a yell. "What the hell was that for?"

Nico propped his elbow on the table and stroked his chin while hitting his friend with an icy stare. "Nothing. Happened. With Trina. We've been over this before."

"Oh, shit!" Kendra grabbed Nico's wrist and twisted his arm to get a better look at his watch. She turned to me then glanced at my half-eaten salad. "We've gotta run. I need to pick up Callie from cheer practice in fifteen minutes. I'm so sorry."

"Not a problem." I hoped my voice didn't show how relieved I was to get out of there. *Better play it down a bit.* "Um, let me see if I can get a to-go container, and I'll finish eating at home." I stood, eager to rush to the counter, but Nico grabbed my hand and stopped me.

"Stay. Finish your lunch."

Fire raced through my veins, radiating from the point where his thumb caressed the back of my hand.

"I'll take you home."

Ben and Logan both froze, staring at Nico with brows raised and concerned expressions.

"I-I'm, um . . . I—" The text alert rang on my phone, giving me an excuse to break free from his hold. I retrieved it from my bag. Guilt sliced through me as Will's words flashed across the screen.

Hey, babe. My schedule's clear, so hurry home—thought we could go out tonight. Get some dinner. Maybe a movie?

As if waiting for something else to appear, I continued staring blankly at the screen. My voice was weak when I finally found it. "I need to go." I struggled to shut down my emotions before raising my face to look at Nico. "But thank you for the offer."

"Huh, maybe Willdo's smarter than I give him credit for." Kendra looked from me to Nico. "Well, doesn't that just suck."

We gathered our things and said our quick good-byes. I tried to ignore the disheartened look in Nico's eyes when I got to him.

He rested his hand on my shoulder and leaned toward my ear, speaking in a low voice that only I would be able to hear. "I hope I'll get to see you again soon." He paused before releasing me.

I closed my eyes and took a long breath, filling my lungs with his fresh scent. My head bobbed in an imperceptible nod. "I think you broke your promise."

He took a step back and let his hand slide down my arm, giving my hand a gentle squeeze before releasing me. A strange feeling washed over me the second he let go. Cold. Empty. Like something was missing. I double-checked my bag and pockets as Kendra and I crossed the room. Everything I'd come with was present and accounted for.

Logan's strangled voice caught my attention. "What the fuck was that? She's married, Nico. Or did you forget that little detail?"

"Logan's right. You don't want to go down that road." Ben's voice echoed the sentiment.

Against my better judgment, I risked a glance back before exiting the deli.

Nico's hands were clasped behind his head, his face raised toward the ceiling. His body language screamed agony.

He looked the way I felt.

CHAPTER 9

DELUSIONS OF LOVE

Spending time with Nico had turned out to be a worse decision than I'd imagined it would be. If I closed my eyes, which I did half the ride home, I could still feel his rough cheek brush against mine and smell the crisp clean scent of his body wash. No matter how hard I tried, I couldn't erase the memory of his touch or the longing in his words.

I waved to Kendra and Callie as their car pulled away from the curb, then I walked to the family room to search for Will. Some random football game played on the big-screen TV, and my sweet husband lounged on the couch. Sound asleep.

As I stood watching him, a conversation I'd had with Jen a few weeks ago came to mind. Advice she'd given for adding some spice to my marriage grew into a perfect plan. Not only would it heat things up with Will, it was also guaranteed to cast aside any residual thoughts of Nico.

I placed my bags and jacket on the side chair, being careful not to disturb Will. Yet.

After removing the barrette from my hair, I bent forward and ran my fingers through the strands, hoping to create a sexy, tousled look. I toed off my shoes and slipped out of my jeans and panties then approached my sleeping husband. Along the way, I undid a few extra buttons on my blouse, just enough to show off my new black lace bra. *Flashing a little extra cleavage never hurts.*

A preview of his reaction played through my mind—Will sweeping me up in his arms and making passionate love to me while telling me how much he adored me.

I dropped to my knees in front of him and slid open the button on his jeans. My heart beat faster. I licked my lips then carefully tugged down his zipper.

He stirred, mumbling something, but he didn't wake.

I freed him from his jeans and gently stroked his warm flesh, loving the way his body instinctively reacted to my touch. A seductive purr echoed in my throat. I lowered my head to his lap, keeping my gaze fixed on his handsome face.

Will's body jerked. His eyes flew open wide. A bewildered expression shifted to one of ecstasy as he realized this wasn't a dream. Twisting his fingers in my hair, he held me in place and pushed deeper into my mouth, hips pumping in a leisurely rhythm.

There were no words, only the sounds of his pleasure filling the room and encouraging me to continue.

His movements became more urgent, but it was too soon to let this end.

I broke free from his hold to regain control and pressed his hips to the couch. With one slow draw, I pulled away then rose to straddle him. He grabbed my waist, guiding me as I lowered myself onto his erection.

Aaah, this is what I needed. I closed my eyes, reveling in the sweet sensation as he filled the emptiness inside me.

I began riding with slow, easy strokes, adjusting my position to get right amount of pressure where I wanted it. Aching with a desperate need to release the tension I'd been feeling all afternoon, I forced my eyes open and focused on my husband's face. My pace quickened.

Will's fingers dug into my hips. He pulled me down and thrust upward one final time, letting out a guttural groan. His muscles shook with the spasms of his release.

He dropped his hands to his sides and let his head fall back against the couch, staring at the ceiling while we caught our breath.

The moment was gone. My tension remained. I pressed my face into the crook of his neck, kissing him gently while waiting for that peaceful feeling of fulfillment that should have washed over me by now. It never came. But then again, neither did I.

"Well, that was unexpected," he finally said without looking at me.

"That was the plan." I skimmed my lips across his jaw then kissed his mouth. "I just wanted to show you how much I missed you today."

Will didn't respond right away. He took a deep breath and blew it out slowly before lifting his head to look at me. "I shouldn't have given you such a hassle about spending time with Kendra."

My insides tightened. "Well, you don't have to worry. I won't be going back to the gym with her." I combed my fingers through his hair and tried to ignore his puzzled expression. "You were right. It wasn't a good idea." I couldn't tell him the real reason I needed to stay away. I forced a laugh. "Yeah, I have a feeling every muscle I have will be aching tomorrow."

Will nodded slowly. Maybe waiting for me to elaborate. Maybe sensing I was hiding something.

"So, dinner." He slid his hands down my thighs, hooking them behind my knees. "We could go to Giardano's, or Marcello's, or that new Thai place that opened in town."

I tapped my chin, considering the options while I reined in

my guilty conscience. "Tough choice. I love Giardano's, but . . . mmm, pizza sounds delicious. Let's do Marcello's."

My pre-holiday starvation diet hadn't allowed for any of my favorite foods, but I'd burned more than enough calories today to treat myself to a few extra carbs. "Give me ten minutes to get ready." I clasped my hands behind his head and held him to me for a deep kiss.

Will pulled away too soon. "Let's get going. You know I'm always starving after sex." He pushed the hem of my blouse between us before easing me from his lap.

"And sleepy. I wouldn't want to risk having you do a face-plant in your pizza." I scrunched my nose and let my face fall into my palm.

"Smart-ass." He gave me a playful swat on my bottom to send me on my way.

I collected my clothes and raced upstairs to wash and dress for our date.

Tonight will be fun. Dinner. Maybe some drinks and a little dancing. And by the time we get back home, I'll make sure he can't keep his hands off me. I hugged myself in anticipation, a huge smile stretching my cheeks.

That faded when I stepped into the bathroom. Will's towel lay in a heap on the floor again. Had he really just dropped it there when I tossed it at him this morning?

I shook my head, grumbling as I picked up the still-wet ball. "I swear he'd never have a dry towel if it weren't for me."

Will cleared his throat. He stood in the doorway, jeans still hanging open. His grip tightened on the shirt slung over his shoulder. He probably expected an argument or at least another lesson on how to pick up after himself, and it took every bit of my self-control not to give him one. Or the other.

I wrestled with the offensive piece of fabric, aggressively untangling it and folding it in half.

Will's posture as he watched reminded me of Nico—the way he'd leaned against the gym equipment this morning. I wanted to trace the lines of his tattoo like Kendra had, feel the grooves in his muscular arms. Brush my fingers along his stubbled jaw to the sweet dimple in his—

Will tugged the towel from my clenched hands. "I said I'm sorry, babe." He hung it over the bar and moved to the vanity, examining his smoothly shaved face. "Just get ready."

"I, um . . ." *What the hell?* "Yeah, I'm gonna take a quick shower." *And maybe while I'm in there, I can figure out what is going on with me.*

CHAPTER 10

STICK WITH THE PLAN

We were able to get a table right away at Marcello's. I had barely eaten anything all day and thought I would pass out by the time our food arrived. Each mouthful of pizza earned my satisfied-hum seal of approval.

I took my last bite, watching Will as I chewed. He'd been quiet all through dinner. Come to think of it, I wasn't sure he had spoken at all. "Hey, you okay?"

His eyes shifted toward me, a slow, lazy movement. "Hm? Yeah, I'm just really tired." He gave a weak smile. "I think you wore me out."

"Hopefully not too much." I leaned toward him and lowered my voice so the couple at the next table wouldn't hear me. "We could head straight home and have . . . dessert."

"Danni, Will, how nice to see you both."

The exuberant greeting from my boss interrupted my proposition. I looked up and reflexively mirrored his infectious smile.

Mr. Jamison was a caring man with a warm heart who reminded me of a teddy bear . . . without all the fluff. Shortly after taking the position as his assistant at Jamison and

Walters, I'd learned he and my dad had been close friends, which explained why he always seemed to watch out for me.

"Hi, Peter. How were your holidays? Did you get to spend them with Alexia?"

"I did. First time since she was a little girl. It was very nice." He looked at Will. "My ex-wife moved to Kansas when we split—wasn't pretty. She took Lexi and didn't let me see her very often."

"Yeah, I think Danielle had told me about that."

"Anyway, she's grown now. Twenty-eight. She came running home last summer after hitting a rough patch with her mom." He chuckled and leaned in, cupping a hand to his mouth. "I've been there—wouldn't even want to put my worst enemy through it."

"Well, I'm sure you're both enjoying the opportunity to spend time together," Will said. His response sounded stiff.

"It's nice having her here. But she's been moping around the house the past few weeks, complaining that she's tired and doesn't feel well. I think she's bored and just needs something constructive to do." He rubbed his palms together, a look of anticipation lighting his face. "So I found a place for her at Jamison and Walters." He tipped his head from side to side, hesitating. "She can be a little shy though, so . . . well, I'm hoping maybe you can help her fit in a little?"

Maybe that explained why she never stopped in the office to see him or have lunch. "I'd love to. Can't wait—"

Will coughed and sputtered, his mug of beer still in his hand.

"Careful there, son." Peter moved closer to slap Will's back.

I grabbed my napkin and wiped up what had spilled. "You all right, babe?"

"Yeah, sorry. Guess I swallowed wrong or something." Will shrugged.

"That happens sometimes. Well, I better get back to my friend before she leaves without me. See you on Monday, Danni. Good seeing you again, Will." He squeezed Will's shoulder. "Oh, I almost forgot to ask, did you two have a good time at Elevations on New Year's Eve?"

I tilted my head at him. "We had a very nice night, but how did you know?"

Peter pulled a hand to his chest and flashed Will an apologetic glance. "I'm sorry. You said it was a surprise, but I just assumed you told—"

"No worries. I meant to, but I guess we were too busy celebrating. It slipped my mind."

"Logan does throw one hell of a party. I'm glad Will remembered the stories I told him back in August. At the company picnic, was it?"

Will nodded. "That's right."

Peter leaned toward me, lowering his voice. "I don't actually remember that conversation, but I may have had a few too many that day." He winked and stood up to include Will again. "Anyway, Will asked if I could get you two on the guest list, and I was more than happy to help out. When I talked to Logan, I believe his response was, 'The more, the merrier,' but that's Logan for you."

"Yeah, he seems like a pretty fun guy," I said.

A crease formed between Will's brows. "I didn't realize you'd talked to him."

"I met him at the gym today. And lunch." I cringed on the inside. Why couldn't I keep my mouth shut?

Peter placed his hand on my shoulder. "I've taken up enough of your time. You folks enjoy your evening."

"Good night." I waited until he was a few tables away then turned back to Will. "How come you never told me you talked to Peter?"

"It wasn't a very exciting story, so I went with keeping it a mystery." Will finished the last of his beer.

"Listen, before I forget, I talked with Mr. Harlow this afternoon. He needs me to go to Chicago for a few days to meet with that potential client about the smart condos. The only day this guy has available is Saturday two weeks from now—I think he's flying back late Friday night from somewhere out west. Anyway, I'll need to leave Friday morning, and I'll catch a flight back on Sunday."

Will had been talking about this project for a few weeks, some huge property with upscale condos—a prototype of a smart building, or something like that. I always got lost on the technical details.

He won't be with the client all the time. I traced the condensation on my glass, deciding if I should make the suggestion bouncing around in my head. *It could be fun.* "You know, I could go with you. Make it a romantic getaway." I raised my eyes to see his reaction. "After you take care of business, of course."

He reached across the table, covering my hand with his. "Not this time, babe. Harlow made it clear that this is an important job to land, and he needs me to really schmooze. Lots of time spent with the client, and I'll need to stay focused. It won't be a fun trip."

"I'm sure it will be fun for you, but . . . I get it." I tried to hide my disappointment.

"It's only two days. Why don't you visit Jen, spend some time with Caden?" Will was talking to me, but his attention was definitely somewhere else again.

Seconds ticked by. He stared past me, mindlessly caressing my hand.

I waved my free hand in front of his face. "Hey. You in there?"

Will blinked several times as he returned to me. "Huh? Oh,

sorry. Guess I, um . . . I'm not sure where my mind went." He released my hand and leaned back in his seat. "You ready to go?" He motioned for the waiter without waiting for my response.

WE WERE BACK HOME by eight thirty. Will had draped his jacket over the kitchen chair and deposited his shoes beside it before I even walked through the door.

He pulled me to him as I passed and wrapped me in a gentle embrace. "I'm sorry I wasn't very good company tonight."

I reached up to kiss him. "We were together. That's all that matters. You okay though? You seem worried or upset." As the words slid out, it occurred to me that he had reason to be. I leaned back to look in his eyes. "Nothing happened at the gym, Will, and I told you I'm not going back."

"I know, babe. I just feel really drained today." He brushed my hair away from my face and kissed the tip of my nose. "Partly your fault. I'm going to call it an early night—maybe watch TV in bed until I fall asleep."

As he walked away, a small part of me wondered if he sensed my turmoil of emotions. *Enough.* This crazy obsession with Nico had to stop. Now. No more behaving like an out-of-control, raging-hormone twenty-something . . . like that little bimbo, Trina.

I need a drink. I poured myself a big glass of wine and carried it to the family room, where I curled up in the corner of the couch to read. By the third time reading the same page, I knew it was useless. My mind kept drifting to Will . . . then Nico . . . then back to Will.

"Hey, Danni. What's up?"

My phone was in my hand. Jen was on the other end of the

line. How did that happen? I didn't remember getting it out of my back pocket or calling her.

"Danni? You there? You okay?"

"I-I'm here. Did I call you?"

Jen laughed, but it sounded tight and laced with concern. "Yeah, are you drunk?"

A quick glance to my glass confirmed I had only taken a few sips. "No. I should be, but . . . no. I didn't even realize I called you. Guess I, um . . . guess I needed to talk." I pushed the book from my lap and slid to the edge of my seat.

"You're kinda makin' me nervous here. You all right?"

Will had said he was going to bed, but I needed to be sure. This was bound to be a conversation I wouldn't want him to overhear. "Hang on a sec."

I crossed the family room and glanced up the stairs, confirming that our bedroom door was closed. Faint voices from the TV on the other side mixed with the rumble of Will's snoring.

"Okay, coast is clear." I pulled the blanket from the back of the couch as I settled into my seat and took a huge gulp of wine.

"Spill, Danni. What's going on?" Her question sounded more like a demand.

Where to start. Resting my elbow on the overstuffed arm, I pressed my forehead into my palm. "Remember that guy I told you about from New Year's Eve?" My words sounded shaky.

"Mmm, yeah. Nico." Her voice had a dreamy quality to it, as she obviously remembered the delicious details I'd shared about how amazing he looked and sounded.

"I ran into him again. Well, more like Kendra made sure I ran into him. Turns out he's a friend of hers."

Jen was silent, and I began to wonder if she'd even heard me. "That sounds like Kendra. It also sounds like it's going to be a problem for you, isn't it?"

"Pretty much." I spent the next fifteen minutes giving her a blow-by-blow recap of my entire day.

"So what do I do? I love Will. I don't want to hurt him, and I would never cheat on him. Never." Thirsty from talking so much, and needing to dull the ache in my chest, I grabbed my wine glass and chugged down most of the contents before continuing.

"But Nico, he makes me feel things I've never felt before—tingles in places I've never felt them. He's like this potent, exotic drug whenever he's around, promising to take my body on a magical journey and make my soul soar, and I just want more. Want to feel more. And knowing I'll never be able to have even a small taste of that is painful. Physically painful. Like a tension headache that's spread through my entire body."

Jen exhaled a heavy breath. "Danni . . . shit. What you're describing is the way I feel around Ryan. And what I imagine it would feel like if I couldn't have him." She was quiet for a few seconds. "Question is, what do you do about it?" She sounded as if she were delivering a terminal diagnosis.

I knew what my answer would be before she even asked the question. "There's only one option. I stick with the plan to save my marriage. It's just . . . sometimes I'm not sure Will's on the same page." I swiped away the tears that fell to my cheeks. "You have your family, Jen. People, besides me, to love you. Will is my family, all I'll ever have. He came along when I needed that most, and I have to believe it's because we belong together."

"I know you do. So it sounds to me like you've made up your mind. Why don't I come up and spend the weekend with you when Will's away? We could both use some good ol'-fashioned girl time."

My voice trembled as I sucked back a sob. "I'd like that. A lot."

"All right then, we have a date." Her voice was back to her

normal cheery sound. "You call me if you need to talk more before then, okay?"

"Yeah. Thanks, Jen. I love you."

"I know. I love you too. Now go get some sleep. You sound exhausted."

"Night, Jen." I pressed the button to end the call and downed the rest of my wine. She was right—I was exhausted. I fluffed the pillow next to me then hugged it to my chest, our conversation replaying in my mind.

"Danielle. Wake up, babe."

Gentle fingers brushed the side of my face, tracing the path my tears had taken earlier. I opened my eyes to Will's face directly in front of me.

"What are you doing down here? It's three a.m."

So much tenderness filled his voice, melting my icy fear of losing him. He slid his arms under me, scooping me up, and carried me to bed.

"I love you, Will."

"I know, babe." He kissed my temple and squeezed me tight.

CHAPTER 11

FRIENDS

I stepped out of my car in the parking garage of Brookdale Tower, not remembering anything about the drive there. Monday morning. Back to work.

I'd barely slept last night. That uneasy feeling I'd been enduring for days continued to gnaw at me. Thoughts of Nico consumed me. Guilt tore at me.

By the time the first signs of daylight had peeked through my bedroom curtains, I had given up any hope of sleeping or relieving the knot of tension in my stomach. I'd slipped out of bed without Will noticing and rushed through my morning routine. Before leaving our bedroom, I set an alarm for him. I shouldn't have. He did say he wanted to "sleep," after all.

The security guard greeted me as I entered the lobby and passed through the turnstiles. The building was quiet now, but it would be a hub of activity in another hour or two.

The elevator ride to the eighteenth floor took less than a minute, delivering me to my second home, the offices of Jamison and Walters, PR. I flipped on the lights, taking a deep breath as I glanced around the office. *Routine. Normalcy.* I didn't have to worry about surprises here.

My shoulders relaxed. My tension eased. Even the cluttered mess of papers strewn across my desk was a welcome sight.

I started my computer and settled into my chair, waiting for the system to come to life. My eyes locked on the framed photo next to the monitor, and my mind drifted to last night.

At some point during the night, I'd tried waking Will for a little romance, something I'd never done before. It made sense to me, in the moment, that relieving a little tension would help me sleep. Plus, I thought guys liked that spontaneous stuff, which meant it fit perfectly with my plan to fix my marriage.

I must have been misinformed, because Will didn't appreciate the interruption. He'd pushed me away before turning to his side, pulling the covers tight to his chin, and grunting that he wanted to sleep.

The photo in front of me grew blurry.

It seemed the only time we had sex anymore was when I initiated it and didn't take no for an answer . . . except for my birthday. Now that night had been amazing.

I picked up the photo, taken in Jamaica on our tenth wedding anniversary. I barely recognized myself with an enormous smile on my tanned face. Will's arms were wrapped around me in a tight embrace, his lips pressed to my temple. I returned the photo to its place then angled it away from me and dove into my work.

It took nearly an hour to find my desk under the files dropped there in my absence and sift through countless e-mails. A quick glance at the clock showed I still had an hour to check the PowerPoint file and set up Peter's office for his eight-thirty meeting with . . .

I clicked on the calendar to open the details. "No way. Logan?"

"Danni!" Kristi Warwick, my coworker and close friend, burst through the office doors. She was a tiny package with a larger-than-life personality. Kristi came to Jamison and Walters about five years ago, fresh out of college, and ran the Outreach Department.

She rushed toward me, arms outstretched. You would have thought I'd been gone for two years instead of only two weeks.

"Hey there, stranger," I said. "Where have you been hiding?" Her mood was contagious, and a huge smile stretched across my face. "Wow, look at you. You're glowing!"

"Oh, Danni, I'm in love! And for real this time." She threw her arms around me, pulling me into her small frame for a lively hug. After a few seconds, she stepped back but kept hold of my hands. "He is so amazing, and hot, and just absolutely perfect. You're gonna love him too; I know you will. His name is Ben, and he plays in a band. Well, it's not his real job; it's just for fun. He's actually the CFO at Elevations, can you believe—his family owns it! But anyway, that's how we met. The band, I mean. Oh, and he has this really sexy voice and incredibly gorgeous eyes that are the most exotic shade of gr—"

"Take it easy." I grabbed her shoulders and looked in her sparkling blue eyes. "Breathe, Kristi." My chest shook with a stifled laugh, and I struggled to get out the rest of my words. "You're going to hyperventilate again. And then I'll have to go steal someone's lunch, again, to get you a paper bag to breathe into."

Her eyes popped open wide. She nodded then took a huge breath, broke into an even bigger smile, and wrapped me in another tight hug. "Sorry. I've just been dying to tell you about him. I guess it all sort of erupted out of me."

"You know, you could have called me instead of sending cryptic text messages all week telling me you met someone."

"I know. And I should have, but I wanted to tell you in person. It's so much more fun. Besides, I was a little too . . . *busy* . . . to spend time on the phone." She giggled, swaying her hips, then grabbed my arm and tugged me forward. "Come with me. I need coffee."

I laughed, following her to the break room. "The last thing you need is caffeine."

She smiled at me with a mischievous grin and lowered her voice. "See, that's where you'd be wrong. Ben had me up—or should I say *he* was up—most of the night." Her cheeks turned a pale shade of pink that almost matched the streaks in her blonde hair. She turned away to fill her mug with coffee.

"Oh, almost forgot . . ." She faced me, leaning against the counter. "You *have* to promise to go with me next time his band plays. I'm sure we can get Kendra to go too—make it a girls' night, you know? We haven't had one in a really long time. It'll be such a blast! Which reminds me—well not really that any of this reminded me, but I just remembered to ask—anyway, how are things going with you and Will? Back to settin' the sheets on fire?" She gave me a playful nudge and exaggerated wink.

Definitely not last night. "Not quite, but I'm working on it. And girls' night sounds fun. Let me know the date."

Kristi watched me, a small pout on her face. Her expression told me she was waiting for details.

"We'll talk about that later. Listen, I need to set up for Peter's eight-thirty meeting with Logan VanBergen. You have anything in the works for that project? It was just added while I was off, and I didn't see a file."

"Oh, now he's dreamy. I have all my files in a shared folder, so you can grab them from there." She took a tentative sip from her mug. "Did you get to meet him at his party? I'm dying to know if he's as charming in person as he looks in his ad photos."

"Not at the party, but Kendra and I met him at The Next Level on Saturday. I think she's got a little bit of . . . a crush."

We both laughed. That seemed like an odd word to use when talking about Kendra.

"Anyway, we went to lunch with him and his friend after the gym, and I've never seen Kendra so focused on someone. Or quiet."

"Seriously? Wow, Kendra quiet is like . . ."

"You depressed?" I rested my elbows on the counter next to her.

"Exactly!" She leaned closer and lowered her voice. "I wonder if they hooked up."

"If they did, I'm sure we'll hear about it." Kendra loved to share every single detail. I rolled my eyes just thinking about it. "Okay, I better get back to work." I paused before leaving. "Lunch later?"

"Definitely! I'll come get you."

A chat with Kristi always cheered me up. But the renewed energy I left the break room with didn't last very long. My pace slowed as I approached my desk. A vaguely familiar-looking woman snooped around it, touching every item as if she were browsing a gift shop. She picked up the picture of Will and me, pulled it toward her face for closer inspection, and brushed a finger across the glass.

What the hell? I never understood why some people couldn't keep their hands to themselves. "Excuse me. Is there something I can help you with?" Keeping my voice polite while watching someone violate my personal space was difficult, but I managed. Barely.

I plopped my coffee mug on the corner of my desk and reclaimed my photo, rubbing it against my skirt before returning it to its place. "Do you have an appointment with someone? I can direct you to—"

"You look so happy." Her pensive comment was barely audible. She shifted her eyes to mine then returned her focus to the photo. "In the picture. I . . . um . . ."

She took a single deep breath. Her shoulders relaxed as she let it out and turned, skimming over me with an assessing gaze. An angelic smile spread across her delicate face. She brushed her long chestnut hair away from her cheek and smoothed it down across her collarbone.

"You must be Danielle. I'm Alexia. Jamison. Peter's daughter." There was a sweet innocence in the melodic tones of her voice. "I hope I didn't offend you. Your lovely picture caught my attention while I was waiting for you to return." She looked down at her hands, clasped tightly together.

I shouldn't have been so harsh. She was clearly uncomfortable, and I could sympathize with that. I put on my best fake smile and greeted her properly. "It's nice to meet you, Alexia. You can call me Danni. If there's anything I can do to help you get settled in, let me know."

I tried not to stare but couldn't stop myself. Maybe I'd seen her in a picture in Peter's office. I couldn't remember. "Your, um . . . your dad is really excited that you're joining the team, so we're glad to have you here."

She stepped closer, her dark green eyes locked on mine like a dog vying for dominance, but her voice remained cordial. "Daddy talks about you all the time. He really adores you, you know. Says you're almost like a second daughter." She gave a nervous laugh. "Guess that makes us sort of like sisters, right?"

"Good morning, Danni. I see you already met Alexia." Mr. Jamison emerged from his office and joined us. "Or maybe you two met at the picnic last summer?"

"Good morning, Peter. Alexia just introduced herself, but I do think I've seen her before."

"I'm going to give Alexia a quick tour of the place and get her set up with Kristi. I should be back in plenty of time for my meeting, but you can have Logan wait in my office if he gets here before I return.”

I EXITED Peter’s office after setting up for his meeting and nearly crashed into Logan.

“Danni? I didn’t expect to see you here.”

“I work here. Mr. Jamison’s assistant.” I smiled. “He had something to take care of, but he’ll be back shortly. Let me take your coat, and you can relax in his office.” I led him to the conference table and gripped the back of the chair across from him. “Can I get you something to drink? Coffee? Tea? Water?”

“Nothing right now, thanks.”

“I’ll be right outside. At my desk. Let me know if you need anything.” Logan had been fun to talk to at lunch on Saturday, but there was a palpable tension between us this time. I was glad for the opportunity to escape and go back to my own space.

“Wait, aren’t you going to keep me company?”

I stopped in the doorway and turned to face him. “Oh. Well, I guess I could.”

It was an unusual request from a client, but I didn’t see how I could refuse. I slid back a chair and sat on the edge with my hands in my lap, tracing the hem of my skirt. An awkward silence hung heavy in the air. Was he expecting me to say something?

“You can relax. Nico won’t be here today.”

I lifted my eyes to look at him, hoping they didn’t betray me. “Why would I—”

“Don’t bother trying to hide it. I’ve seen the way you two look at each other.” He propped his elbow on the table and stroked his chin, continuing to watch me.

Kristi's earlier remark about Logan popped into my head. I hadn't taken a close look at him on Saturday—no doubt because I hadn't been able to pull my eyes off of Nico long enough. I wasn't sure dreamy would be my choice to describe Logan though. A small scar below his right eye added character to his rugged face. And a bump near the bridge of his nose suggested it had been broken at one time. Together, they gave him a distinctive bad-boy charm.

"He's a really good guy, you know." Logan let out a heavy sigh and leaned back in his chair. "I'm just not sure where his head is right now. I mean—" He rubbed his hands over his short-cropped hair and seemed to struggle choosing the right words. "I'm just sayin' that Nico knows you're married. And I know him well enough to say he would *never* cross that line."

"Well, I'm certainly not looking for an affair. But I am curious how you can be so sure about Nico." I folded my arms over my churning stomach and waited for his response, hoping his reason would make me as confident as he appeared to be.

He hesitated, a conflicted look on his face. "That's not my story to tell. You'll just have to trust me on it."

And that wasn't the answer I needed to hear. "Honestly, I'm not sure why you're telling me any of this. I barely know him, and I'll prob—"

"That's exactly why I'm telling you." He leaned toward me. "You see what he wants you to see—the image he works so hard to portray. I don't want him to get hurt."

"Then maybe you should tell him to stop hitting on a married woman." I placed my palms on the table and leaned forward to look him in the eye.

"Yeah well, we covered that pretty in-depth on Saturday." Logan paused to rub his hand. "He's really upset about the way he behaved."

I got the impression that meant Logan had torn into Nico

until he realized he was wrong. Maybe because I'd overheard Logan's initial remark when Kendra and I were leaving the deli.

"I guess what I'm trying to say is just cut him some slack. Give him a chance to work it out." He raised his hands. "And—don't take this the wrong way—but I have a feeling you need to work out a few things yourself."

"I already—"

"Logan! It's so good to see you again." Mr. Jamison entered the room.

"He's all yours, Peter." I jumped from my seat, eager to escape. "Logan, it was . . . interesting." I was through the doorway before the words were completely out of my mouth.

"Thanks for the company, Danni. I enjoyed our chat."

THE FRONT OFFICE door opened at quarter to twelve, and my skin tingled. Nico entered, looking incredibly sexy. He wore a navy suit with a crisp white shirt, and his usual air of confidence. His eyes caught mine as he approached, but they lacked the playful spark they'd had the other times I'd seen him.

"Looks like you've changed the dress code at The Next Level." A nervous laugh slipped out, but I tried to pass it off as laughing at my own joke.

Nico seemed to relax a bit. "Good to see you again, Danni. Logan gave me some papers that Mr. Jamison needed me to sign." He held up a folder I hadn't noticed before. "I'm just dropping them off."

Apparently Logan also told him to behave. I hesitated, trying to make sense of Nico standing in front of me at work, my surprise-free zone.

He dipped his head, meeting my stare. "I'm Logan's business partner. Sorry, I assumed he told you."

"Oh, I think he forgot to mention that one tiny detail." *Deep breaths, Danni. You're at work. Be professional.* "Do you need to see Peter about any of them?"

"We already discussed them over the phone last week." He tapped the edge of the folder on my desk, hesitating before handing it to me. "Listen, it's just about lunch time. I thought maybe you'd like to grab a bite?"

I was glad to be sitting right now. My legs might not be able to support me if I were to stand. "I'm really sorry. I have other plans." *Now or never. You know what you need to do.* "But even if I didn't, I don't think it would be a good idea."

Nico looked as though he'd been slapped. His jaw tensed. He closed his eyes and took a deep breath. "I'm sorry. I realize the way I acted before isn't acceptable. And I'd really like to be friends—I need at least that much." He watched me, waiting for my answer.

I picked up his folder. "I-I don't think I can. Thank you for dropping these off. I'll see Peter gets them." I stood to escape to his office, hoping Nico would be gone by the time I came back out.

He grabbed my wrist as I stepped away. "Please stop running."

I turned to look at him but didn't know what to say.

"Give me a chance. Friends, Danni. Nothing more. I promise I won't hurt you."

I swallowed hard and looked to his face. The right thing to do was tell him it wouldn't work. Why couldn't I make those words come out? "I need to think about it."

"That's better than no." One corner of his mouth turned up in a lopsided grin. "I'll take it." He stepped back and let his hand slide to mine, squeezing it gently before releasing me. "Bye, Danni." He winked then turned to leave.

Kristi emerged from the back section of the office suite as

Nico walked toward the door. Her eyes popped, and her mouth opened slightly. She looked between the two of us as she approached my desk.

"Holy hell! Who . . . was that?" Her voice was a little louder than need be. But at least the door had closed, with Nico on the other side, before her words flew out.

I groaned and grabbed my coat. "*That* was trouble. Let's get lunch."

CHAPTER 12
TEMPTING OFFER

The brief encounter with Nico at my office on Monday was the only time I'd seen him all week. In person, that is. He still made nightly appearances in my dreams—gazing at me with his warm chocolate eyes, his dark hair perfectly messed and looking like he'd been rolling around in bed with me for hours.

I let out a faint sigh and shook off the fantasy before his soothing, deep voice started whispering seductive promises again.

And now I've got this to deal with. I couldn't stop staring at the e-mail that arrived a few minutes ago.

"Danni!"

My head snapped up as Kristi approached my desk, bubbly as always and wearing a huge smile that screamed *weekend*. Her pace quickened, and her rushed words started spilling out before she reached me.

"I've got great news! And you are going to be so excited—at least you better be. So I just talked to Ben. Well, technically we texted, but that part doesn't matter. Except to me, of course, because I didn't get to hear that sexy voice of his." She paused and gave a wistful sigh. "Anyway, the important thing is that his band is scheduled to play next Friday night at Metro Sky. Which means . . . girls' night out!" Kristi gave a restrained squeal, quietly clapping as she bounced in her wedged heels. "But, even better, you don't have to wait that long to meet him, because he's going to join us for happy hour tonight. You did get my message about that, didn't you?"

She stopped rambling long enough to scan my cluttered desk and gave me a questioning look. "Why aren't you cleaned up and ready to go?"

"Sorry. I just told Peter I'd stay late to help him with some last-minute changes on the VanBergen account." I grabbed her hand and gave it a gentle squeeze. "Kendra will still be there, but shoot, if I'd known Ben—"

"Don't worry." She covered my hand with hers. Her look of disappointment was gone as quickly as it had appeared. She leaned down to give me a hug. "I plan on keeping this one. You'll have plenty of other chances to meet him. Like next Friday?" She pulled back to look at me.

I'd never been to Metro Sky. The trendy nightclub, located on the top floor of a high-rise downtown, had opened over the summer and had quickly earned a reputation for being "the place" for the upscale crowd to hang out. Flashbacks of the guests at Logan's New Year's Eve party flooded my mind, reminding me how uncomfortable I felt among people like that —so out of place.

Kristi waited for me to answer, her hopeful expression pleading with me to agree.

How could I refuse? "Sure. Next Friday. Sounds like fun." I smiled, a lame attempt at looking enthused. *Maybe she didn't notice.*

She released me but didn't straighten up. My stomach

clenched as her gaze locked on my computer screen and the open e-mail I should have deleted. *Damn.*

"Danni?" Kristi drew my name out in long, tense syllables. She turned her head toward me and lowered her voice. "I thought you said you were focused on Will? That Nico had just been a temporary distraction—a little bump on your road to happiness?

"But this?" She waved her hand at the screen. "Well, it sounds to me like he plans on sticking around until you come to your senses and pick him. *Not* that I'm saying that's what you should do . . . although he sounds *really* hot, and Will can be a total ass at times." Her hands flew to her mouth, and she gasped before offering a muffled apology. "Inner voice—I didn't mean for that to come out. Oh God, Danni. I'm so sorry!"

I hated that she said it. I hated more that it all was true. "You're entitled to your opinions. And I'm glad you share them so freely. That's what friends do, right?"

"I just want you to be head-over-heels, sappy in love. Like me." She gave me another tight squeeze. "Speaking of which, I better get going. Don't want to give Ben time to shop for a replacement." She giggled as she walked away. When she reached the door, she turned back to throw me a kiss.

After she was gone, my eyes wandered to the e-mail I'd already read six or seven times.

I'll be at The Next Level tomorrow morning with a clear sched-ule. Hope you'll join me. We can put together a custom workout for you while we get to know each other better. Looking forward to spending some time with my new friend. ~Nico

"Shit." My finger hovered over the Delete button as I read through the message one last time.

"Everything okay, Danielle?"

Great. I let my finger drop to the keyboard, deleting the e-mail before I got wrapped up in another conversation and forgot about it again. "Alexia, hi. I didn't realize you were still here."

"I was in one of those comfy chairs in reception. I think I may have dozed off waiting for my dad to finish." She gave a dainty stretch then casually smoothed the fabric of her peplum top. A faint smile lit her face when she returned her attention to me. "Guess I'm not used to working. I'm just so exhausted by the end of the day."

"There's still some coffee in the break room if you'd like a little pick-me-up."

"Oh, no thanks. I need to stay away from caffeine." She shrugged but didn't elaborate.

I studied her, wondering what her life had been like growing up without her dad. Had *her* mother loved and nurtured her? She was so beautiful and sweet but apparently very shy. I hadn't seen her talk to anyone in the office all week.

"You know, some friends and I are having a girls' night next Friday. You're welcome to join us if you'd like."

She bit her lip, making her smile barely noticeable. "I have plans for that weekend, but thanks for inviting me." Her green eyes sparkled over rosy cheeks.

I recognized that look, the same one I'd seen in the mirror when planning my night away with Will a few weeks ago. "Okay, maybe the next time."

"That would be nice. I'd like us to be friends." She brushed her chestnut hair away from her face, tugging at the long strands in what appeared to be a nervous habit.

"Since we are kinda like sisters, right?" I said.

She laughed.

"Well, I better get back to work so you can go home and get some rest."

CHAPTER 13

EXCUSES

Running errands Saturday morning gave me a valid excuse for passing on a trip to the gym. When my phone vibrated on the kitchen counter, I wasn't the least bit surprised to see Kendra's name on the screen. Actually, I would have been shocked if she *hadn't* called.

I pressed the button. "Hi, Ke—"

"So you bail on happy hour, and you blow off Nico's invitation to the gym. You avoiding your friends for any particular reason? Or are you just trying to hide from the truth?"

"Jeeze, who wound you up already today?"

"He was looking for you, you know. The whole time. And he looked pretty damn hot too."

I rolled my eyes at her melodramatic rant. "So did you meet Ben last night?"

Kendra laughed. "You're not getting off the hook that easily, sweetie. But I'll concede for now."

"Because you love me," I teased.

"Because I'm feeling generous." Kendra never could stay mad at me, and I could hear the smile in her voice already. "Ben got delayed in some board meeting, and I had to leave to pick up Callie from cheer practice, so I missed meeting him. Anyway, I told Kristi we'd go with her to Metro Sky. *All* of us. So don't bother trying to come up with some lame-ass excuse to get out of it."

"Yes, dear. Besides, I already promised Kristi I'd go. It's just—"

"Nope. Don't you dare say it."

I sucked in a breath and forged ahead. "It feels wrong going out while Will's away."

Kendra groaned. "That makes it perfect. It's a *girls'* night. And this way you don't have to feel all guilty about leaving Willy-nilly home alone, or whatever. Enough about him though. I need to run. Just called to see what brilliant excuse you came up with for avoiding Nico today, but I see you don't have one yet. You're gonna have to face him sooner or later, you know."

"I vote for later. Much, much later."

"Oh, sweetie, you can't hide from love. See ya." The line went dead.

I stared at the lifeless phone in my hand. "I am not in love with Nico, and I can ignore him for as long as I want."

She did have a point about Will though. It wasn't like he'd be going with us if he were home. *So why does it feel like such a bad idea?*

Resignation setting in, I typed a quick text to Jen.

Me: *Hitting the club Friday night with Kendra and Kristi— bring your party dress.*

Her response came a few seconds later.

Jen: *Awesome idea! But how pissed is Will?*

He didn't trust Kendra and hated when I went out with the girls, which Jen knew from my years of complaining about it.

Me: *He doesn't know. Probably won't tell him.*

Jen: *You sure that's a good idea? Sounds more like looking for trouble than fixing a relationship.*

I groaned, hating that she was right.

Me: *Not sure about anything lately. See you Friday.*

CHAPTER 14

REJECTIONS

How did Friday morning get here so fast? I missed Will already, and he didn't even leave for his trip yet.

Hot water pulsed against my body, failing to ease the tension that had been building for days. It was getting late. I turned off the faucet and pushed aside the steamy glass door.

Will stood brushing his teeth, his back to me. He seemed oblivious to my presence as I dried off and secured the towel around my chest. I moved behind him and wrapped my arms around his waist, tracing my fingers across his abdomen. My chest heaved as I snuggled against him, starved for physical contact.

"You know, I could still call off work today—take a personal day and go with you."

His body tensed.

I raised my head enough to catch his reflected gaze in the small section of mirror he'd wiped clear. Will looked away after only a moment. He leaned forward to spit his toothpaste into the sink then dragged the back of his hand across his mouth.

"Drop it, Danielle." A weary undertone clung to his flat voice.

He'd been under a lot of stress—putting in a lot of hours in preparation for tomorrow's presentation and meetings. I could help him relax if he'd stop shutting me out.

"I ju—"

"How many times must we go over this? I can't have any distractions on this trip. I can't take you with me. Period." He pushed away from the counter, easily breaking free from my hold. "I need to get ready."

His image grew blurry as he stormed from the room. *Don't you dare cry.*

I sucked in a shaky breath, biting the inside of my lip to steel myself. Following him into our room, I sat on the foot of our bed and watched him get dressed. "Did I do something wrong?"

He continued buttoning his shirt without looking at me. "Other than piss me off when I'm trying to get ready to leave on a trip? No."

"It's just . . . well, you've seemed off all week. Distracted or something." I hated the vulnerability, the weakness, in my voice.

His shoulders slumped forward, as if deflated by the rush of air he expelled. He crossed the room and took hold of my arms, pausing to study me. "I've got a lot on my mind, Danielle, but I'm not mad at you."

He tucked my hair behind my ear then slipped a finger under my chin, raising my face toward him. "The car will be here for me any minute. I need to go." He placed a chaste kiss on my mouth. "I'll be back on Sunday."

After picking up his bag, he headed toward the door.

"Will?"

He stopped and looked back without saying a word.

"Did you leave your flight and hotel information for me?"

His eyes closed. "I don't have it. Harlow's secretary forgot to give it to me in advance. I'll need to send it to you later." His voice was restrained, cautious, as though he expected a fight. The doorbell rang, and he escaped toward the stairs.

"Have a good trip. I love you."

The front door opened. It closed. Will was gone.

Guess he didn't hear me.

The silence, an ominous weight of loneliness, crushed in on me. I grabbed the corner of my towel to dry my eyes. *Jeeze, Danni. Get a grip.* I gave myself a mental shake and continued to get ready for work.

WILL's cold departure left me feeling scattered, emotionally and mentally. Instead of heading straight to the elevator when I arrived at work, I took a detour to the little coffee shop around the corner.

Several people were in line ahead of me. While I waited, I tried to come up with a way to back out of going to Metro Sky that wouldn't make my friends mad. I hoped Jen would be able to help me sort things out and needed to spend time talking with her.

The bell on the door jingled—a warning to all inside that another burst of cold winter air was heading our way. The chill that rushed down my spine came from more than a mere temperature change.

I turned to look behind me. Just as I'd suspected . . . trouble had walked in, looking sexier than usual in his graphite wool overcoat and burgundy scarf. His ever-messy hair was wind-blown, making me want to run my fingers through it—return it to its normal haphazard state.

Nico's eyes sparkled. "Well, isn't this a great way to start my day. Good morning, beautiful." He pulled off his leather gloves and tucked them into the pocket of his overcoat.

His contagious energy gave my mood an instant boost. "Good morning."

He moved close, making it easier to hear each other over the conversations around us. Close enough for me to smell his fresh clean scent. Close enough to feel him brush against me. Every touch, every breath fanned the embers that lingered inside me since our first meeting.

Easy, Danni. You can do this.

"I was looking for you at The Next Level last Saturday. Guess you didn't get my e-mail about working out together." He paused briefly. "You'll need to give me your correct address. You know, in case I need to contact you about Logan's account . . . or other things." He placed his hand on the small of my back, guiding me forward as the line moved.

I didn't know how to respond. He seemed like a bright enough guy. He must have at least *suspected* I'd ignored him last week.

"Listen, if you don't have plans tonight, maybe—"

"Sorry, my sister's coming into town tonight to visit for the weekend. We're just going to hang out at home. Ice cream. Movies. That kind of stuff." My response was probably a bit too hasty and enthusiastic, but I was relieved to have an honest excuse to turn him down. The last thing I needed, especially today, was to spend the evening with Nico.

"Can I help you?"

Saved by the barista. I ordered my latte and reached into my bag for my wallet. Nico's hand rested on my forearm, stopping me.

"I'll get this." He looked at the barista without waiting for my response. "Good morning. Can we also get a large dark roast coffee, black?" He released my arm and retrieved his card to pay.

"Thank you. That wasn't necessary though."

"You're very welcome. Next time you can get mine."

"Sounds fair enough." Too bad there wouldn't be a next time since I would be adding this to my list of places to avoid. But he didn't need to know that.

He collected our drinks from the counter. "So do you have time to hang out here for a few minutes, or do you need to get to work?"

I lifted one shoulder and tried to play it cool, determined not to give in to my surprising urge to sit and chat. "Afraid I need to run."

"Not a problem." He handed my cup to me and motioned toward the exit, guiding me through the crowd again with his hand on my back.

When we reached the door, he stepped forward and held it open for me to pass through first.

"Guess this is where I leave you. Thanks again for the latte." I hesitated, not quite sure of the proper protocol for leaving someone who'd just bought my morning shot of caffeine.

"I don't have any meetings this morning, so I don't need to rush. I can walk with you." He hesitated, looking at me. "That is, if it's okay with you. I don't want to make you uncomfortable."

My head tilted as I studied him. This was a different side of Nico than I'd seen before. He really was trying to keep his promise; I had to give him credit for that. I smiled, nodding. "Sure. Why not?"

He fell in step beside me, close enough to carry on a conversation but not touching me. "So, that invitation to help you with your workout program still stands."

"Oh, I . . . um, I'm not sure about that. I only went that one day because Kendra insisted. I'm really not a very athletic person." *And I don't think having your hands all over my half-*

naked body, controlling every movement, would be a good idea. Fun? Sure. But not too smart.

"Danni?" Nico was looking at me with an odd expression on his face. "Did you hear me?"

"Hmm?" *Damn overactive imagination.* I bit the inside of my lower lip, trying to focus. "Sorry, I think I may have zoned out. Not enough caffeine yet." I raised my cup to emphasize my point.

God, I suck at cover stories. My cheeks grew warm despite the cold air around us.

He smiled. "I just said you can call and talk to my secretary if you'd like to give it a try. Or I could give you my personal cell number." He angled his head slightly to glance at me from the corner of his eye. "That way you could call me directly. Yourself."

We arrived at Brookdale Tower. Nico opened the door for me to enter and followed me into the lobby. The past fifteen minutes with him had been very nice, but I still needed to avoid spending time with him if I planned to revive my decaying relationship with Will.

The answer was clear.

"If I change my mind, I'll call your secretary. But I doubt that will happen. Thanks for the offer though."

He pressed his lips together and nodded, clearly understanding the message. "Well, I guess I better let you get to work." He took my hand, giving it a gentle squeeze as he looked into my eyes. "I really enjoyed spending time with you—hope we get to do this again."

"It was nice." *Nice* was the best I could offer. I didn't dare to tell him how much I'd truly enjoyed it. But something in my smile may have given it away.

A familiar lopsided grin broke out on his face, revealing that single dimple in his left cheek. Mischief sparkled in his eyes as he gave a playful wink.

"Have a good day, Danni." His thumb brushed across my hand before he let it slip from his, then he turned and exited the building.

CHAPTER 15

SHOULD'VE STAYED HOME

It'd been forty-five minutes since Jen called to tell me she was on her way for our girls' night in, and I'd been pacing the house ever since. I knew the drive would take close to an hour, but I couldn't stop myself from looking out the window every few minutes. As I fluffed the couch pillows for the tenth time, a flash from headlights in the driveway grabbed my attention and sent me sprinting to the door.

I burst outside, eager to greet my sister. Shivering on the stoop, I waited for her to climb out of her car then rushed to meet her halfway. "I'm so glad you're here."

My enthusiastic hug nearly knocked her overnight bag from her hand. She wrapped her free arm around me, squeezing tight, and rubbed my back as I shook with restrained sobs.

"Shh . . . it's okay. Let's go inside." She stepped back and took my hand, pulling me toward the house. "Things were crazy at home, and I was beginning to wonder if I'd be able to escape alone," Jen said, chuckling as we closed the door behind us.

I loved that she was giving me time to re-collect myself before bombarding me with questions about my breakdown.

"Caden insisted he was coming along." She opened her bag

and carefully retrieved two pieces of paper. "He put up quite a fight about not getting to deliver these himself."

I smiled, easily recognizing my nephew's familiar artwork. The first had a neon-green blob with a black stripe and four black "wheels" along the bottom. A small face smiled from the middle of the blob—Caden behind the wheel of Will's Challenger. He loved to tease Will about his car, saying it looked like slime. But I was convinced he just loved the hearty tickling it always earned him while Will forced an apology.

The next was a picture of Caden and me, holding hands and smiling. "Aww, this is perfect. I love that little guy."

Jen followed me to the kitchen, filling me in on the latest adventures of raising a four-year-old boy. She grabbed two bottles of Smirnoff Ice from the fridge and popped them open. While she chatted away, I took down the pictures Caden had made for me last month and replaced them with his new masterpieces.

After a few minutes, Jen set her bottle on the counter and turned to look at me. "So . . . are you ready to talk about it yet?"

Where to start. "I don't know what I'm doing wrong." My voice tapered off. "With Will, it's one step forward, two steps back. We have great sex . . . well, most times it's not so great, but at least it's sex, right?" I lifted one shoulder, hoping to brush it off as *no big deal.* "I mean, we can't all be like you and Ryan."

A slight blush shaded Jen's face, and she rolled her eyes. "Get back to your story."

"It's just that he withdraws so often—becomes really distant. Uninterested. Like I don't . . ." I sucked in a shaky breath. "Like I'm not enough."

Jen crossed the room and took my hands, squeezing gently until I made eye contact. "Hey. No one can make you feel inferior without your permission. Remember?"

The familiar words sent a comforting warmth through me. "Eleanor Roosevelt. I used to tell you that all the time growing up. I'm surprised you remembered."

"I remember a lot. Like the way you always stood up for me. Protected me. After Dad . . . well, you were all I had. And I remember what you went through with Mom—the way she treated you—and how much you gave up to take care of me."

I shrugged. "You're my sister. I love you, and you needed me."

"And now you need me. Danni, you need to stop blaming yourself for every problem in your marriage. And you need to talk to Will about the way he's been treating you—you've been through enough of that crap, and he knows it."

My eyes fell closed, squeezing out the tears that had pooled. "I can't—what if he leaves me?" I opened my eyes to look at her. "I don't know if I can take that chance."

"Then just promise me you'll think about it. No matter what, you've always got me, Ryan, and Caden." She gave my hands another gentle squeeze before releasing them. "Now I'm pretty sure I was promised a fun night and a pint of Chunky Monkey."

After giving Jen a huge hug, I grabbed two pints of Ben & Jerry's and a couple of spoons.

"So what movie are we watching first?" I asked as we moved into the family room.

Jen laughed, digging into the bag she'd dropped by the couch. "You're gonna love it! Ready?" She pulled out *Grease*. "Ta-da! Bring back memories?"

"Oh, wow. A few. How many times did we watch that?"

"I don't know—every Friday night for probably a year? But I haven't seen it in ages." She crossed the room and popped it into the DVD player.

We settled in on opposite ends of the couch, singing along despite mouths full of ice cream.

About ten minutes into the movie, Jen turned her attention to me. "So, have you heard from Will at all today?"

"Only the text letting me know he'd arrived safely. I tried to call him when I got home from work, but the call went straight to voicemail. And he hasn't gotten back to me." I paused, thinking about what that meant, then let out a quiet sigh. "He was mad this morning—guess he's not over it yet. I don't really want to talk about it right now though."

"Okay. New topic then." She tapped her temple, thinking for a moment. Her mood shifted, and she gave a scandalous smile. "Why don't we talk about Nico? You hear from him since his e-mail last week?"

I groaned and rambled off a quick summary of our encounter this morning. "So that's it, and enough talk about Nico too. I'm trying to forget about him. Remember?"

Jen simply nodded, an odd expression on her face, and we went back to watching the movie. More accurately, I went back to watching the movie. Jen became obsessed with watching her phone.

"You have better plans or something?"

"Hmm?" Her response had the tone of someone who'd been caught daydreaming.

"Your phone." I pointed with my spoon before digging in for another bite. "You've been checking it every two minutes for the past ten."

Jen gave a sigh. "I'm just worried about Caden. He was so upset earlier, and it's soon his bedtime."

"I'm sure he and Ryan are having fun, but why don't you call him? It'll make you feel better."

"Yeah. I think I will." Jen pressed a button on her phone as she stood, moving toward the kitchen.

The doorbell rang, startling me, but I chose to ignore it. The bell rang again, a series of impatient dings this time, prompting Jen to interrupt her call.

"Are you going to get that?"

"Wasn't planning to." I took another bite of ice cream. "I'm not expecting anyone."

She narrowed her eyes at me.

"What? It's probably someone selling something that I don't want."

Jen swept her fingers forward, motioning for me to answer the door, then continued with her call.

"Fine . . ." I took Ben and Jerry with me, waving my spoon at Jen. "But I'm giving them your name and number." I crossed the room and peeked through the glass panel. "What the hell?" I turned the lock and pulled the door open.

"Surprise!" Kendra and Kristi shouted in unison.

"We're here to kidnap you," Kristi said. She cupped her hand by her mouth and leaned toward me, giggling. "Not really *kidnapping,* just borrowing you for a night of fun. Didn't want you to call the cops on us or anything." She gave an exaggerated wink.

I leaned back, fanning away the smell of alcohol. "Did you leave the club to come here?"

Kristi waved dismissively. "No, silly, we're on our way there now. We can't have *girls' night* without *the girls.* Jeeze. But we did sort of start the party without you." She paused to give an apologetic pout. "Sorry. We tried to wait for you, but that bottle of moscato was just too hard to resist and oh, so yummy!"

"Wait . . . you were drinking on the way here?" I couldn't believe they'd been so irresponsible.

"Relax. Ben arranged for our ride tonight." Kristi's face glowed, and she poked her thumb over her shoulder without turning around.

I looked past them at the sleek black limo waiting by the curb. *How could I have missed that?* "Wow. Impressive."

"I know, right?" Kristi said. "It's from his family's resort. Remember I told you they own Elevations? Anyway, the driver's this sweet old guy named Ernesto, and he even wears one of those cute little chauffeur hats."

Kendra pinned me with an impatient stare. "I hate to break up this fun little chat session, ladies, but how much longer are you planning to make us stand in the cold?"

"Actually, I was hoping you'd come to your senses and leave without me." I groaned, realizing that wasn't an option as her stare intensified. Stepping aside, I pulled the door open farther and motioned for them to enter. "What are you even doing here? I told you I'd changed my mind about going out tonight." *Shoot, that came out harsh.*

"Intervention, sweetie," Kendra said. "Kristi told me you were really upset about dirtbag Will this morning and that Jamison sent you home early because you looked like shit."

"Kendra! That's not what I said."

"Fine. Because you didn't look well." A dramatic eye roll accompanied Kendra's patronizing tone, then she continued with an air of determined confidence. "What you need is a night out with the girls."

"I can't. I mean . . ." I glanced at Jen as she joined us, knowing she'd have my back. "We don't have anything to wear even if we wanted to go."

"Actually . . . we do." Jen's voice held a cautious tone. She bit her lip, eyes focused on me. "Our dresses are in my car."

"You were in on this? And that's why you kept checking your phone." I shook my head, looking between my sister and friends who'd conspired against me. "Un-freakin'-believable." *There is no way in hell I'm getting out of this.*

Jen shrugged. "Sorry. Kendra was worried and called this

afternoon to sell me on her plan. And after our conversation tonight, I'm even more convinced she's right. You do need a night out, so we're going." She grabbed my face and gave me a huge kiss before rushing out the door. "I'll be right back."

It only took a minute till she returned, carrying a long black garment bag and wearing a huge grin. "You are going to look *amazing!*" She practically sang the words.

Lord help me.

They all swarmed toward my bedroom, dragging me with them, and dumped their bags on the bed. When Jen uncovered our dresses, squeals of approval rang out. Not from me, of course. Her beautiful blue wrap dress matched her eyes. The other dress, presumably mine, was a little . . . no, make that a *tiny* black dress.

"You're joking, right? Because there is no way in hell I'm going out in public wearing that thing. Assuming I could even fit into it."

"Relax, sweetie. It's got spandex. Guaranteed to hug you in all the right places." Kendra demonstrated by dragging her hands across her body. She picked up the dress and held it in front of me. "And Jen's right, you're going to look sexy as hell in this."

I rolled my eyes. Arguing was pointless. I was outnumbered, three to one.

Jen threw herself together then joined the tag-team makeover Kendra and Kristi were putting me through. Hair, makeup. . . the works. Last, and most dreaded, was the dress. It reminded me of pulling on a snug leather glove. I kept tugging at the bottom, but it stopped moving mid-thigh.

Kristi's bubbly laugh caught my attention. "It's not gonna grow if you keep tugging on it." She pushed my hands away and motioned for me to turn. "Let's see how you look."

All three gave enthusiastic oohs and aahs while I spun in a gradual circle in front of the mirror.

"Enough, already. You all need to stop, because you're making me really uncomfortable."

"Danni, you're beautiful—inside and out—and you deserve to feel that way." Kendra gave me an air kiss then eyed me with a wicked grin. "And trust me, every horny guy in that club is going to love your outer beauty so much they'll wanna get inside."

I gasped. "I'm not looking to pick up guys, horny or not. That's your agenda."

"Ignore her." Jen pushed Kendra aside with a laugh. "Danni, you deserve to be treated with respect. Going out doesn't mean you don't love your husband or you're looking to screw around. You said yourself that you admire Ryan's and my relationship, and I'm going out too. So relax and enjoy."

Jen grabbed her bag. "Okay, finishing touch." With a dramatic flair, she pulled out a pair of bright-pink-and-black stilettos and a matching handbag. "Ta-dum. A little pop of color guaranteed to make you feel pretty."

I wasn't about to admit it to any of them, but I did feel pretty . . . and kind of sexy. I missed Will though and wished he could see the way I looked right now.

We all piled into the limo for the short trip into the city. Fifteen minutes later, we were in an elevator, climbing to the twenty-first floor and Metro Sky. Kristi rambled on at hyper speed, filling Jen in on all the qualities that made Ben the perfect catch.

As we stepped out of the elevator, Kendra moved beside me, bumping her shoulder against mine. "Hey. Have fun tonight, okay?"

I turned to her and nodded. "I'll try."

We paid our cover charge and passed through the entrance

into the most amazing club I'd ever seen. Pale gray floors with mirrored flecks sparkled under the blue and purple neon lights that ran around the ceiling and glowed from large pillars wrapped in bands of nickel. White crescent-shaped chairs surrounded gray marble tables. An elevated VIP section with roped-off luxurious private seating areas rose above the perimeter of the large dance floor, ending next to the raised stage where Ben's band, The Executives, was playing. Their upbeat alternative rock filled the club and energized the group on the crowded dance floor.

My steps faltered before I froze in place, eyes locked on the man singing—black hair, dressed in all black. I didn't need to see Ben's eyes to know they were an exotic shade of jade. My stomach clenched. My heartbeat quickened. My skin tingled with a now-familiar awareness as I scanned the room.

Kendra grabbed my wrist. "Oh shit." She stared at the stage, obviously making the same connection I had a moment earlier. She leaned close and shouted over the music. "Danni, I swear I didn't know. Do you think *he's* here?"

I needed to stay focused on my search and didn't look at her. "I don't see him, but he's here. Somewhere. It's like I can feel him, if that makes any sense."

"Hey, you two. What are you waiting for?" Kristi called as she came up behind us. She burst out laughing when Kendra and I turned toward her. "Look at your faces. I knew you'd love him. But what's not to love, right? I mean, isn't that the sexiest voice you've ever heard? Mmmm . . . makes me just wanna run up there and jump him. Anyway, I'm sure you've already figured it out, but that gorgeous creature is Ben."

"Yeah . . . we've, um, already met. Kristi?" I looked at her. "Don't you think you should've mentioned that he's Nico's brother?"

"What?" Her outburst drew the attention of several people

nearby. She threw her hands over her mouth before continuing in a quieter voice. "*My* Ben and *your* Nico are brothers? No way. I mean, what are the odds? This is just so exciting!"

My jaw clenched, and I let out an exasperated groan. "He's not mine. And this is a nightmare, not exciting. How could you not know they were brothers?" I shook my head.

"Jeeze, give me a little break. I've only known Ben two and a half weeks." A rosy blush crept into her cheeks. "What can I say? He's a man of action. And what amazing action it is." She cringed when her eyes locked on my icy stare. "But, you don't want to know about that right now. Let's just say we haven't exactly spent a lot of time talking, if you know what I mean." Her smile returned. She gave an exaggerated wink, driving home the obvious point.

Jen finally caught up to us. "Ladies, compliments of Ben, our VIP table is ready." She narrowed her eyes as her gaze flicked between the three of us. "Something's wrong. What did I miss?"

My words erupted in a panic. "Ben is Nico's brother, and I have a feeling he's here too."

"Oh, shit!"

"Exactly what I said." Kendra threw her palms up.

Jen studied my face. "So what are we doing? Do you want to leave?"

Yes! Definitely. Get me the hell out of here! I can't believe you even dragged me here in the first place!

I looked at Kristi's pleading eyes. She'd been so excited about tonight. They all had.

After a few deep, calming breaths, I knew what I needed to do. I forced a cheerful smile and attempted to sound confident. "It's fine. We should stay." I nodded, trying to convince myself. "I want to stay."

"You sure you're okay with this?" Jen watched me closely while waiting for my answer.

"Yeah. I'm sure. Let's find our table, because I need a drink."

As I moved forward, the massive bar came into view. Brushed nickel and neon lights carried through the theme of the rest of the club. Only a single row of tables stood between me and a giant margarita. *Do I really need to wait until I get to our table?*

Several patrons were seated along the bar, some with their stools turned to face the large dance floor and stage beyond. My attention drifted to a group of beautiful young women blatantly flirting with the men seated closest to me.

A tiny-waisted blonde with hair halfway down her back wedged herself between the first man's legs, her hands on his chest. He grabbed her waist as she leaned close, her lips to his ear.

A phony giggle accompanied a skillful flip of her hair before she took the drink from his other hand and stretched across him to place the glass on the bar. The exaggerated movement caused the hem of her ridiculously short dress to rise even higher.

Another inch, and we'll all know her panty preference. I shook my head, wondering why I cared . . . about any of it. But I couldn't tear my eyes away from the infuriating scene.

The man slid his hand over her hip to her exposed thigh, skimming just below the hem of her dress. Blondie wagged a finger at him as she stood up straight, but she didn't bother to move the offending hand. Taking hold of his tie, she turned and pulled him toward the dance floor, pausing to toss a seductive look over her shoulder.

As he wrapped his arm around her waist, shifting his body to pull her closer, his face came into view.

I sucked in a sharp breath, realizing why I was so drawn to this couple. He looked toward me, and our eyes met. The heat of his gaze burned through me.

My chest tightened. An uncontrollable, possessive anger coursed through me as the woman turned in his arms and pressed every goddamned inch of her body against him. He didn't move. He didn't release his virtual hold on me.

I reached for Jen, needing her to drag me away. Now.

"Ouch, what the . . ." Jen tried to pry my fingers away, failing to ease my tight grip on her arm. "Danni, what are you doing?" With a questioning look, she followed my line of sight. "Oh, damn. Now that guy is seriously hot."

I managed to close my eyes, breaking the connection, and turned to my sister. "Oh, Jen . . . that guy is Nico."

CHAPTER 16

LOSING CONTROL

I rushed toward the exit with Jen in tow, my heart pounding at a frantic pace.

"Danni, slow down." She dug in her heels and forced me inside a ladies' room along the way. "Where are you going?"

"Home. Where I should have stayed in the first place." I paced the narrow space. "I can't do this. I have a husband I love and a marriage to fix. I don't need this—whatever it is that happens around Nico—interfering."

She took my hands. "Relax. I'm not gonna deny you two have some intense chemistry. But you said yourself, several times, that you're committed to Will and your marriage."

I nodded.

"This is a girls' night. It's okay to let yourself have some fun with your friends. We'll all stick together, and you'll be fine."

"I don't know about that."

"Besides, Nico's date looked like she plans to keep him entertained. I don't think he'll be a problem tonight."

My fists clenched every time I thought about Nico and that little tramp. "Will would want me to stay home."

"That's not very fair, is it?" She tipped her head and stared, daring me to argue. "Come on, Danni. We're already here, this place is amazing, and I *really* want to dance. Please?"

I never was good at saying no to Jen. The long silence and her pleading expression weakened my resolve to flee. "Fine. I'll stay." I gave her a weak hug. "Let's go, before I change my mind."

We made our way to our spacious VIP section, right near the stage and dance floor. I would have loved to stop at the bar first, but I didn't dare risk running into Nico.

Kendra and Kristi had settled in and were already on their first round of drinks. Jen called out to them several times before they turned around. Their stunned expressions as they rushed toward us told me I must look as awful as I felt.

"Where have you been?" Kendra said.

"Oh my, Danni. What happened?" Kristi grabbed my hands. "Are you okay?"

Jen motioned for them to move closer. She took a deep breath and paused. "Nico's here."

"You ran into him?" Kendra grinned. "I would've liked to see that."

"He and Danni spotted each other. You should have seen the way he looked at her. Practically stripped her with his eyes . . . *while* he was wrapped around some other woman on the dance floor." Jen waved her hand dismissively. "Anyway, Danni just needed a few minutes to pull herself together before we joined the party."

"Hi, there!" A petite redhead poked her head into our tight huddle. "I'm Leah, your server for tonight."

She took a step back and smoothed a hand down her long ponytail, an amused expression on her face. "What can I get you started with?" She hugged her empty serving tray, focusing on each of us as we placed our drink orders. She quickly repeated them to us then turned to leave.

"Hold on a sec," I called after Leah as she walked away. "Can you add a shot for me? Anything strong."

"Sure thing. I'll be right back." She tipped her head to the side and smiled sweetly, a sympathetic look, then slipped through the crowd toward the bar.

I looked at Jen, who was staring at me from beneath arched brows. "What? I can't waste time sipping girly drinks and waiting patiently for them to calm my nerves." I walked past without giving her a chance to reply and collapsed in one of the plush chairs. My arms dropped over the sides, and my head fell back on the top edge, leaving me to stare at the ceiling.

"What the hell is wrong with me?" A muffled groan escaped me, and I wondered if the band would be loud enough to cover the raging scream brewing inside. *Probably shouldn't try to find out.*

"I mean, seriously . . . I have no damn clue what happened to me down there. The sight of that sleazy little bitch hangin' all over Nico made my blood boil. I wanted walk over there, grab her bleached-blonde hair by its dark roots, and physically drag her off of him."

"Sounds to me like someone's jealous." Kendra's voice held a smug, gloating tone. "Does that mean you're finally ready to admit you have the hots for Nico?"

I lifted my head and narrowed my eyes at her. "Not in the mood for your meddling right now. And for the hundredth time, I *don't* have the *hots* for Nico. I love my husband."

"Okay, fine. Whatever." She threw her hands up in surrender, but I could tell she wasn't buying my story.

Kristi took over, her words hesitant at first. "Well, then it's no big deal that he's here, right? I mean, you said Nico wanted to be friends, and well, friends hang out together. So . . . we can still have a fun night. Can't we?"

It seemed like an easy enough request. At least it should have been. Except for the fact that I planned to avoid Nico.

I leaned forward, pressing my fingers to my aching forehead. "You know Will doesn't like me going to clubs without him. Sneaking out while he's away was . . . it was a bad decision. Maybe I should just—"

"Oh, come on . . . do you really believe that dear, sweet, asshole hubby of yours isn't out having a good time right now? Has he even taken a minute to return your call or bothered to send a quick text?"

"Kendra, shhh. Back off a little. She's already upset enough." Jen's calming voice was barely audible over the music.

"Maybe she needs to get upset for a change." Kendra pulled my hands away from my face, squeezing them as she looked in my eyes. "You know I love you, sweetie, but when are you going to realize you deserve more? Someone who's gonna treat you better."

My chest tightened. My throat burned. It hurt like hell that Will had brushed me off all day—I knew that's what happened. *I'm not stupid.* That didn't mean I wanted to share my humiliation—not even with my best friends—so I needed to be strong. I'd assumed he was punishing me for upsetting him this morning, or all week, but . . . what if Kendra was right?

Stop it. How could I even let myself think that way? Will was working, winning over an important client. Period.

Leah returned with our drinks.

"This is just what I need." I threw back my shot, drowning my internal dispute.

My eyes fell shut on a slow, heavy breath. I shuddered as the liquid burned a trail down my throat. The fire cooled to a soothing warmth that spread throughout my body and eased my anxiety, even if only a bit.

When I opened my eyes, I reached for my margarita and

locked my lips around the straw. "Mmmm." The cool, sweet liquid went down so easily.

My friends stared, concerned expressions etched on their faces.

"I'm fine. Or I will be in a few minutes anyway." I raised my glass and forced a goofy smile. "To girls' night!"

All three ladies tapped their glasses to mine and chimed in with their toasts. We downed our drinks then slammed the empty glasses on the table.

"That's more like it. Let's get this party started." Kendra's voice boomed, and she rubbed her hands together. "All I need now is a hot, sexy guy to rub against on the dance floor, and everything will be perfect."

As if on cue, Logan ducked under the velvet rope and entered our private section. "Well, that's the best offer I've had all night. Hello, ladies." He looked at each of us before lingering on Kendra. "You look stunning. I'm going to be the envy of every guy out there."

I'd have sworn Kendra blushed, but I didn't think she was capable.

"You're damn right you will be. So you better not disappoint, because you can easily be replaced." She winked as he moved toward her.

Logan placed a hand on her arm and leaned to her ear, but he didn't bother whispering. "You're trouble, aren't you?"

Kristi fanned herself. She silently mouthed the words, "Oh ... my ... God. Dreamy."

Remembering our conversation about Logan the other week, I knew Kristi was dying to have him join us. But that would undoubtedly mean spending the night with Nico.

"He'll be here any minute, Danni." Logan studied me for a moment before giving a slight shake of his head. "Should be an interesting evening."

Interesting. I had a hunch that would turn out to be a major understatement. "Good to see you again, Logan."

The music stopped, and Ben's voice filled the room, announcing the band would take a short break. He introduced the DJ who would keep the party going until they returned.

Jen and Kristi moved next to me, talking while casually observing Kendra with Logan.

"Wow, Danni, you were right," Kristi said. "Guess there's a first for everything."

Kristi's face lit up. She let out a squeal as Ben rushed toward her, scooping her up in a huge hug and planting a kiss on her mouth.

My skin tingled from the happiness radiating from them. I leaned back in my chair and pulled out my phone. No messages. No missed calls. No relief for the uneasy feeling in the pit of my stomach.

Jen grabbed my arm and shouted over the music. "I think I'm going to slip out for a minute—call home to check on Caden." She glanced over at Logan then back at me. "You'll be all right?"

"Yeah, I'm feeling better." I slipped my phone back in my dress.

Ben pointed out an exit beyond the bar to a rooftop patio. "It's cold, but that's probably the only place that will be quiet enough to hear."

"She can borrow my jacket."

My heart skipped at the sound of Nico's deep voice. I tried but couldn't take my eyes off him as he approached carrying two drinks. There was something inherently sexy about a confident man in a suit, but I had a feeling Nico looked incredible no matter what he wore . . . or didn't. I sucked in a quiet gasp, pulling a hand to my chest. *Get a grip, Danni.*

"Your choice of poisons, I believe." Nico smiled and leaned past me to set a very large strawberry margarita on the table.

I took a slow breath, intending to calm myself. It only managed to fill my head with his potent scent. "I'm surprised you remembered." My voice shook. I returned his smile but couldn't look into his eyes. "Thank you."

He placed his tumbler filled with an amber liquid next to my drink before removing his jacket, his eyes fixed on me the whole time. "My pleasure."

Jen stood watching, her arms folded across her chest. "So this is Nico?"

I could barely resist laughing at my younger sister's parental tone, but I managed to stay composed and introduce them.

She accepted his jacket and pinned me with a wary look before leaving. "I'll hurry back."

Nico didn't move. His gaze slowly skimmed every inch of me, burning me with its intensity. A lopsided grin spread across his face, complete with the single dimple that added to his charm. The easygoing confidence I admired seemed to be returning.

Without saying a word, he grabbed a chair and dragged it to mine. As he settled in across from me, he took a long, leisurely drink from his glass.

"What happened to your date?" I reached for my drink, watching him from the corner of my eye, and hoped my question sounded casual enough.

Just because I was curious, it didn't mean Kendra could be right. *Why would I be jealous?* A snort of laughter slipped out just thinking about her crazy idea.

Nico rested his arms on his thighs, both hands wrapped tightly around his glass. He absentmindedly swirled the liquid inside. "You look . . ." He lifted his head to glance at me again and took a deep breath before continuing. "Wow. Absolutely amazing."

He let out a low groan and straightened in his seat, rubbing the back of his neck. "I'm here alone. That girl . . . she's just someone . . . just some girl I know. She's not important." His eyes locked on mine as he leaned forward again. "What about you?" His voice had a slight edge to it. "Your husband wander off again?"

"Will's away. On a business trip."

I stirred my drink, concentrating on the tiny rivulets left behind by the straw, while sneaking an occasional peek at the incredibly gorgeous man in front of me. Looking at Nico was sort of like looking at the sun. If you stared too long, you'd get burned . . . or something like that. I took another long sip and a brief glance.

He narrowed his eyes, giving me a suspicious look. "Hmm. Well, that's too bad . . . for him. But it means I don't have to worry about you chasing me off before he comes back this time, so it's a good thing for me." He leaned closer, reaching out to brush a curl from my face. "And maybe you'll even relax enough to look at me."

A trail of heat remained where his gentle fingers touched my cheek then skimmed along the side of my neck and shoulder.

He took another slow drink from his glass, draining the last of its contents, and placed it on the table. He scrubbed a hand across his face, making it difficult to understand his mumbled words. "Dammit. I'm not playing this well."

I stood to push past him. "This isn't a game, Nico." He reached for my wrist, but I pulled it away and continued to the rail near the stage.

Nico followed and stood behind me, reaching past me on

one side to grab hold of the post. His chest occasionally brushed against my back as I watched the crowd dance.

I was trapped.

"Turn around, Danni. Look at me."

I shivered as his warm breath caressed my ear, his low voice rumbling through me.

"You can trust me. I promise I won't hurt you."

I turned slowly, expecting him to step back and give me some space, but he didn't move. Seconds ticked by, my eyes locked on his solid chest, his broad shoulders, the dark stubble that covered his jaw.

"We have got to come back here this summer." Jen's voice rang out beside me, snapping me from my daze. "That patio is amazing. It's this beautiful garden, complete with a stream and waterfall—on the roof of a city building." She pulled off Nico's jacket while she rambled on about plants and lighting and cozy seating areas. A crease formed between Jen's brows as she paused, looking between Nico and me. The rush of words she didn't say were all clear in her expression. "Everything okay here?"

Nico cleared his throat and seemed to regroup. His voice was calm. Relaxed. "Yeah. Everything's good." He gave me a playful wink then collected his jacket from Jen's arms, folding it in half before he moved to drape it over the chair he'd been sitting in a few minutes earlier.

He returned, carrying my margarita. "We were just talking about her husband's business trip and how it's too bad he couldn't be here. Right, Danni?"

I gave a noncommittal nod while I sucked down the rest of my drink.

Ben stepped in front of me and touched my arm. "Hey, sorry to interrupt," he shouted. "I need to get back for our next set. It's good to see you again, Danni. You look beautiful, by the way." He turned his full attention to Nico and slapped a hand on his brother's shoulder. "Stay out of trouble." The stare that followed told me there was more to that message than the casual taunt implied.

Ben caught Kristi by the waist on his way past her. She giggled as he lifted her petite body and spun her around, kissing her when he returned her feet to the ground.

"I expect to see you ladies on the dance floor," he said, pointing at each of us as he walked away.

CHAPTER 17

DANCE WITH ME

We watched Ben weave his way through the crowd, dodging several women's attempts to grab him. They screamed his name, along with a few propositions, as he hopped up on stage. Their reaction didn't surprise me—he was almost as hot as Nico. But a quick glance at Kristi's face told me she hadn't anticipated the attention and wasn't at all happy about the situation.

Ben looked up at our section as he strapped on his guitar, a huge smile on his face, and tipped his head toward Kristi.

She grabbed Jen and me as the band started playing, tugging us toward the dance floor. "Let's go, ladies."

I needed some distance from Nico, a chance to regain control of my traitorous body. Heading to the dance floor with the girls would be the perfect escape.

As Kristi pulled me along, I waved over my shoulder and shouted to Nico, "Gotta run. Thanks for the drink. Enjoy the rest of your evening."

"Get a move on, Kendra." Kristi blurted out the demand without slowing to wait for her. "Plenty of hot guys on the dance floor for you to hit on."

The determined look on Kristi's face was almost comical. She danced her way through the crowd until reaching the front of the stage, hips swaying as she turned in a slow circle.

Ben moved closer, beaming with his approval.

"That's more like it." A satisfied grin filled Kristi's face. "I need to make sure the only suggestive moves my man's watching are mine." She looked past me and waved a hand in the air. "About time you . . . oh." Her smile faded. She twisted her lips and shifted her eyes to me.

I turned to follow Kristi's line of vision. Kendra was walking toward us with Logan and Nico following close behind. *Damn!*

We all danced as a group, Kendra keeping her promise of grinding on Logan.

I did my best to avoid Nico, but he occasionally made it clear that he wasn't dancing alone by taking my hand or shifting behind me with his hands on my hips. The provocative way he moved that sexy body of his and the flirtatious expressions on his face when our eyes met were chipping away at my willpower, melting my self-control.

I needed to be responsible, force myself to think about something else. *Okay, I can do that.* And what could be more responsible than thinking about Will? I closed my eyes, trying to imagine him here—not exactly the best plan. I lost my balance and fell against Nico.

Mental note to self . . . keep eyes open when mixing alcohol, dancing, and stilettos.

Nico didn't seem to mind. He pulled me closer for a hug, his mouth pressed to my ear. "I knew you'd fall for me sooner or later. Guess I just had to be patient." He laughed and released me, but his smile didn't fade.

Maybe I couldn't imagine Will here because he didn't really like to let loose and dance. If he'd had enough to drink and I begged relentlessly, sometimes he'd join me on the dance floor.

Even then . . . well, there was just no comparison between his tense movements and Nico's relaxed sensuality.

Ugh! Focus, Danni. Will . . . Will . . .

His meetings for the day should be finished by now. I wondered if he missed me, what he was doing. *Probably not trying to distract himself from adulterous thoughts.*

I pulled my phone from my dress and pressed a button, eager to see a message or missed call from him. Nothing.

Cheers erupted as the band finished the debut of their original song, snapping me from the heartsick daze I'd drifted into.

Kristi grabbed my arm and pressed a hand to her throat. "I'm parched. Let's take a break and grab a drink."

"Sounds good." I nodded. The last thing I needed was another drink, but I could definitely use a break.

She tapped on Kendra's arm and motioned toward our table while I reached for Jen, intending to pull her with me. But Nico caught my extended wrist, his gentle fingers wrapping completely around it with just enough pressure to stop me in my tracks.

Ben's deep voice echoed through the room. "Thank you. We're gonna slow things down, do a little Coldplay for you now. This one's from a few years back. It's called 'Sparks.' "

His head shifted toward us as he stepped back and adjusted his guitar. It was too dark to see his eyes, but I could feel him watching. *Judging.* The music began, a sultry rhythm.

"Stay. Dance with me." Nico's voice recaptured my attention.

Logan stepped closer. He clapped a hand on Nico's shoulder and attempted to tug him away from me. "Nico. Come on, man, you don't want to do this."

A worn, weathered edge marked the practiced tone of his voice. He'd clearly been down this road before with his best friend.

Nico turned, without releasing his hold on me, and shrugged away from Logan's grasp. His face tensed, and he narrowed his eyes at him. "I got this." His voice was firm and decisive. Dismissive.

Logan seemed to expect his reaction and didn't back down. "You *think* you got it. You're drunk, Nico, and you know what's gonna happen? You're gonna fuck things up. And then I get to deal with your shit about it for however long it takes you to screw your head back on."

Nico paused, his head bobbing as he considered Logan's words. After taking a slow breath, he continued in a calmer voice. "It's all good. I'm good. I'm just going to dance with my new friend, nothing more." He smiled at me and relaxed his grip on my wrist enough to brush his thumb across my skin.

The simple movement ignited a tingling sensation in the pit of my stomach.

"Right, Danni?"

The two men stared at each other in silent conversation until Logan held up his hands and stepped back, shaking his head. "I hope you know what you're doing." He glanced between Nico and me. "Both of you."

Logan called past me to where my friends and sister stood watching. "Care to join me, ladies?" He motioned toward our table then walked away without waiting for their response.

Kristi hesitated. "I think we should stay with Danni."

"She's a big girl. We don't need to babysit her." Kendra draped an arm across Kristi's shoulders. "Let's go find Logan, and you can have another drink while you lust after your insatiable sex machine and pity all the slutty bitches who think they're going home with him tonight." Before ushering Kristi away, Kendra gave me a wicked grin. "Have fun, sweetie."

So much for sticking together and having my back.

Jen lingered, pausing in front of us. "Danni?"

Her face clearly expressed concern over leaving me alone with Nico. She was the only one who knew how deeply conflicted my feelings for him were. She also knew this wasn't the path I'd chosen, regardless of my husband's apparent lack of interest.

"I'll be right there. Go ahead." I touched her arm, gave my best reassuring smile, and sent her away. *Don't leave me.*

Nico turned his attention to me, his eyes searching mine. He extended his free hand and waited for me to accept it. "It's just a dance, Danni. What are you afraid of?"

You. Me. That look in your eyes. The way it makes me feel. The truth. My chest constricted, closing in on my lungs and making it difficult to breathe.

He continued to wait patiently, his eyes pleading.

I swallowed hard against the lump in my throat and opened my mouth to respond, turn him down, but nothing came out. Every cell in my body screamed *this is a huge mistake* as I placed my hand in his and allowed him to pull me against his solid chest. I couldn't stop myself—didn't want to—and caved to the overwhelming need to know how it felt to be wrapped in his strong arms.

He released my wrist and pressed his palm to the small of my back, the heat of his touch radiating through me. I closed my eyes and relaxed into him, breathing in the crisp scent of his cologne mixed with the intoxicating scent that was purely Nico.

Our bodies moved in time with the seductive tune Ben's band played as his raspy voice sang out the poignant lyrics.

Nico's chest lifted in a deep inhale. His warm breath caressed the side of my face when he spoke, his voice regaining its familiar soothing tone. "See, Danni? Just two friends sharing a dance." His fingers flexed against my back before sliding to grab my waist, pulling me tighter against him. "Perfectly in control."

His heart beat harder against his chest as if trying to escape, or maybe it was mine. Blood coursed through my body, pulsing deep in my core and waking unfamiliar sensations that were best left dormant.

Nico released my hand, allowing it to drop to his chest. The gentle brush of his fingers as they skimmed the length of my arm, then across my shoulder, sent an electrifying shiver through me. He let his hand come to a rest at the base of my neck but continued stroking my exposed skin.

My emotions raged out of control. I was completely enveloped in Nico's embrace, consumed by him. The music faded to a muffled hum, and the other couples disappeared. Nothing existed beyond Nico and me. In that moment, nothing else mattered.

I lifted my head to search his face. Hunger. Desire. Need. His eyes mirrored my feelings.

I hesitated, moving my hand from his chest to touch the side of his face with trembling fingers. The rough surface did little to mask the gentle warmth of the man beneath it.

His eyes closed as he leaned into my touch.

I continued exploring, my fingers weaving through the lush texture of his jet-black hair and pulling him closer as I stretched on my toes to close the distance. I forced my eyes to stay open, watching his troubled face. My heart raced. I paused then brushed my lips across his.

Nico's body tensed at the contact. His hand slid from my waist to my hip as his arms tightened, pulling me closer. The full length of my body pressed into his warm, muscular frame, discovering the enormous effect I had on him.

His eyes remained closed—a conscious effort, I decided. Was he hiding from me? Or from himself?

I pulled in a shaky breath and covered his mouth with mine, moving my lips gently against his. My grasp on his hair tightened as I strained to be closer to him. Letting my tongue skim along his lower lip, I tasted a hint of the scotch he'd been drinking earlier.

You're drunk, Nico. You're gonna fuck things up. I pushed Logan's words away as quickly as they surfaced. For the first time in my life, I didn't want to care about responsibility or consequences. I only wanted to feel. And nothing else had ever felt this amazing.

Nico's soft moan vibrated against my lips. "Danni." His single word a whisper before he returned the kiss, gentle at first then becoming more fervent. When his lips parted on a ragged breath, I seized the moment and let my tongue slip past.

He welcomed the intrusion, pulled me in deeper. Releasing his tight hold on me, he raised his hands to frame my face, the possessive gesture luring me further into this sensual dream.

Cool air brushed against my abandoned mouth. Nico had pulled away. His forehead rested against mine, his breaths erratic.

"Christ, Danni. I don't . . . I didn't . . ." He gave a muffled groan of frustration, running a hand through his hair. "I'm . . . I'm so sorry."

Sorry. The kiss of death. My senses returned to me. Couples surrounded us on the dance floor. The band had moved on to a different song. Humiliation. Disgrace.

Betrayal. *Oh, God! What have I done!*

Distance. I needed distance from him. Now.

Fighting back tears, I pushed away from Nico and turned to run, wobbling on my damn stilettos.

He caught my waist, saving me from further embarrassment at least, but I pushed him away.

I kicked off my shoes and stooped to grab them. "Freakin' slut heels. You sure earned your title tonight."

Nico called after me as I raced toward the patio exit, bumping into several people along the way.

The brutal January air assaulted me like a harsh slap across the face, one that I fully deserved. I leaned against the brick building, letting my head fall back against the hard surface. A deluge of tears streamed down my face, but there could never be enough to wash away the damage I'd done tonight. The weight of the situation was suddenly too much for my legs to bear. I collapsed, my back scraping along the rough brick wall.

It didn't take long for Nico to find me. Rather than face him, I stayed on the ground and stared at his designer shoes. His weight shifted from one foot to the other as he stood silently in front of me.

After several seconds of uncomfortable silence, he drew a shaky breath. "Danni . . ."

"Please. Leave. I just want to be alone."

He crouched down and lifted my chin, forcing me to look at him. His warm chocolate eyes seemed to melt as they scanned my tear-streaked face. A weary sigh escaped him. "I really did fuck things up with you." He gently wiped away my tears. "I never meant to hurt you."

My eyes snapped wide open. I was willing to accept full responsibility for my actions, but he needed to own up to the consequences of his own. "Well you did, Nico. What the hell did you think was going to happen?" I pushed to my feet, nearly knocking him over.

He stood, crowding me even though no one else was near. "I thought I could . . ." He scrubbed a hand down his face, but it didn't erase his troubled expression.

"Could what, Nico? Handle it? Suck it up? Take one for the team?" The words were like acid on my tongue.

"What are you talking about?"

"You rejected me. Pushed me away." My hands balled into

tight fists. I rubbed them along the side of my legs as I fought back the next onslaught of tears.

"I didn't—"

"I had no right kissing you. Or even dancing with you, but that part was your fault." I poked his chest, shoving aside the memory of how he'd held me against it a few short minutes ago, and choked out the rest of my words. "Do you have any idea how humiliating it was—"

"Shut up, Danni." He closed in on me as he spoke, forcing me to back into the wall. The frustration in his voice weakened the severity of his harsh words. His eyes closed, and he shoved his fingers through his hair again.

I was beginning to understand why it always looked so unruly. Seconds passed; the wait became awkward. I glanced toward the entrance, hoping someone would come out to check on me. Rescue me.

Nico's voice, calm again, interrupted my thoughts. "Do you think you can stay quiet long enough to let me talk?"

I couldn't imagine he had anything to say that would make me believe he wasn't disgusted by the way I'd behaved, but curiosity won out. I pinched my thumb and forefinger together, dragged them along the line of my lips, then crossed my arms, waiting. *This should be good.*

He closed his eyes and lowered his head, a hint of a smile on his lips. When he looked back at me, the humor was gone, replaced by a tender expression. "You're married."

"No sh—"

He placed a finger over my lips, the gentle contact reminding me of his initial response to my kiss. "You said you'd be quiet." His whispered words were slow, teasing.

I sucked in a shaking breath, nodding. Relief rushed through me when he pulled his finger away. I dropped my arms to my sides and pressed my palms against the brick for support.

"It may look to you like I'm some sort of a player who never turns down an opportunity to get laid, but I don't sleep with near the amount of women people seem to think I do. And I would never"—he lifted my chin to look into my eyes—"never screw around with a married woman. That's a line I've never crossed."

He released my chin and rubbed the back of his neck as he paced in front of me, glancing over occasionally as he spoke. "Everybody thinks I've got it all under control. Everything goes my way." He let out a short bitter laugh. "But then you came along. And now I'm so fuckin' screwed up inside—I don't know what the hell I'm doing half the time. You're all I think about. You're all I want. And knowing I can't have you, or even spend time with you, is driving me insane."

He paused, shoving both hands in his hair. Even though his face was partially obscured, I could still see his pain—his eyes squeezed shut, his jaw tense.

He lowered his hands and continued. "It's just . . . I've never felt like this, not even when . . . let's just say it's been a long time since I've even come close."

This had to be a dream. His words swirled around in my already fuzzy head, making me dizzy. Never before had a man poured out his feelings like this. Not even Will. The mere thought of him trying caused a puff of laughter to slip out.

My hand flew to my mouth as I gasped. "I wasn't laugh—"

Nico stopped pacing to face me, silencing me with a look. I recoiled at his tortured expression.

He shook his head and laughed before continuing. "I've had too much to drink. Listen to me spilling my guts like some goddamned pathetic, lovesick teenager."

He moved closer and placed his hands on my arms, warming me and giving me chills at the same time. I opened my mouth to speak, tell him that I thought he was amazing . . .

damn near perfect actually. He didn't give me the chance to get even the first word out.

"I thought I could handle a simple dance. And it was wrong, I know that." He closed his eyes and rested his forehead against mine, pausing as he drew in a ragged breath. "But it felt so damn good to hold you." He pulled back, studying my face. "I trusted you to defend that line in the sand, to protect your marriage in case I screwed up. But you didn't. *You* kissed *me*."

He dropped his arms and turned away from me, a hand tugging through his hair again. "Dammit! You're supposed to honor your wedding vows. Even if the bastard doesn't deserve you."

This time when he turned to me, he maintained the distance between us. "I never meant to hurt you, Danni, but I'm not the lone villain here. Yes, I kissed you back. I'm crazy about you, but I'm not crazy. So yeah, I pushed you away; because what we were doing was wrong."

"Hey . . . everything okay here?" Jen's voice startled me. She moved closer, drilling Nico with a threatening glare.

I knelt to collect my shoes, taking a moment to wipe away my tears. "I, um . . ." Swallowing hard, I looked between the two of them as they stared each other down. "I gotta go."

I ran toward the door, shoes clutched to my chest. It was the cowardly thing to do. I knew that. But I didn't let it stop me.

CHAPTER 18
MELTDOWN

Back inside Metro Sky, I pushed my way through a group of people and skirted the crowded dance floor, glancing at our VIP section before darting in the opposite direction. My friends would be angry, but they'd get over it. I couldn't go back and risk being coerced into staying. After collecting my coat from the attendant, I ran toward the elevator, calling out for the man exiting it to hold the door.

"Made it." Trembling and short of breath, but I'd escaped.

I pulled on my coat and stepped into my shoes during the quick ride to the bottom, where I hoped to catch a cab before anyone realized I was missing.

No such luck. My phone vibrated sooner than I'd anticipated. I needed to avoid everyone right now and rejected the call without looking at the display. Even if Will had finally decided to call, I was in no condition to talk.

The elevator doors opened, and I crossed the lobby at a brisk pace. A few people sat talking or watching the news, but I was only interested in the exit. Straight ahead.

"Ms. Danni." Ernesto approached from the lounge, waving his chauffeur hat. "You leaving so soon?"

"Yes, I'm . . . I'm not feeling well." I lowered my head and kept walking, but he stepped in front of me when I tried to move past.

"Sit. I'll go get the car. The others, they're coming too?"

"No, just me." I turned to him with pleading eyes. "But I need to hurry."

The wrinkles on his forehead deepened as he searched my tear-streaked face. He dragged his free hand through his silver hair then patted my arm and gave a reassuring nod. "How 'bout you come with me. We get the car together."

"Thank you, Ernesto. I appreciate it." I managed a faint smile then latched onto his extended arm.

We no sooner entered the garage when my phone vibrated again. I ignored it this time, letting the call go to voicemail.

Ernesto opened the limo door and took my hand to help me climb in the back. As I settled into my seat, anxious to make a speedy getaway, he reached in his jacket pocket and pulled out a handkerchief. He leaned in and handed it to me without saying a word, but the look in his eyes when they met mine spoke volumes—kind words of empathy and compassion.

"Thank you. For everything." My voice trembled when I spoke.

He nodded then took his seat behind the wheel. When the car pulled away, I listened to the message from Jen and read the text messages from Kristi and Kendra that I hadn't even realized I'd received. They all wanted to know the same thing.

Where are you?

I typed a quick text to Jen.

Me: *Going home. Don't worry. Stay and have fun.*

She wouldn't stay, but it was worth a try. I pressed Send then paused, my finger hovering over the power button. *What if Will calls?*

My grip on the phone tightened, mirroring the crushing

force of the truth on my heart. He wouldn't call. I let my finger fall on the button but continued to hold my severed lifeline. Never letting go.

The ride home was quick, and Ernesto escorted me to my front door. When I moved to step inside, he gripped my shoulders, turning me to face him. He didn't speak until I lifted my eyes to meet his.

"A pretty young girl like you shouldn't have such a heavy heart. Makes me sad." He paused, eyes closed. A peaceful expression seemed to erase years from his face. He looked at me wearing a lopsided smile, accented with a single dimple. "Sleep. My Lorena, she always said, 'Things, they always look better in the morning.' *Buona notte*, Ms. Danni." He tipped his hat before returning to the car.

Once inside, I threw my coat across the couch and went straight upstairs. Sleep was exactly what I needed.

I closed the bedroom door, kicked off my shoes as I crossed the room, grabbed the box of tissues from the night table, and crawled under the covers. My fingers ached when I opened my hand, releasing the tight grip I'd had on my phone since turning it off in the limo.

Too bad I couldn't turn off my brain as easily. No matter how hard I tried, I couldn't stop thinking about Nico. About that kiss. Raising my fingers to my mouth, I brushed them along my lips, remembering the perfect moment they'd touched his—warm, soft, moving gently against mine. The taste of him. The sound he made when he gave in to the passion, claiming my mouth, my heart . . . maybe even my soul.

If he hadn't stopped us, come to his senses and pushed me away, I'd have lost myself in him. *Why? Why does he make me feel this way?* I squeezed my eyes shut, anxious for sleep to fade the memory, stop the constant replay of my reckless actions that had pushed me across that moral line, breaking the promise I'd made to Will fifteen years ago. My promise to be faithful.

My body shook with ragged breaths and heavy sobs as I let out all the pain and confusion I'd kept locked inside.

THE CREAKING of my bedroom door woke me, but my nightmare didn't end. My eyes burned from the tears that wouldn't stop flowing. Groping blindly in front of me, I shoved aside my lifeless phone and found another tissue to wipe my face.

Jen cursed under her breath as she tripped crossing the room and crashed into the side of the bed. The far edge of the mattress dipped down.

"Danni?" Her gentle voice wrapped around me, an invisible hug, and she rubbed my back. "You awake?"

I lowered my shoulder and turned my head toward my sister, squinting through the darkness at her silhouette. "After that graceful entrance, how could I be asleep?" The raspy tone of my response betrayed my true emotions.

"Nico told me what happened . . . guess I don't have to ask how you're handling it?" She brushed my hair from my face and let out a heavy sigh. "You made a mistake, Danni. It happens sometimes."

"Don't. Not tonight." Every muscle in my body tensed. The way I'd behaved was deplorable—it couldn't be swept aside as a meaningless mistake. I wished I could erase the last few hours of my life, but I couldn't. "I don't deserve to feel better."

Jen crawled in bed and snuggled up against me. "You do, Danni. And you will. We'll work it out in the morning." She stroked my hair in silence for several minutes before wrapping me in an embrace. "I let you down. I'm so sorry. I never should have left you alone, knowing how you feel about him."

I reached up, grabbed my sister's hand, and held on.

DAYLIGHT PEEKED between the gaps in the curtain panels, the bright light further irritating my stinging, swollen eyes. I sniffled, trying to breathe in through my stuffy nose, sore from being rubbed with tissues most of the night.

I found my phone and powered it on, waiting impatiently for the screen to come to life. There were several missed calls and messages from Kendra and Kristi but nothing from Will. The phone fell to the mattress, leaving my hand as empty as my heart.

Still wearing the dress I'd worn to Metro Sky last night, I slid out of bed and headed toward the stairs. The smell of bacon lured me to the kitchen, where Jen had made herself at home.

She turned off the burner, setting the pan aside, and watched as I approached, an inquisitive look on her face. "A little overdressed for brunch, don't you think?"

"Figured black was appropriate for my funeral, so I decided to leave it on." My stomach roiled as I glanced at the plates of food on the counter. "You can eat without me. I'm not hungry. Sorry."

I grabbed a mug, filled it halfway with coffee, then added a copious amount of my favorite amaretto creamer and a huge mound of sweetener. I could feel Jen's gaze on me as I stirred and turned to find her watching with an amused grin.

"Can you even taste the coffee in there?" She motioned to my now-full mug.

"Not if I made it right." I took a sip as I crossed the room and climbed onto a stool at the breakfast bar, letting my head drop to my folded arms. A painful groan echoed through me. "How am I gonna face Will?" I lifted my head, hoping Jen had some sort of miracle answer. "He's gonna know. See right through me."

"You'll be fine." Jen carried a large mixing bowl filled with chocolate chip cookie dough and placed it on the bar before settling onto the seat next to me. "Dig in."

I poked at the batter, pushing the chips around, but I didn't think my stomach could handle it. Jen pushed my spoon out of the way and scooped some for herself.

"Look, you'll pull yourself together, and he'll never know. It was only one kiss." She waved her spoon in the air, continuing to talk around a glob of batter. "I get that it was a huge mistake, but—"

"It doesn't matter if it was one kiss or one hundred, it's still cheating! God, I *cheated* on my husband!" I tossed my spoon in the bowl as the tears started again and pushed the words out between heavy sobs. "I'd be able to tell." I pressed my palms to my eyes, wiping them dry. "If it was Will, I'd know in a heartbeat."

She studied me for a moment. "Would you? People hide that kind of stuff all the time. I mean . . . I'm not saying *he* has, but . . ."

"What *are* you trying to say?" A sharp pain clawed at my chest, making me gasp. "Do you know something you're not telling me?" The pitch of my voice rose as an icy chill tore through me.

"Shhh." She reached across the counter, taking my hands. "I'm not hiding anything. Promise. I'm just not sure I tru—if it were Ryan, I'd like to think I'd be able to tell. But lots of people are fooled every day."

She released my hands and sighed, picking at a piece of chocolate on the rim of the bowl. "Look, my point is that you can move past this. You have to. It's your only choice if you still want to rekindle things with Will."

I squeezed my eyes shut. *Great. Cheating, and now lying to cover it.* "What's the plan?"

The doorbell rang, followed immediately by a steady rapping and Nico's faint voice. "Danni? Answer the door. Please."

Jen turned toward the sound, but I didn't move. After a few seconds, she hopped off her stool and crossed the room.

"What the hell are you doing?" I called after her, trying to keep my voice low.

"I thought it was pretty obvious." She shook her head in amusement. "I'm going to open the door and see what he wants."

I scurried around the bar and back through the kitchen to hide in the small mud room by the garage. My heart skipped at the sound of his voice. Even muffled, it had that soothing, melodic tone. I smiled, remembering the effect it'd had on me the first time I'd heard him speak. It still didn't put me at ease . . . probably never would.

Jen's restrained voice called out from the kitchen. "Danni, where are you?"

I didn't respond, deciding to wait until she found me. Hoping she wouldn't.

She rounded the corner and stopped directly in front of me, crossed her arms over her chest, and pinned me with a judgmental stare. "Nico's here. He's worried about you and wants to talk."

"And you just let him come in? Are you crazy?"

"He seems really upset. Looks like hell too. Poor guy."

I seriously doubt that's possible. "Exactly whose side are you on?"

"I'll be right here. Just talk to him, Danni." She rested her hands on my shoulders and looked me square in the eyes. "Get things straightened out with Nico, and it may help you—"

"No. Absolutely not." I turned Jen around and pushed her toward the door. "You let him in; now you can get rid of him. I don't care what you tell him, just make him go away."

Jen hesitated then let out a huff and trudged back the way she came. Hushed voices filtered from the entrance again, followed by the door closing.

"Coast is clear, chicken. You can come out now." A hint of frustration filled her voice.

Not fully trusting her, I crept through the kitchen and peeked at the front door. Only Jen stood there. Feeling confident, safe, I closed the rest of the distance in a few long strides, pushed forward by a rush of adrenaline. "What the hell were you thinking?"

"Talking to him might help you figure this mess out. Give you a chance to ease your conscience."

I threw my hands up in the air. "Not likely! I'm guilty. Remember? What else is there to figure out?"

"I'm sorry for pushing Nico on you, but you need to get a grip if you don't want Will to get suspicious." She wrapped me in a calming hug. "Come on, let's watch the rest of our movie. Give your mind a rest, and we'll work on a plan a little later."

The doorbell rang. We both jumped then pulled back to look at each other.

"Nico?" I whispered, terrified by the possibility even though I couldn't imagine he'd come back so soon.

Jen shrugged. "I don't think so . . . but only one way to find out." She leaned to the side and peeked through the glass. "Oh, this won't be good."

She turned to me with a guarded expression as the bell sounded again, followed by knocking and Kendra's muffled shouts.

"Dammit, Danni. How long do you think you can hide from me? Open the damn door!"

Jen cringed. "She was pretty pissed when you ran off last night without even telling anyone you were leaving. And then you wouldn't answer your phone, and Logan left to deal with Nico. Hopefully she's calmed down by now."

I raised my brows and looked at Jen. "Does it sound like she's calmed down?" I moved past her to open the door. "Might as well get this over with."

Kendra stormed inside. "What the hell happened last night?" She swept her gaze over me, a strange expression on her face. "Wait a sec. If you ran off on Nico, why are you still dressed from the walk of shame?" She looked between Jen and me. "Someone needs to explain to me what the hell is going on."

I turned to Jen, my voice low. "Didn't you tell them anything last night?"

"Only that you were upset, and I was going home to keep you company."

Grabbing my sister's hand, I gave it a gentle squeeze and silently thanked her with my eyes. "Nico and I had a little . . . misunderstanding last night. I needed to get away, and I didn't want to ruin everyone else's night." Hoping to both calm and comfort my best friend, I reached out and rubbed her arm. "Jen just told me Logan ditched you to deal with him. I'm sorry. I didn't mean for that to happen."

The corners of Kendra's mouth turned up. A spark flashed in her eyes. "Oh, no need to worry about that." She winked then leaned to the side enough to bump her shoulder to mine. "He came back. And he *definitely* made up for leaving."

It took a few seconds for her message to sink in. "Wait . . . what? Did you go home with him?"

Kendra waved dismissively. "Long story. Very long." A suggestive grin spread across her face. "Anyway, Logan dropped me here and ran on a quick errand. He should be back any minute to take me to lunch before he heads home to New York, so we'll talk about that later. Tomorrow afternoon . . . whatever you want to do."

"I-I can't. I think I'm going to plan a special 'welcome home' for Will. Let him know how much I missed him." My voice faded; and I steeled myself, expecting her to tear into me again about the way he'd been acting and the fact that he still hadn't called me. I lifted my eyes to meet hers. "I need to focus on my marriage and stop thinking about Nico. And I need you to cooperate. Please."

Kendra groaned, shaking her head. "Look, sweetie, you know I just want you to be happy. And if you can somehow manage to find that with *him*, then fine, I'll do my best to support you. But you light up around Nico like I have *never* seen you do before. Right, Jen?"

Jen shrugged and gave a reluctant nod, mouthing the word, "Sorry."

Kendra continued with her last-ditch effort. "Just think about that. Okay? Sometimes love fades . . . or maybe it never really existed in the first place." She stared off in the distance a moment before closing her eyes. When she opened them, she continued in a somber voice. "Not the passionate kind of love anyway. Trust me."

Logan's car pulled into the driveway, and Kendra snapped out of whatever that odd moment was. A huge smile returned to her face.

"Love to stay and chat, ladies, but there is an incredibly sexy man waiting for my charming company." She gave us each a quick hug before rushing out the door.

Jen closed the door and turned to me. "So. We can try watching our movie again, or we can head to the kitchen for brunch first. Take your pick."

I caught my reflection in the glass by the door—ratted hair, smeared makeup, and Jen's little black party dress. "I think I'm going to go take a shower." *Wash away the memory of last night. Of Nico.* "And then maybe you can help me plan something special for Will?"

Jen's face lit up. "Oh, I think we can come up with something that will make him very happy to be back home."

Emotionally drained, I took two steps toward the stairs before stopping. How did everything get so off track? New Year's Eve had been perfect—the way Will treated me, and the way he worshiped my body when we made love that night. It was everything I wanted. Less than three weeks had passed, and I'd allowed myself to become so consumed by Nico that I'd lost sight of my goal—my resolution to spice things up in my marriage.

I turned and threw myself at Jen, wrapping her in a tight embrace. "Thanks. You're the best, you know."

"I know." She laughed, returning my enthusiastic hug. "But that's only 'cause I learned from the best."

CHAPTER 19

ROOM FOR DESSERT

The clock on the stove read 7:24. According to the text Will had sent earlier, he should be home any minute. My pulse pounded an erratic beat, a combination of nerves and anticipation.

Jen had talked me out of confessing, telling Will about the kiss I'd shared with Nico, a decision I still had serious doubts about even though it was "only one minor indiscretion," as she'd put it. According to Jen, I'd already punished myself enough, and "there was no point jeopardizing my marriage over a momentary lapse in judgment that would never happen again."

In my mind, a lie of omission was still a lie, and the only thing worse than living with that lie would be getting caught in it. I had to hope my body wouldn't betray me and make Will suspicious.

Fear that he might still be angry with me intensified my guilt over the secrets from Friday night. I wrapped my arms tighter across my churning stomach as I paced the kitchen floor, waiting for the car to bring Will home. The clicking of my heels on the tile echoed in the otherwise silent house. I needed to get things back to the way they'd been on New Year's Eve, get our relationship back on the right track and remind him how good we were together. Discover how passionate our sex life could be. Jen's plan had to work.

The dining room table was set for an intimate dinner for two, complete with a chilled bottle of champagne and some fresh strawberries with whipped cream. The aroma of Will's favorite dish, an herb-crusted beef tenderloin, filled the air. Candles burned in every room, the only source of light.

I clenched my fingers around the remote for the sound system, ready to begin playing the romantic songs I'd picked to tell Will how much he meant to me. Headlights flashed in the driveway, followed by car doors closing and the house door opening.

"Danielle?" The door closed. "What's with all the candles? Did we lose electric or something?"

I didn't answer, waiting patiently in the kitchen for him to come closer.

"Mmmm . . . something smells good. Danielle? You down here?" He paused when he reached the dining room then continued in a cautious tone. "Wow . . . what's the occasion?"

"Welcome home, sweetheart." I stepped into the dining room, beaming at my husband and realizing how much I'd missed him.

He'd only been away two days, but so much had happened during that time that it felt much longer. Of course, not hearing from him the whole time didn't help. My chest tightened at that thought, but I pushed aside the heartache for now.

I strolled across the room, a provocative sway to my hips, enjoying Will's expression as he watched. A casual glance at the table as I stopped in front of him reassured me the silver serving platter was within my reach.

I rested my hand on the back of a chair for support and

returned my eyes to my handsome husband. "See something you like?"

His head tipped to one side, a single eyebrow arched, and an appreciative grin spread across his face. The heat of his gaze scorched me as it swept over every inch of my body. My chef's apron covered me from my collarbone to my knees, but it left exposed my bare arms and shoulders, pale silk stockings, and my jeweled gold stilettos—the same shoes I'd kept on, at Will's request, when he made love to me on my birthday.

"You seem to be . . . underdressed." He slipped his hands in his pants pockets, tugging at the fabric while adjusting himself. "Aren't you cold?"

"Actually, I'm feeling rather *hot* tonight." I stepped closer, loosening his tie as I spoke. "I was thinking we could have dessert before dinner tonight." I pressed my hips against him, a subtle check to make sure I had raised his attention. "And then again after dinner."

"I—"

"Shhh." I placed a finger over his mouth then traced it along his lips while speaking in a seductive whisper. "I wasn't finished. Now, in case you were wondering what you're having for dessert . . ." Stepping back, I reached behind myself, untied the straps on my apron, and let it fall to the ground.

"Nice." He brushed the backs of his fingers along the top of my pale pink bra then explored the matching panties and garter belt, tracing the lace ruffle that ran around my hips. "Very nice."

His feathery touch made my skin tingle. I closed my eyes, anxious to get lost in the arousing sensation. My body tensed when my mind filled with an image of Nico standing in front of me, touching me—an unwelcome interruption from my guilty conscience. I forced it aside, reminding myself to stay focused on Will.

He slid his hand up my torso and captured the gold heart

pendant that dangled between my breasts, tracing his thumb over the diamond accents of the gift he'd given me on our wedding day. His eyes closed, and his brow furrowed. "You stole a piece of my heart the first day we met, but today I willingly give all of it to you. Now you can wear it next to yours . . ."

Heat from his palm as he pressed the pendant against my left breast sent a chill through me. I drew in a shaky breath and finished the words he'd first spoken nearly fifteen years earlier. "And always remember how precious and beautiful our love is."

My jewelry box held the handwritten note with the message he'd whispered in my ear while fastening the clasp behind my neck that night. Every time I wore his heart, I took a moment to remind myself what it represented. Could he possibly remember the words so clearly, or had he read them again too?

A single tear fell, landing on Will's hand.

"I'm so sorry, Danielle. I never meant to hurt you." He tipped my face toward his and placed a tender kiss at the corner of my eye.

It warmed my heart that he realized how much I'd suffered this weekend, but I worried he was seeing my guilt instead of the pain he'd caused by ignoring me. Either way, we were veering away from my plan to seduce him.

"So, getting back to dessert." I took a strawberry from the plate, dragged it through the whipped cream, and raised it to my mouth. Keeping my eyes locked on his, I swirled my tongue around the tip of the berry then closed my lips over it and gently sucked at the cream. "Mmmm . . ." I took a bite. "So sweet. Want some?"

The strawberry left a sticky trail as I skimmed it along his lower lip. His tongue darted out, gathering the juices and licking a dollop of cream from the corner of his mouth.

"Let me help you." I held his face and traced my tongue

along his lips before letting it sweep into his mouth, tasting the odd combination of strawberry and Will's favorite mints.

The kiss was warm. Familiar. The way it should be, I supposed, even though I craved more. More excitement. More passion. More . . . something.

He grabbed my wrists and pulled away. "I'm pretty worn out from my trip, babe." He brushed his hands across my breasts, down my torso, and up my arms. The light contact gave me goose bumps. "And I already ate. I'm sorry. You went to so much trouble too."

Such a jokester. I raised my brows, challenging him, waiting for him to crack a smile. It didn't come.

"Not a chance, mister. I'm not taking no for an answer tonight." I rolled my hips, grinding on his erection. "Seems to me you're up for some fun. Tell ya what, I'll even do all the work. All you have to do is lay back and enjoy."

"Christ, you're stubborn," he mumbled, pushing farther away from me.

"I prefer to think of it as persistent. Determined." Stepping forward, I leaned in and nuzzled against his neck, letting my lips glide along his skin before placing a lush kiss below his ear. "Getting what I want."

He groaned, sounding defeated. "Fine, but let me grab a quick shower first."

"Deal. I'll meet you upstairs." I smiled at him, satisfied with my small victory. His reaction was less enthusiastic than I'd imagined, but it would have to do for now. At least he hadn't turned me down. Again.

It had been almost three weeks since Will made love to me, and nearly as long since the last time I'd successfully seduced him. Of course, I'd had the advantage that day, sneaking up on him while he slept.

I stopped at the bottom of the stairs, a fun idea springing to mind, and dashed back to the dining room to grab the bowl of whipped cream before following Will upstairs.

WILL'S DRAWN-OUT "QUICK SHOWER" gave me plenty of time to get ready. I lit the candles I'd placed on every dresser then laid towels across the bed before kneeling in the middle to wait for him, the bowl of whipped cream by my side. We had never played with food before, and this wasn't part of the plan Jen helped me put together, but it could be romantic.

Sensual thoughts of caressing his body with my mouth filled my mind. A soft sigh slipped past my lips. I wiggled restlessly, trying to ease the gentle pulsing between my legs. Will hadn't even entered the room, and my panties were already damp.

Soft music drifted up from the sound system downstairs, and the scent of lavender slowly filled the air. Flickering light reflected off my pendant. I grasped it the same way Will had earlier. Hearing him recite the sentimental message had given me hope, shown me that he wanted to save our marriage too. Tonight would be perfect. *We belong together.*

After what felt like an eternity, the shower finally stopped. I straightened my garter belt, smoothed my panties, and adjusted my bra to show off the girls. My pulse quickened, anticipating his reaction to my surprise. I repositioned the bowl beside me then dragged my finger through the fluffy white cream and raised it to my lips.

Will emerged from the steamy bathroom, completely naked, pausing to watch as I sucked the cream off my finger. "Oh, now that's hot."

His body's instant reaction was clearly visible . . . not to mention a complete turn-on. My core clenched, anxious for his touch. But my needs would have to wait until I'd blown his mind, as promised.

"Why don't you join me?" I extended my arms toward him as he sauntered across the room.

He grabbed my hands, placed a tender kiss on each palm, and allowed me to pull him onto the bed. We knelt facing each other, our bodies pressed together.

I skimmed my fingertips along his smooth face as I gazed into his eyes, drowning in the ice blue pools. "I am gonna rock your world and make sure you never want to leave me again."

His eyes grew wide with a shocked expression, making me laugh. I weaved my fingers through his damp hair and guided his mouth to mine. There were no sparks like . . . the other night, but that didn't mean there wasn't a fire burning somewhere deep inside.

Will smoothed my hair away from my face. He pulled back to look at me and brushed his thumb across my lower lip. "So. This is nice, but I thought I was going to lay back and relax while you enjoyed your dessert." One side of his mouth pulled up in a suggestive taunt.

I gave him a gentle shove, and he fell to his back with an excessive amount of dramatic flair—hand on his chest, feigning a wounded heart. He slid toward the headboard and reclined against the mound of pillows there.

I shook my head, laughing at his lighthearted mood. Business trips were usually stressful events, but he seemed different this time. Relaxed. Things must have gone better than he'd expected, and I really wanted to ask him about it, but that would mean passing up the opportunity stretched out in front of me. News of his trip would have to wait.

Propped there, waiting with arms spread wide, he hooked his fingers, motioning for me to come to him. "Okay, babe.

Bring it on. I'm ready to be rocked." He folded his hands behind his neck and leaned his head back, eyes closed.

I collected my bowl and straddled his legs, climbing to sit on his thighs. After pausing to study my canvas, I swiped a finger through the whipped cream and painted a heart near the side of his neck, just below his jaw.

He winced, as I expected. It was a sensitive spot for him. But a few nibbles there could get his motor revving.

I bit back a grin. "Okay to go on?"

A smile eased his scrunched up face, and he nodded. "I'll be brave."

I continued dipping into the cream and drawing hearts along his jawline, down his neck, and at random places on his chest, giggling as he flinched with each cool touch.

"What are you doing?" He drew out the words with playful curiosity, peeking at me through one opened eye.

"Frosting my dessert." I beamed at him, thoroughly enjoying myself.

"Didn't anyone ever tell you not to play with your food before you eat it?" He bounced his eyebrow suggestively and wiggled his hips.

I took a moment to enjoy his amused expression before returning to my work of art. "Nope. Now, where was I?"

He squirmed, laughing, as I painted a trail of small white hearts down the center of his abdomen and along the length of his erection.

"So what happens after you finish frosting me?"

I leaned across the bed to place the bowl on the night table. "You already know the answer to that." I slid my finger along his lips, depositing one last dollop of cream, then covered his mouth with mine, pushing the whipped cream across his tongue as I kissed him. I pulled back to admire him, devouring him with my eyes. "You look delicious."

His smile widened. He tipped his head, exposing his neck and the first heart. "Dig in, babe."

I nibbled at his neck, licking and sucking the sweet cream from his fresh, clean body. When the first heart was gone, I continued with the second one and lapped up every drop. Will's breathing increased with each heart I moved to, following the order in which I'd placed them.

His occasional gasp or sigh as my lips and tongue explored every inch of him increased my arousal. A tingling energy spread throughout my body. A deep desire to be touched, loved.

Will shifted his hips when I reached the line of hearts that ran down his abdomen—my own version of a happy trail, paving the way to my prize.

"Oh damn, babe. This is sweet torture." His voice was tense, thick with anticipation.

"Patience, sweetheart."

Only one frosted body part remained. He moaned his approval as my mouth glided along the silky surface, my tongue swirling to hit all the right places to take him higher. One last heart to savor. Will hissed as my tongue slid down over it.

I pressed my thighs together, trying to appease the pulsing that begged for his touch. But there was only one way to satisfy my need to be filled by him. I dragged my lips up his stomach, eager for him to indulge me.

His eyes opened as he reached for me, sliding his fingers through my hair to grasp it and hold me in place. "Don't stop."

He stretched across the bed, grabbed the bowl from the nightstand, and scooped out the last of the whipped cream. "I think you missed a spot." A wicked smile spread across his face as he smeared the cream along the length of his erection. He wiped his finger across my mouth before slipping it past my lips, removing the excess. "Aren't you gonna finish me off?"

What I really wanted was to have him inside me. To find

that connection between us that I'd been missing. I gave him a sweet smile then licked my lips. "Of course. I was just teasing you."

I picked up right where I'd left off, and it didn't take long for Will to find his rhythm again.

He was getting close, and I swore only one touch from him would put me over the edge too. I clenched my thighs tighter, trying to relieve the throbbing. Each long stroke I drew on him vibrated as I purred with unfulfilled need as much as with the satisfaction of driving him wild.

"Yeah, right there, babe." He twisted his fingers in my hair, tightening his grip as he held my head where he wanted it, pulling me harder against him as his pace quickened.

I pressed his hips to the mattress, pinning him and taking full control of his pleasure with my mouth and hands.

"Damn, babe, you're killing me." A low steady moan echoed in his chest and grew in intensity. "But it. Feels. So. Fucking. Good."

His abdomen tensed. His head fell back against the headboard. A feral growl emanated from him, and his body shuddered as he rode out his release.

I fought against my gag reflex, taking what he gave me until his body relaxed. He eased his fingers from my hair, finally allowing me to disengage. I sat back on his legs, dragging the back of my hand across my mouth as I watched the man I love.

A satisfied smile covered his peaceful face, and he let out a contented sigh. His eyes opened, meeting mine. He leaned forward to grab my shoulders and pulled me along his chest until our mouths met, rewarding me with a deep, lush kiss. "Now that's one hell of a welcome home."

"I wanted to show you how much I missed you . . ." I settled into his lap, still aching for relief, and rubbed myself along his withering erection. "And how happy I am to have you back home."

"And you succeeded. That was amazing." He pulled me closer, wrapping me in a tight embrace.

I nuzzled his neck, still grinding against him. "Will?" Desperation laced my voice as I pleaded with him.

He pressed his lips to the top of my head. "But I think I need another shower now." Grabbing my hips, he shifted me off his lap then slipped from the bed and crossed the room.

What the hell? That's it? Is he freakin' serious? "Um, Will? Are you coming back?"

"Of course." He turned in the doorway to face me, leaning into the trim. "You don't think I'm going to spend the whole night in here, do you?" He chuckled and shook his head, but he strolled back to me.

It was a mean joke, making me think we were finished, but I probably deserved it after torturing him. I knew he wouldn't really leave me hanging.

He brushed back my hair and lifted my face toward his. "Why don't you go get dinner set up while I shower." His words were soft and sweet, like the kiss that followed. "Then we can come back upstairs."

He returned to the bathroom and closed the door.

I let out a deep sigh and tried to adjust to the hollow spot where my heart used to be. "Well that didn't go as planned, did it?" I slid off the bed, grumbling under my breath as I crossed the room to collect my robe from the closet. "Well, Danni, you can give up, or you can keep on trying. What's it gonna be?"

The bathroom door opened just enough for Will to pop his head out, a huge smile on his face. "Oh, and don't get dressed. You look incredibly sexy like that."

CHAPTER 20

MORE LIES

The pop of the champagne bottle greeted me when I entered the dining room carrying the last of the serving platters. Will watched me with an amused smile as I placed the food on the table, barely able to pull my eyes away from him. Loose-fitting lounge pants hung low on his lean hips, tempting me. One tug would have him completely naked again.

His muscles flexed with each casual movement as he filled our glasses then sat at the end of the table and slid my place setting close to his.

He barely managed to eat as he rambled on, unusually animated, sharing every minute detail of his trip. The whole time he spoke, he touched my arms or let his hand drop to brush along my legs. After a few minutes, he shifted in his seat, moving closer, and progressed to sliding his fingers along the straps of my garter belt and stroking my thighs above my stockings. His constant attention distracted me and made it difficult to focus on his words or perform even the simplest tasks, like cutting my food or chewing.

I uncrossed my legs and allowed them to ease apart, gasping when his teasing touch rose higher, sending shockwaves through my already aroused body. His occasional chuckle told me he knew exactly what he was doing and the effect it was having on me.

I didn't know how much more I could take before I cleared the dining room table and threw myself across it, begging Will to take me there. All I could think about was our next round of dessert.

We stood at the same time when we finally finished . . . sort of eating. He grabbed my wrist, stopping me as I reached for his plate, and pulled me to him. The kiss began slow and gentle, his hands framing my face, then grew deeper and more intense, taking my breath away.

He leaned back, looking at me. "You're so beautiful. You know that?" He rolled his hips, demonstrating the effect I had on him, before claiming my mouth for another kiss.

My only response was a soft moan as my body collapsed into his.

He brushed his cheek along mine. "Why don't you clean up here while I go unpack?"

I nodded as he peeled me away from him. The moment he left the room, I rushed to complete my task in record time, shoving covered plates of uneaten food into the fridge. I couldn't wait to join him upstairs.

Will was already in bed when I entered the room. He greeted me with a smile and patted the empty spot next to him. "Been waiting for you, babe. What took you so long?"

He laughed when I narrowed my eyes at him before sliding under the covers. Will was on me immediately—kissing me, fondling me, overloading my senses. It had been weeks since he'd touched me like this.

By the time he moved his hand between my legs, I could barely contain the explosion building inside me. It took only a few strokes for him to push me over the edge, crying out with relief as my body trembled. He held me, continuing to kiss me, as waves of my amazing orgasm washed over me.

"Wow! That was just . . . wow." I closed my eyes and sighed, still enjoying the aftershocks.

"I aim to please." Will kissed me then rolled to his back and swung an arm above his head—his normal sleeping position.

"Hey. That's it?" I leaned over him, poking at his chest.

He didn't open his eyes. "Christ, Danielle. What more could you want?"

"Well, I thought Little Will might want to come out to play." I tugged at the sheet, exposing his chest, but he grabbed my wrist to stop me.

His eyes opened and locked on mine, pleading. "Babe, I had a really busy weekend. This was a nice welcome home, but I'm exhausted. Let's get some sleep."

I fell to my back and stared at the ceiling, feeling suddenly empty. Okay, so tonight didn't go exactly as I'd planned. Why couldn't I be satisfied with the incredible orgasm I just had? I breathed out a heavy sigh, unable to relax enough to fall asleep. We didn't actually have sex, but at least he didn't turn me down. Didn't blow me off . . . tonight.

"Will?" I shifted, propping myself on my elbow to look at him.

"Hmm?"

"Why didn't you call or text me all weekend? Were you so mad at me for wanting to spend time with you that you needed to cut me off? I was worried about you, you know. I didn't know where you were staying. And I couldn't even reach you on your phone."

He turned his head to look at me with a confused expression. "Didn't Kim call you? She felt bad about not getting the information to me before Friday and said she'd take care of calling you with my arrangements. I'll have to talk to her about it when I get to the office tomorrow. Find out what happened." He returned to his relaxed pose, staring at the ceiling.

"You could have called me yourself, you know?"

"I'm sorry, babe. I didn't mean to upset you. I was having trouble getting a signal for some reason."

"Really? That seems a little hard to believe. Two whole days and no signal? Not one tiny opportunity to send a text?" I shook my head, amazed. Did he actually think I was stupid? "Even so, I'm sure there was a phone in your room. You could have called from there. But I'm sure you had another good excuse not to. Why don't you just admit you were avoiding me?" My voice faded. Saying the words out loud was more painful than I'd imagined it would be.

He turned on his side to face me. "Because I wasn't. It was late when I got back to my room both nights. I didn't want to take a chance of waking you." He brushed my hair from my face, wrapping a curl around his finger. "But you're right—I should have, and I'm sorry. It won't happen again." He leaned forward, placing a kiss to my forehead. "Why don't you tell me about your weekend—what did you and Jen do?"

His question caught me off guard, and I struggled to remember what Jen told me to say. "Um . . . nothing exciting. You know. Just the usual. Boring sister stuff." I stretched, forcing a yawn and rolling to my back. "You're right. It's late. We should probably get some rest."

He leaned over me, a deep furrow between his brows. "You okay?"

"Yeah." My voice squeaked. I cleared my throat. "Yeah. I'm . . . I just don't feel so good all of a sudden." I lifted my head and gave him a quick kiss before turning to lay with my back to him. "I think I just need some sleep."

The mattress shifted as Will settled back into his pillow and heaved a heavy sigh.

CHAPTER 21

SET UP AGAIN

"A note. Can you believe it? A goddamned freakin' sticky note on the bathroom mirror telling me he couldn't sleep and went into work early." Keeping my voice down as I finished recapping my unsuccessful attempt to seduce my husband was nearly impossible but necessary if I wanted to avoid becoming the latest bit of office gossip.

A few overachievers had already wandered in and continued to conveniently pass by my desk for no apparent reason. Yeah, I looked a wreck. So what? They needed to get a life of their own and stop eavesdropping on mine. My grip on the receiver tightened as I hunched over my desk and braced for Kendra's reaction.

Applause drifted through the phone line. "Well, it's about damn time you get angry at him for treating you like shit."

"I hate feeling this way. Jen called on my drive in, tried to calm me down, but even she said something's off." I picked up the picture of Will and me, a daily reminder of how happy we'd once been . . . and could be again if he would only cooperate. "I don't get it. He was really into it, having fun, you know?" I plunked the frame facedown on the desktop with a little more force than intended, but I'd worry about the possibility of cracked glass later. Maybe.

"Of course he was into it. He's a guy. You really think he'd turn down a blow job? Personally, I think you were too generous, finishing him off when it wasn't what you wanted." She gave a bitter laugh. "Seriously though, what kind of selfless ass thanks his wife by throwing her a quickie O just to shut her up so he can sleep? And don't even get me started on his pathetic excuses for not contacting you all weekend. Like he can't get a signal in Chicago . . . give me a break. You have every right to be pissed."

I hated that I actually agreed with her assessment of Will for a change and kept my mouth shut.

"Next time, instead of greeting him in sexy lingerie, you should show up at the door with a meat cleaver, a fist full of sausage links, and a crazed look in your eyes. Tell him you've been thinking about him. That'll get his attention."

"Or get me arrested."

"You're no fun." The laughter in her voice eased some of my tension.

"I don't know what I'm doing wrong."

"No, I'm . . . pretty sure it's him." A strange dismal tone crept into her voice, but the sudden bout of melancholy didn't last. She cleared her throat and carried on, her usual brazen attitude back in place. "What is his fucking problem anyway? I mean, he must have a problem to keep turning you down, right? Maybe he just needs a little trip to the pharmacy." Kendra chuckled. "I bet Nico wouldn't—"

"Stop. You promised not to push anymore."

"Okay, fine. Sorry. You're right." She gave a wicked laugh. "But you're curious now, aren't you?"

"Kendra!" Great. With that thought planted in my mind, I'd

be fantasizing about him most of the day again. *I should probably be angry with her.*

"All right. Stopping. But seriously, you do need to sit Will's ass down and find out what the problem is. Trust me, it's the only way to make it work. No more games. You gotta let him know what you want from your marriage and find out if he's on the same page. Tonight."

"Can't. His eloquent sticky note ended with a reminder that he would be working late tonight. It's probably best to give it a few days to settle anyway. And I may even turn in early tonight. Get some rest, you know?" *Avoid him.*

A long pause preceded Kendra's quiet reply. "So, you believe him?"

"Yes. Maybe . . . hell, I don't know." I blew out a heavy sigh. "I have to."

Kendra didn't respond, which created possibly the first ever awkward moment of silence between us.

"Hey, my boss just walked in. I gotta run. Talk to you later?" He'd be here any minute, so it wasn't a total lie.

"Sure. Um, later. Love you, sweetie."

The line went dead a few seconds before Peter entered the office, Alexia lagging far behind.

I pushed the past three days aside and slipped into professional mode. "Good morning, Mr. Jamison."

"Danni, good morning to ya." He paused at my desk. "You feeling okay?"

I raised my chin and gave a confident nod. "Bit of a rough night, but I'm good to go. Briefing at eight?"

"Long as you're up to it. Sure. I just need a few minutes to settle in." He studied me a moment longer then moved on to his office.

I turned my attention to his agenda for the day, making sure I had everything organized.

"Good morning, Danielle. Isn't it a beautiful day?"

Alexia's syrupy greeting made me want to barf or hurl something, but I did the right thing and painted on my best fake smile. "Good morning. You're in an awfully good mood for a Monday morning." It should be illegal, or at least kept to herself. "Did you have a good weekend?"

"Amazing!" Her smile threatened to take over her entire face. She clasped her hands, pulling them to her chest as she floated to the side of my desk. "Would you like to hear about it?"

Nope. Not at all. I presumed I didn't have a choice though. A quick glance at the time on my computer confirmed that I still had five minutes to kill. "Um, sure. I have a few minutes."

She pulled her long chestnut hair to one side, tugging on it as she talked. "My boyfriend took to me to New York City for a romantic weekend. I'd never been there before. We took a limo and stayed in this beautiful hotel on Fifth Avenue." She paused, biting at her lip. Her cheeks turned a rosy shade. After peeking at our surroundings, she continued in a whisper. "We barely left our room the whole time."

Her shy innocence was endearing and uncommon for a twenty-eight-year-old. I almost felt guilty about tuning out half of what she said, but an odd sense of *déjà vu* distracted me—the same sense of familiarity I'd had when we met on her first day.

She rambled on about a carriage ride in Central Park and watching ice skaters. Maybe on another day, in a better mood, I would have found it interesting. Not today.

"It sounds fabulous. No wonder you're so excited." I checked the time again. Only a minute had passed. "I really hate to cut you short, but your dad is expecting me for a meeting."

Alexia traced the edges of my upside-down picture frame and talked on about the beautiful view from their room and seeing the city lit up at night. She lifted the frame, turned it over, and smiled as she glanced at the photo. Her eyes flashed to mine. "Uh-oh. Trouble in paradise?" She adjusted the stand and placed it back on my desk, angling it toward me. "Hope it's nothing serious. I'd be happy to listen, you know, if you need someone to talk to."

I tipped my head, a futile effort to avoid seeing that damn photo. It was impossible to look at Alexia without catching a glimpse of Will. She didn't seem to notice my unease, or maybe she was just too polite to acknowledge it as she waited for my response. Her doe-eyed expression and sweet smile reinforced the sincerity of her offer, but it didn't feel right to rant about my screwed-up love life with someone I barely knew. Especially after hearing how happy she and her boyfriend were.

"Oh, I'm sorry," her angelic voice interrupted. "I-I should have realized you—I didn't mean to pry." She moved away from my desk, glancing back at me with sad eyes. "Well, I better get to work, and you have your meeting."

"Alexia . . . wait." It seemed being an ass might be contagious. But, unlike my husband, *I* couldn't let someone go on feeling unappreciated. Now all I had to do was figure out what to say.

She turned to me, an expectant smile on her face. "It's okay, Danielle. I understand." She stepped closer and placed her hand on my arm. "I hope your day gets better." She walked away, humming a cheery tune.

Between worrying about talking things out with Will and imagining Nico in place of him last night, my mind had created its own nonproductive agenda this morning.

Fifteen minutes and counting until my lunch break, but stress had my stomach in too many knots to deal with food.

That would leave plenty of time for a brisk walk on a frigid winter day to clear my head.

The cursor on my blank screen blinked a steady beat. The slow rhythm of a dance, rousing the intoxicating memory of being wrapped in Nico's strong arms, pressed against his solid chest. Surrounded by him. Consumed by him. My fingers twitched, tracing the ridges in his sculpted body, exploring the impress—

"Hey, you in there?"

Kristi's hand waving in front of my face registered around the same time I realized she was hanging over the reception counter on my desk, practically shouting at me. I blinked a few times, drifting back to reality.

"Wow! You were totally zoned out there for a minute. Reminded me of one of those goofy sci-fi movies Ben loves to watch. Well, we don't actually *watch* too much of it, ya know?" She giggled and hugged herself. "But anyway . . . hmmm, where was I going with that?" She shook her head. "Doesn't matter. I just wanted to see how you're doing, post Friday night meltdown and all."

I pressed my brows together, trying to focus on her scattered babbling while the images of Nico slowly faded. "What are you talking about?"

"You, silly. Your mind was a million miles away." She swept her hands through the air as she spoke, fingers wiggling. "Care to share? I mean, Kendra already filled me in on last night, but . . ." She pushed out her bottom lip in an exaggerated pout.

I couldn't tell her she'd interrupted my latest fantasy about Nico or that I'd spent most of the morning lusting after him. "Sorry, I was just thinking about Will. Kendra and Jen both told me I need to talk to him about—"

"Oh, my. Showtime." Kristi drew the words out, sounding amused.

I twisted in my seat to follow her line of sight straight to Nico. He crossed the room, adjusting his tie and checking the buttons on his suit coat, his eyes locked on me the whole time. His pace slowed as he approached, and his lips twitched with a hesitant smile.

"Hey there, Nico! Isn't this a nice surprise?" Kristi's exuberant greeting demanded attention.

He cast a quick glance in her direction. "How's it going, Kristi?"

"Oh, you know. Nothing too exciting. At least not so far. But . . . I have a feeling that's about to change." She practically sang the last sentence.

Nico swept his gaze over me, a concerned expression on his face. "Good to see you, Danni. You look . . . very nice today."

Clearly not, but he deserved credit for trying. "I—that's—" *Not this again.* I rubbed my temples, trying to remember how to form a sentence.

Maybe it was his casual, sexy demeanor or the way his tailored suit accentuated his perfect body that rendered me speechless.

Or it could have been the mental images of him in his birthday suit still lingering from my latest fantasy.

"What are you doing here?" The question erupted with more force than I'd intended.

His expression steeled, and he retracted from the verbal slap. "Well, I'm sure I deserved that." He dragged a hand through his hair and took a deep breath. "I'm here to see you."

Kristi's faint sigh reminded me of our audience. Nico and I both turned toward her. She'd settled in quite comfortably, elbows propped on the reception counter and her chin rested in her palms. She watched intently, a dreamy smile covering her face, as she listened to our conversation.

I cleared my throat to get her attention.

"Oops. Sorry. Just thinking about something Ben and I were talking about this morning. Carry on." She motioned for us to continue.

Nico chuckled, returning his attention to me. "I came to apologize for the other night. Thought we could have lunch together, which would give me plenty of time to grovel and beg you to forgive me." He shifted uneasily, twisting and tugging at his signet ring.

A lunch date with Nico? I didn't dare put myself in that situation. "Sorry, I already have plans." He didn't need to know my plans involved only me and a brisk walk.

"Actually . . ." Kristi interrupted, beaming at me. "I came up to tell you I need to cancel. Sorry." She shrugged then faced Nico with a satisfied grin. "So, it turns out she's free."

I wanted to kill her, but shooting her with a menacing glare would have to do. Right now, I needed to think of a way to get out of the trap she'd sprung on me.

"Guess it's my lucky day then. As long as you agree to go, that is." Nico fidgeted, waiting for my response. "Danni? Please say yes."

"Sorry. I have work to do." I grabbed a stack of folders and stood, preparing to flee to Peter's office before I gave in to the growing urge to jump into Nico's arms.

He lifted his hand to stop me but retracted it, gripping the back of his neck instead. Eyes closed, he raised his face toward the ceiling. I ignored his faint troubled groan and took advantage of the opportunity to slip past him. That small amount of distance made it possible to breathe again. I managed to pull in several calming breaths by the time I reached Peter's office.

Nico appeared at my side. He touched my arm, stopping me from opening the door, then slid his hand to mine. "Don't run off. I know I don't deserve it, but give me one more chance to prove myself." He looked into my eyes, pleading. "I promise I'll keep my hands to myself."

The desperation in his voice cut through me, resonating with the need for him that I'd been trying to suppress. Maybe talking things out would give me closure and allow me to move past this crazy infatuation. I gave a gentle nod then lowered my eyes to stare at our joined hands.

Nico released me and surrendered. A playful smile spread across his face, revealing that familiar single dimple. "Starting now."

"Well, my work here is done." Kristi blew me a kiss before bouncing off. "Toodles! And make sure you call me later, Danni."

"Oh, you can count on it," I said. She had a lot of explaining to do.

Nico shoved his hands in his pockets and leaned into the doorframe. "I have a reservation at Giardano's."

Well that was a bit presumptuous. But Giardano's? I blew out a short huff. *Nice touch, Kristi.*

Nico bent his knees, lowering himself to my level. "Is that okay? I have lunch there every Monday, but we can go somewhere else."

I blinked, trying to focus. "No, that's my favorite restaurant, but I suppose you already knew that."

His smile grew wider, and his chest expanded. "Why, thank you. I'm sure the owner will be very pleased to hear that." He reached past me and knocked on Mr. Jamison's office door.

At Peter's muffled response, Nico opened the door and strode inside with his normal air of confidence.

"Nico. Good to see you, son." Peter rose from his desk and crossed the room, meeting Nico midway for a hearty handshake. "I never got to thank you for New Year's Eve. I really appreciate you filling in last minute like that."

"You know me . . . never too busy to spend the evening with a lovely lady. Anyway, the reason I'm here, and I'm sorry to show up unannounced, but I wondered if I could borrow your assistant for a business lunch. I could use help with some of the additional forms you sent over, and my assistant is off this week."

"That's fine by me, as long as Danni doesn't have other plans."

"Nope. Already checked with her."

"All right then, just don't go trying to steal her away from me with that legendary charm of yours." Peter's boisterous laugh echoed in the room. "I'm expecting you to give her back when you're done."

"Will do, sir. And thanks." Nico emerged wearing a satisfied smile. "You're all mine. Well, temporarily." He swept his arm through the air in front of me. "After you."

CHAPTER 22

SWEET GESTURE

The elevator doors opened, freeing me from the confined space. I needed air—fresh air that didn't fill my head with Nico's scent every time I took a breath. I rushed across the vast lobby, eager to get outside. Nico caught up to me midway and brushed his hand across my lower back, guiding me toward the exit. The brief contact made me shiver, which earned a questioning glance from him.

"Caught a chill." I shrugged and pulled my scarf higher on my neck. "It's not usually this drafty in here. Must really be cold outside." I added a forced shiver to reinforce my point.

He gave a single nod, but I got the impression he didn't believe me.

How did I get myself into this? I drew in a shaky breath and tapped my thumb against my leg. *It's just lunch, Danni. Get a grip.*

When we reached the exit, my feet froze, refusing to cross the line and leave with Nico. He held the door open and waited patiently, watching me. There was a call to "keep it moving," and someone bumped me from behind, but I couldn't go.

"Danni?" Nico leaned closer and touched my arm. "Is something wrong?"

"I-I can't. We shouldn't—" I wrapped my arms across my churning stomach and took a step back, shaking my head. "Tell me what we're doing here, Nico. The truth." I pleaded with my eyes, wanting him to tell me it was fine, that I was overreacting.

"Come with me." He took my hand and eased back into the lobby with me in tow. We stopped beside a large planter, and he lowered himself to look in my eyes. "The truth, Danni, is that we're two friends going to lunch together. And there's nothing wrong about that." He continued studying me, searching my face for something. "Wait here. Okay? I'll be right back."

He reached into his breast pocket, pulled out a small platinum case, then turned to leave. Crossing the marble floor with long, smooth strides, Nico headed toward the nearby security desk. The clerk seated there smiled as he approached, twisting a finger in her long blonde hair. He leaned across to talk to her then borrowed a pen and wrote something.

I glanced across the lobby at the steady flow of people going into the cafeteria. It would be so easy to slip in there and get lost in the crowd while Nico was preoccupied. If I wanted to.

So why am I still standing here?

Nico returned. He took my hand and pressed a business card into my palm. "This is your insurance policy. If I cross the line, even slightly, you can call Ben and Logan." He chuckled and rubbed his jaw. "Trust me, they'll be more than happy to kick my ass for hurting you again."

Most people wouldn't have cared about my unease, so I appreciated his sweet gesture. I hooked my finger, motioning for him to come closer. "You do realize I could have just asked Kristi to call Ben, don't you?" I smiled at him, teasing. "But thanks."

I reclaimed my hand and looked at the card. Three numbers

were written on the backside, the last without a name beside it. "Who's the other number for?" I raised my eyes to wait for his delayed answer.

His lopsided grin greeted me. "That's mine. My personal cell." He turned the card over in my hand. "And that's my office number. You can call me anytime, for anything. 'Cause that's what friends do, right?"

I already heard his voice too often in my fantasies. Actually calling him—the *real* him—was definitely not a good idea.

My attention drifted back to the card. *Domenico Giardano, COO.* "This is you?" Stupid question, but I needed to be sure since I'd expected his card to be for The Next Level. "I mean, what about your gym? I thought—well, I remember Kristi mentioned that Ben's family owns Elevations, so . . . wow. You're a busy guy." Yet he'd managed to make time for me. I bit back a grin. "Probably too busy for lunch."

Nico chuckled. "Nice try, but even us busy guys have to eat."

"Wait." I glanced at the card again. "Giardano? As in the restaurant?"

"Yep. My parents' baby."

"And that's why we're going there." I drew out the words, feeling foolish about the way I'd reacted outside Peter's office.

"Yes. *If* we can ever manage to leave the building." He swept his arm toward the exit.

"Sorry, I just assumed Kristi—and then you picked there because—uh, never mind." I held up the card he'd given me, wishing it were large enough to hide behind. "Thanks for this."

"So . . . we're good?" He spoke the words with caution, but his voice held a glimmer of hope.

I hesitated, still not confident I trusted him. Or myself.

My chest vibrated with a low groan as my resistance crumbled. Again. "Fine. Let's get it over with."

CHAPTER 23

DELICIOUS COMPANY

If I thought the confined space of the elevator was unbearable, I should have known better than to get into Nico's little sports car with him; but here we were.

His magnificent scent and the palpable energy radiating from him brought all of my senses to life. My body pulsed with an intense beat that rivaled the rock music from his playlist. Even the skillful way he shifted and maneuvered through the speeding traffic aroused me.

While he drove, Nico told me the history of Elevations and how his grandparents had grown it from a small ski lodge to the exclusive resort we knew it as today. Focusing on his story kept my mind occupied—prevented it from following my body's lead and becoming fully consumed by him. But I had to admit, and only to myself, that I could learn to love the effect he had on me.

"Nonno, my grandfather, is supposedly retired now, only serving as the head of the board." Nico let out a laugh. "But he 'gets bored sitting around waiting to die,' so he says, and likes filling in at various positions throughout the resort. We never know where he's going to show up from one day to the next.

But it makes him happy, and that's really all that matters to any of us."

"So you and Ben run the place now?"

"And our sister. Gabriela is the CEO. She'll tell you it's because she's the smartest and most responsible, but it's really because she's the oldest." He bobbed his head. "Then again, she may be right."

The teasing tone of his voice made me smile.

As he zipped into the parking lot at Giardano's, I let out a long, exaggerated breath. "Wow, that was . . . some ride." I peeled my aching fingers away from the seat and armrest where I'd been clinging.

Nico's face lit up. "What fun's a toy if I can't play with it?" He laughed as he cut the engine and hopped out.

The amazing aroma of Italian cuisine greeted us when we entered the restaurant.

"Mmmm . . . smells delicious." My stomach grumbled to life as my appetite returned.

"Welcome to Giardano's." A beautiful young woman, mid-twenties at most, hopped off her stool behind the hostess station. Her interest in me vanished the moment Nico appeared beside me. She shifted her full attention to him, devouring him with her eyes. "Hi, Nico. I was beginning to worry you weren't coming." She adjusted her low-cut white blouse and watched him with an anxious smile.

"Good afternoon, London. You look nice today." His response was very business-like . . . almost too practiced.

I looked between them, suddenly aware that London might have a reason to expect a special greeting from Nico.

"Do you know if our table is ready?" he asked as he took my coat.

She slipped from behind her podium and moved toward him. Her short black skirt revealed long slender legs, accented by spiky red shoes that weren't made for standing all day. She scanned me with an inquisitive glare while answering him, but her voice didn't waver. "Yep, your usual spot. I took care of it personally." She stroked her sleek ebony hair, letting her hand skim over her breast and down her torso.

Nico seemed oblivious to London's performance. Without even glancing in her direction, he thanked her and moved to the coat room on the far side of the elegant waiting area. She sagged against one of the Tuscan pillars, a disappointed expression on her face.

"Wake up, London," Nico teased when he returned a moment later. He joined me by the arched stone entry to the dining area and extended his arm. "Shall we?"

As he to led me to our table, my gaze darted around the room. It hadn't occurred to me before that someone might see us and get the wrong impression. Sure, Peter would back me up if Will were to question me about it, but I'd prefer to avoid an uncomfortable situation. Especially with the way things were between us lately.

A group of female guests watched us cross the room, reminding me of the attention Nico garnered making his entrance at Elevations on New Year's Eve.

I cast a sideways glance at the gorgeous man next to me and tried to ignore the knot in my stomach. "So, do women fall all over you *everywhere* you go?"

He moved closer, fixing me with a mischievous smile. "What can I say? It's a curse." He laughed and bumped his shoulder against mine.

Images of the women I'd seen throw themselves at Nico crowded my mind, and the knot in my stomach pulled tighter.

He directed me to a table tucked in the back corner near the kitchen, pulled out my chair, then took his seat across from me. Without saying a word, he studied me briefly, brushing his thumb along his lips. His eyes locked on mine as he leaned forward, a satisfied grin spreading across his face. "You're not jealous, are you?"

What? "Of course not." My cheeks grew warm, and I gained a new appreciation for the dim lighting in restaurants. I tore my eyes away from his to take in my surroundings, focus on anything other than him.

A privacy wall isolated us from most of the restaurant, except for a small, unoccupied bar directly ahead of me. This eased my concerns of being discovered, but it did little to help with my effort to avoid facing him.

A bottle of wine and plates of bruschetta and caprese salad filled the center of our table, an arrogant display of his confidence that he wouldn't be dining alone. Was I that weak and predictable, or was he just used to women always caving in to him?

Before I had a chance to question him, the waiter appeared. He greeted Nico by name then introduced himself to me, opened my napkin, and placed it on my lap. After taking our orders, he served the wine then disappeared toward the kitchen.

"Here's to new friends and second chances." Nico tapped the rim of his glass to mine before taking a drink.

Not wanting to be rude, I followed his lead and took a tentative sip of wine, which turned into downing half my glass. If Nico noticed, he didn't let on.

"I hope you're hungry." He motioned to the plates before taking a hearty bite of bruschetta.

I rearranged my place setting and smoothed out the imaginary wrinkles in the linen tablecloth. The weight of Nico's stare grew uncomfortable as I slid my fingers along the stem of my glass.

"You're quiet," he said.

I lifted my eyes to meet his. "You brought me here to apologize, grovel, and beg for my forgiveness, if I remember correctly. I'm not the one who should be talking."

He rubbed the stubble along his jaw. "Fair enough." After blowing out a slow breath, he leaned toward me, resting his forearms on the table. "Look, Danni. The other night—I don't know what got into me, but I promise it won't happen again. My parents raised me to be a gentleman, and I hope you'll give me a chance to show you that's who I really am."

I waited for him to continue, but he didn't. "That's it? You didn't need to drag me across town for that. Hell, you could have even sent it in an e-mail. A very *short* e-mail."

He groaned and leaned back in his chair, keeping his eyes locked on mine. "You're not going to make this easy on me, are you?"

"Why should I? You knew I was married, but that didn't stop you from coming on to me."

He leaned forward again, his eyes reaching into my soul. After a quick glance around the room, he continued in a hushed, sultry tone. "Correct me if I'm wrong, but the way I remember it, *you* kissed *me*. I was just out having a few drinks and a little fun."

"Right, you were just an innocent victim. Well, I guess that explains the huge erection that kept pushing against me, so don't go acting—what?" The mischievous sparkle in his eyes distracted me.

"Nothing." He gave a low chuckle. "I'm just glad you were impressed."

I let out a frustrated groan as I realized what I'd said. When would I learn to keep my mouth shut? I narrowed my eyes and struggled to make my voice stern. "This isn't funny."

His lips pressed together and managed to contain his playful grin, but the sparkle in his eyes remained. He held up his hands. "You're right, and I'm sorry. I acted like a jerk Friday night."

"No argument from me." I crossed my arms and continued to stare at him, choosing to ignore the surge of energy that shot through my body when his gaze flashed to my chest.

"Logan likes to hang out at Metro Sky when he's in town. I'd never seen you there before. Didn't expect to see you there that night. And I'd already had a few drinks." He hesitated, massaging his palms. "I let things get out of hand, and I'm sorry. Not about the way I feel about you, but for the way I acted and for hurting you. I want you to—" Nico looked toward the kitchen then straightened in his seat. "We'll finish this later."

He pushed to his feet as a man wearing a black chef's coat approached our table. He was a few pounds heavier than Nico and had graying hair, but the resemblance was clear.

"Papa."

The older man's face lit up, and he extended his arms, pulling Nico into his embrace. "It's about time you show up." He laughed and took hold of Nico's head to place a kiss on each cheek. "How's my boy?"

"Good as always. This is my friend Danielle." Nico looked at me with a warm smile. "And this is my father, Angelo."

Angelo looked between Nico and me with a doubtful expression. "Friend. Hmm . . . if you say so." He pulled me from my seat and greeted me with the same type of enthusiastic hug he'd given Nico.

"Danni here is a big fan of your restaurant."

"She has good taste. I like her already." Angelo laughed, squeezing me again.

As soon as he released me, I returned to my seat and allowed the two men to chat. I picked at my salad while sipping my wine, enjoying the animated way they spoke, joking and laughing. The obvious depth of Nico's love and respect for his father warmed my heart. Theirs was the type of relationship I'd imagined having with my parents and always dreamed I would've had with my children.

After a few minutes, Angelo draped an arm across my shoulders. "Danni, it's so nice to meet you. You make sure Nico brings you around again soon."

"The pleasure was all mine, and thank you. I'd like that."

Angelo placed his hands on Nico's shoulders and looked into his son's eyes. He tipped his head toward me. "You be a good boy, yes?" He gave Nico an affectionate tap on his cheek then walked back toward the kitchen, waving as he went. "*Ciao.*"

Nico laughed, shaking his head. "Friend, Papa," he called after his father, the smile never leaving his face.

As Nico settled back into his seat, the waiter returned with our entrees. He topped off our wine glasses and made sure we had everything we needed before leaving us to enjoy our meal.

"So is your mother here too?" I glanced toward the kitchen, trying to imagine what she looked like.

Nico hesitated then shook his head. He kept his gaze fixed on the table as he spoke in a tender voice. "She's gone. Ten years now."

"I'm so sorry. I didn't know."

He lifted his eyes to meet mine and gave a faint smile. "How would you? She was the heart and soul of our family, and so beautiful—dark wavy hair, warm brown eyes, and always smiling. Except for when she was yelling at Ben or me for getting into trouble, of course . . . mostly Ben."

"Of course."

"Gabriela's the one who keeps everything together now—at Elevations, here, and with the family. She likes to think she keeps Ben and me in line too." He gave an affectionate laugh.

"We just don't tell her half the crazy shit we've done over the years." Nico picked up his fork then pointed to my plate. "You better eat up, or Papa's gonna think I lied to him."

I followed his orders, pausing with the fork at my lips. "Wouldn't want to get you in trouble, would we?" After just one bite of eggplant piccata, I closed my eyes and let out a satisfied hum.

"That good, huh?" He laughed low and reached for his wine.

I shrugged. "Sorry. It's been a while. Will and I used to come here a lot, but we haven't gone out much lately."

A crease formed in his forehead, and he studied me for a moment.

"I'm afraid to ask, but what's wrong?" I took a large sip of wine and another bite of my meal.

"I have an idea, but hear me out before you say anything. Okay?" He raised his brows as though expecting an argument.

I nodded.

"My parents' restaurant, this one, is really the second Giardano's Ristorante. The original is at Elevations—Lorena's, named after my grandmother. The menus are the same, for the most part, and the food's just as good. If you don't already have plans for Valentine's Day, you and your husband should go there. We're having a guest chef from Italy all month, a childhood friend of my father's, and the club will be open for dancing."

"That sounds perfect, but I—"

"It's the least I can do after ruining your night out on Friday. And, of course, I'll be there to make sure you get the full VIP treatment. All you need to do is pick a time and enjoy yourselves. I'll take care of everything else."

Nico hovering over a romantic evening with Will . . . doesn't that sound like a recipe for disaster?

"I don't know. It's—Will may have something planned

already. He likes to surprise me. But sure, okay. It sounds like fun, so I'll see if he'd like to go." Nico didn't need to know I had no intention of mentioning his ridiculous idea to Will. Or that I doubted Will even realized it would soon be Valentine's Day. "Thank you."

Nico did most of the talking as we finished our meal, entertaining me with stories of unusual guests they'd had at Elevations over the years. I would have been content to only listen to him, but he always managed to pull me into the conversation.

He drank the last of his wine then stared at the empty glass. "I'm really glad you came." He lowered the glass and focused his attention on me. "I can't remember the last time I enjoyed someone's company this much."

I didn't want to admit how much *I'd* enjoyed myself, despite a few tense or awkward moments. Talking with Nico was easy. Natural. And I couldn't remember the last time I'd laughed so much. "Lunch was delicious. Thank you. But . . ."

Nico nodded. "I know."

He stood and led us back through the restaurant. While he retrieved our coats, I dug my phone out of my bag and found the number for the local taxi service. I didn't think I could handle a repeat of the sensory overload I'd experienced on the way here. I moved toward the vestibule to place my call.

"Where are you going?" Nico held up my coat for me.

"I'm fine with waiting for a cab. You go ahead."

He stepped in front of me, shaking his head. "That's not the way I do things. I brought you here. I'm taking you back to your office." The corner of his mouth lifted. "And I promise to drive the speed limit and stay in one lane . . . and not just because I'll get to spend more time with you that way."

I turned my head, unable to resist the playful gleam in his eyes.

He leaned to the side, putting himself back in my line of

vision, a full-blown dimpled smile in place. "Come on. You know you want to."

I exhaled slowly, weighing my options. "Fine, but only because it makes the most sense and will get me back to work quicker."

He held my coat up again, and this time I stepped into it.

As he lowered it onto my shoulders, his lips brushed against my hair. "Thank you."

I followed Nico in silence through the parking lot, concerned by my inability to say no to him.

He helped me into the car before going around to the driver's side and grabbing a folder from behind his seat. "The file for Mr. Jamison," he said as he got in and handed it to me.

My stomach lurched. I'd forgotten all about the excuse he'd given Peter for my extended lunch break. "But we didn't—"

"Everything's in order. My assistant took care of it, but Peter doesn't need to know that."

I stared at the folder in my hand as if it were a test I hadn't studied for. "What if he asks me about it? Is there anything I need to know? What if he knows I'm lying and this wasn't a business lunch?"

Nico started the engine then reached over to touch my arm. "Hey, relax. First of all, you have time to look over everything while I drive. And second, this *was* a business lunch. We had important personal business to tend to." He twisted in his seat to face me. "Before we head back, I want to finish our discussion that got interrupted." He took a deep breath. "There's something about you, an attraction that I can't explain. But it's impossible to ignore."

My breath hitched as he described the way I felt about him. I lowered my head, certain my eyes would give me away. "I'm married."

Nico held his index finger in front of my lips. "Shhh . . . let me finish, please." His voice remained gentle. "I know you're married, and that's a commitment, a promise to love someone forever. I'm not asking you to break that—I don't *want* you to break that."

I risked looking at him again. "Well that's good, because—"

An amused grin stretched across his face. "You really can't stop talking, can you?"

The laughter in his voice made the words harmless. I narrowed my eyes, pretending to glare at him, which only made him laugh more.

"You're so damn cute." He shook his head. "Let me try again. Friends, Danni. I know that's all you can give me, and I'm not asking for more. So . . . what do you say? Am I forgiven?"

My grip on the folder tightened, causing it to bend. I wasn't sure I trusted either of us to settle for being only friends. I could lie to him, tell him I didn't want anything from him, but I worried only the truth would come out if I attempted to speak.

He let out a sigh as he faced forward and shifted the car into gear. "Let's get you back to work."

CHAPTER 24

BREAKING THE SILENCE

Between Will's long work hours and my self-imposed early bedtime, we'd managed to avoid each other for three days . . . four days if you counted dinner tonight.

You'd think we'd have plenty to say after not seeing or talking to each other all that time, but you'd be wrong. I asked questions about his week and managed to extract a few details about the project he'd spent those late nights working on. After a few minutes, I lost interest in forcing a conversation and settled for interminable silence.

As soon as Will finished his meal, he escaped to the family room. While he lounged on the couch, tapping away on his laptop and watching ESPN, I cleaned up the kitchen. The two rooms were only separated by a breakfast bar, but it might as well have been a brick wall.

I'd had plenty of time alone this week. Time spent thinking about the two men playing tug-of-war with my heart. Comparing them—the way they treated me and the way they made me feel. The only thing I'd managed to figure out was that I was still confused.

I stacked the last of our dinner plates in the dishwasher and gave the door a fierce shove, cringing at the rattling noise of toppled glasses. A frustrated growl rumbled through me. I needed to find a better outlet for my pent-up frustration.

Kendra always raved about the calming effects of her regular workouts, even though I believed her adventurous sex life deserved the credit. Maybe I should give the gym another shot. And if I accidentally bumped into Nico there, well . . . I smiled, imagining him flirting with me while his skillful hands guided my body through the exercises. *Probably not a good idea.*

I lifted my hair from my neck and blotted at the dampness. A shower. That would calm me and help clear my head.

A little wine wouldn't hurt either. I grabbed a bottle of my favorite moscato and filled my glass. On my way to the stairs, I passed in front of the couch, apparently invisible.

I retraced my steps and stopped in front of Will, desperate for him to show a little interest in me. A warm tingle grew in my chest, foolish hope springing to life yet again. Maybe he just needed a nudge. I could invite him to join me. Unbuttoning my blouse, I let it slip from one shoulder.

"Hey, babe. While you're standing there, would you mind grabbing the remote for me?"

I practically dropped my glass. Following his line of vision, I discovered the remote control perched on the arm of the chair a few feet away. *You have got to be freakin' kidding me.* My teeth ached as my jaw clenched to hold the words inside. I didn't have the energy for another argument, and I wasn't sure I even cared anymore.

"Here you go." *Bastard.* I managed to keep my voice sweet and tossed the remote next to him on the couch with a little more force than necessary. Not nearly as much as I'd have liked to use, but fear of damaging the innocent laptop prevented me from pegging the damn thing at his chest. It bounced on the cushion, landing just beyond his reach. A small consolation, but I'd take what I could get. "I'm going for a shower."

"What the hell was that about? Danielle?"

I climbed the stairs, ignoring his shouts. Once inside our bedroom, I closed and locked the door then let out a frustrated groan. I downed most of my wine by the time I reached the bathroom and wished I'd thought to bring the bottle.

Some women liked to soak in a tub full of bubbles to unwind, but I preferred a long, hot shower. Therapeutic steam pervaded the room in a matter of minutes. Each deep, calming breath I drew filled my lungs with the soothing effect of the warm, moist air. I opened the shower door and stepped inside, humming as the water pulsated against my skin. It eased my tension. Allowed me to relax. To think.

Maybe I expected too much. Will and I'd never had that intense carnal attraction that some couples had, but we were happy together . . . most of the time. At least I'd always thought we were.

I rolled my neck, letting the hot water hit the tight muscles along the sides and down my back. Four, maybe five months ago, we'd started drifting apart. I'd even worried he was having an affair. When I asked him about it, he promised he could never do that to me. To us.

Maybe our relationship had just run its course. It happened to Kendra and Nate, and they'd always been so passionate and in love. I guessed anything was possible.

Whatever the reason, this past week had been hell. Will was gone before I woke up every morning. He worked past dinner and well into the evening. And I made sure to be in bed, feigning sleep, by the time he came home. He never bothered to try waking me, didn't even kiss me goodnight. And if he noticed my face buried in my soggy pillow, heard my muffled sobs, or felt the tremors from my stuttered breathing, he never let on.

I heaved a heavy sigh and turned to let the water wash away my tears as they fell.

What surprised me most though was my complete lack of interest in seducing Will. After all my determination and the hard work I'd put into rekindling our marriage the past month, I finally felt defeated. "Can't start a fire where there isn't a spark."

I squeezed the shower gel into my hands and worked it to a lather, breathing in the soothing scent of lavender.

Thoughts of sparks always led to thoughts of Nico and the raging inferno that threatened to erupt whenever he came near. I didn't understand my body's reaction to him, and it seemed I couldn't control it either.

Spreading the shower gel over my body, I massaged my arms, my shoulders, my throat. Nico's face flashed in my mind—the desire in his eyes when his gaze fell to my chest during our lunch. I imagined how my skin might burn under his touch.

My eyes fell closed, and I let my hands skim the length of my torso, down my thighs. Surrendering to the fantasy, I envisioned Nico's hands as they retraced the path and discovered my breasts, caressing them with feather-light strokes. My breath hitched when he caught my nipple between his thumb and forefinger, the gentle pressure sending a bolt of electricity straight to my core. My head fell back, a low moan escaping me, as his hand slipped between my legs.

THE GENTLE THROBBING from my powerful orgasm lingered nearly ten minutes later. I pulled on my satin nightgown. The fabric skimming over my taut nipples sent an unexpected jolt to my core that threatened to send my body into another uncontrollable state of arousal. As amazing as that might feel, I didn't want to let it happen.

I hated my utter lack of self-control when it came to Nico.

My phone chimed, announcing a new text message. *Perfect timing. I could use a distraction.*

Kendra: *Happy hour tomorrow?*

Finally, an allowable reason to smile. Kendra and I had begun kicking off our weekends with drinks at The Oasis nearly fifteen years ago. Back then, we went every week, but now we were lucky to get there once a month. The trendy little bar, located midway between our two office buildings, had a lively atmosphere and was usually packed with hot guys in expensive suits looking to blow off steam from a long, stressful week. It was the perfect environment for a little harmless fun.

Me: *Definitely! Meet you there. It's been a rough week.*

Kendra: *Aw, sweetie. We'll cheer you up. You'll tell Kristi?*

My fingers hovered over the keys while I thought about my response.

After my lunch with Nico on Monday, I'd paid Kristi a little visit to *thank* her for setting me up. She'd explained, saying Ben had told her Nico planned to stop by my office after his weekly meeting at The Next Level because I'd refused to talk at my house on Saturday. Of course, she'd promised to make sure I didn't turn him down again—the little traitor.

Truth was, I'd enjoyed spending time with Nico, but I didn't dare tell her that. Instead, I'd struggled to act mad, and she'd apparently bought it.

Me: *Maybe you should text her. Coward is still hiding from me.*

I hit Send then quickly typed another message.

Me: *Just us girls, right? No surprises this time!*

I grabbed the laundry bag from the closet and gathered clothes for the dry cleaner, nearly missing Will's suit coat that was slung over the chair by our bed. *I swear he never puts anything away.*

My phone chimed again. I read Kendra's response while checking Will's pockets, pulling out a crumpled ATM slip and a pack of his favorite mints.

Kendra: *I'll make sure she plans to drag her boney ass to Oasis. And I promise, girls only.*

The inside pocket contained a folded piece of pink paper. I pulled it out, letting his jacket fall to the bed. A strange shiver ran up my spine as I opened it.

The elegant logo for Carmela's Jewelry stretched across the top of the page. I gasped and quickly folded it back up. My heart raced as I stared at the pink square, torn between putting it back and taking another peek.

I drew in a shaky breath and peeled back one edge with trembling fingers, revealing a sale's receipt from today with Will's signature and a pick-up date of February 14. The words ruby and diamond caught my attention before I pressed it shut.

I bit my lip, holding back a squeal. "He remembered."

Giddy relief bubbled through me, escaping as bursts of laughter. I sank to the mattress, trying to recall the last time he'd surprised me with jewelry. It had been years. A lot of years.

I wanted to rush downstairs and throw myself at Will, show him how happy he made me, but that would ruin his surprise.

How could I have given up so easily? *Nico.* I'd overreacted to Will's silence last weekend because I'd allowed Nico to get inside my head. *Well, that won't happen again.*

I returned the receipt to Will's pocket and draped his suit coat over the chair exactly as he'd left it. If he asked, I'd just pretend I hadn't noticed it when I gathered the laundry.

I went downstairs, a bounce in my step, and sneaked up behind Will. He hadn't moved. At all. I leaned down to kiss his neck.

He startled at the contact but continued to scroll through his Facebook news feed. "What's up?"

I moved to the front of the couch, closed his laptop, and placed it on the table before snuggling in next to him. He gave me a sideways glance but didn't protest, which surprised me. Maybe he thought I was still angry. After I nudged his arm several times with my shoulder, he raised it enough for me to slip under.

He let out a heavy sigh as his arm draped across my back, settling into the notch of my waist. "Danielle, what are you doing?"

"I thought that was obvious. I missed you." I twisted my finger in the string to his sweatpants. "Is it so horrible to want to spend quality time with my husband?"

"No, but less than an hour ago, I'd have sworn you wanted to kill me." He kissed the top of my head. "What's on your pretty little mind?"

"Well. Since you asked." I climbed across his extended legs to straddle him, wiggling as I settled into his lap. The friction caused an unexpected gasp.

Will tilted his head to look at me, a smile playing at his lips.

I ignored his unspoken question but couldn't ignore the stirring beneath me. I drew in a slow breath and pressed on. "Valentine's Day is next Friday."

"Oh, I—you're right. I guess it is next week." He rubbed the back of his neck. "I guess we should probably do something."

It was hard not to laugh at his performance. "Do you want to go out somewhere? Or, if you'd prefer to stay home, I can make a special dinner."

"How about I call Giardano's. See if they still have reservations available." He pushed my hair from my face.

I should have expected his response, and he probably already had a reservation. But Giardano's held a different memory for me now. Saying no to my favorite restaurant wasn't an option though.

"You having fun?" Will laughed and looked down to my hips, rocking against his erection.

"Oopsie." I smiled and shrugged but didn't stop my movement. "What can I say? You feel good."

He pushed his hands under my nightgown, caressing my sides and stomach.

"Giardano's is perfect." I placed a kiss below his jaw. "And I was just thinking, that will be the fifteen-year anniversary of our first date."

His chest lifted on a heavy breath. "That's right, I suppose it will be."

"Mm-hm. You rescued me back then, you know. Loved me when I thought no one ever would."

"I'll always love you, babe. No matter what." He brushed his thumbs across my breasts then sealed his mouth over mine with a tender kiss that turned passionate.

He lifted me from his lap and stood. I expected him to move away, but he cradled my face and reached into my soul with his beautiful ice blue eyes.

I stepped closer, pressing my body to his. "Make love to me."

He kissed me again, tender and sweet, wrapping me in his gentle embrace. He broke away and rested his forehead on mine. Without a word, he took my hand and led me toward the stairs.

CHAPTER 25

BEHAVING BADLY

"Okay, ladies, what are we drinking?" Kendra asked while she flagged down the waiter.

"Oooh . . . let's do snowflake martinis." Kristi drummed her hand on the table. "I saw an interview with that slutty little blonde actress. You know who I mean—always has her boobs hanging out . . ." She waved a dismissive hand. "Doesn't matter. Anyway, she said modern twists on classic drinks are the hot new trend that all the celebs are drinking. Snowflake is her go-to, and it sounds absolutely yummy, if you ask me. We definitely need to try it."

I laughed. "Well, who are we to argue with yummy trends?" I leaned closer to our waiter and made a looping motion with my finger. "A round of snowflake martinis."

Alexia held up her hand. "Make that three. Sorry, I don't drink." She shrugged, glancing at me before placing her own order with the waiter. "I'd like cranberry juice with a splash of orange. Easy on the ice."

Kendra crossed her arms on the table and pinned me with a curious stare. "Okay, what's going on? You are entirely too happy for someone whose husband treats her like shit." She sucked in a sharp breath. "Oh, my God. You finally slept with Ni—"

"What? No!"

"Well, something happened. Last night your text said you'd had a rough week." Kendra tipped her head and gave a look that dared me to deny it. "So?"

I was relieved she'd asked; because if I had to keep this news to myself much longer, there was a good chance I'd explode. We all leaned in, huddling together over the small table so I wouldn't have to shout and share my story with everyone.

"You know things between Will and me had been awful since a few days before his trip to Chicago. Right? And my welcome-home surprise didn't go as planned." I wrinkled my nose at the memory. "So by the time we'd suffered through last night's dinner in bitter silence, I was convinced we were finished."

Alexia gasped, pulling a hand to her chest. "Oh, no."

I realized she didn't know about my troubled marriage, but I wasn't going to give a recap. She'd catch up.

I told them about Will ignoring my last-ditch effort at a little romance and Nico joining me in the shower, courtesy of a very vivid fantasy.

Kendra and Kristi let out cheers and catcalls, attracting the attention of a group of businessmen gathered by the bar.

"Then I found a jewelry receipt in Will's suit coat."

"Really?" Alexia straightened. "I mean, that's just so romantic."

I continued my story—telling them how Will had teased me by pretending to forget about Valentine's Day, the way he'd touched me and kissed me, and that he'd said he would always love me. "Then he took my hand and led me to the bedroom. It was perfect." I closed my eyes, enjoying the memory replaying in my mind.

Kendra slapped her hand on the table. "It's about fucking time."

Alexia eased back in her seat, her voice barely audible. "So . . . you had sex then?"

Kristi mimicked Alexia's sweet voice. "Well, I doubt they were cleaning the bathroom."

"Okay, ladies, we have three snowflakes and one cranberry." The waiter placed our drinks on the table and looked at Alexia with a playful smile. "Just grab me if you need anything else."

Kendra lifted her glass. "Here's to Will finally getting his head out of his ass."

"Kendra!" My emotional high allowed me to laugh even though I was sure the message came from her heart.

Kristi nudged Kendra's shoulder. "Aw, don't be mean. Danni can't help she has better taste in men in her fantasies than she does in real life."

Kendra gave a wicked laugh. "How about to really hot fantasies coming true?" She smiled, fanning herself.

I attempted to glare at her but couldn't keep eye contact without laughing. "Nope. Finally winning my husband back, and he's all I need."

"Fine. Party pooper. To Danni's success."

This time we all raised our glasses.

"Excuse me." Alexia stopped our waiter and pushed her glass into his hand. "Take this back to the bartender and tell him if I wanted a glass of ice, I'd have ordered one. What I *asked* for was cranberry juice with a splash of orange, *easy* on the ice. That means only a little bit." Her snarky complaint easily rose above the noise in the bar.

He apologized and turned to leave, but she put her hand on

his arm. "Be sure to tell him I'll be watching. And if he even thinks about spitting in my drink, he'll find himself out of a job. Like that." She snapped her fingers then leaned forward, finishing with an ominous tone in her voice. "And I know people who can make it happen."

The sinister way she bit out the words sent an icy chill down my spine, and the message wasn't even directed at me. I glanced at Kristi and Kendra, who had the same stunned expression I imagined I wore.

Alexia's gaze swept over each of us. She pulled a hand to her chest, gasping with laughter. "Did you see his face? Oh, my. I've always wondered what it would feel like to do that."

"And?" Kendra asked, sounding confused as she drew out the word.

"I felt like such a badass." She covered her mouth and giggled.

Kristi's eyes grew wide. "Wow. I didn't think it was possible, but you have even less self-control about blurting out inappropriate stuff than Kendra does."

I looked at Kendra, silently pleading for her to save the conversation.

"Speaking of asses"—Kendra smiled at me—"is Will taking you out for Valentine's Day?"

I glared then told her about our plans to have dinner at Giardano's, without mentioning my concern that I'd spend the whole time thinking about my lunch date with Nico.

"You're not going to Elevations?" Kristi pouted. "Ben told me Nico invited you."

"He invited me *and* Will. And it was to apologize for ruining my last night out, so don't jump —"

"Semantics." Kristi wagged a finger at me. "You know it's because he wants to spend time with you."

I didn't want to consider whether that could have been his

motive. "I'm sure you're wrong, but I'm glad you and Ben will have a nice romantic night."

Our second round of drinks arrived, and our conversation shifted to safer subjects—which meant anything that didn't include my love life. After a lot of laughs and some harmless flirting with a group of lawyers who offered to buy us drinks, it was time to head home.

Alexia slipped off to use the ladies' room while I settled our tab and apologized to the waiter for her scene earlier.

Kristi scooted her chair closer to mine as soon as he walked away. "I cannot believe you brought that bitch here. I mean, what were you thinking?"

"What are you talking about? She's always been sweet to me." Sure, she acted a bit odd at times, but that didn't make her a bad person.

"Even Jolly Jodie in Accounting, who absolutely adores everyone, doesn't like Alexia."

"She's still new, trying to fit in. Give her a little break."

Kristi shrugged. "Well, I'm just telling you I wouldn't be too quick to trust her."

"So," Kendra interrupted, "here's the plan. Since you ladies both have big plans for a hot Valentine's roll-in-the-sack, and I just always like to be at my best, I say we plan a little spa day tomorrow. Whole nine yards—facial, mani, pedi, and waxing." She gave a suggestive bounce of her eyebrows. "Gotta clear the runway, ya know. And then we can do a little shopping at Sasha's Closet. They got in a whole new line of lingerie last week, and some of it's pretty hot."

"As long as we don't include our new psychotic BFF, I'm in." Kristi looked at me with a questioning glare.

"Jeeze, I was only trying to be nice," I grumbled under my breath.

I liked the idea of doing something special to surprise Will.

Last night proved things were back on track, with both of us working to save our marriage.

"Well?" Kendra drew out the word.

"Yes. Definitely in," I said.

Kendra's jaw dropped, and Kristi's hands flew to her chest, both over-dramatizing their disbelief.

"That's it?" Kristi laughed. "No multiple rounds of persuading or bribing, and no need for Kendra to threaten you? Wow. Never thought I'd see the day."

Alexia rejoined our group and slumped in her chair. "Well, that sucks. My boyfriend called earlier and left a message to cancel our dinner plans."

Having been turned down and tossed aside by Will more than enough times lately, I knew how she felt. "I'm stopping for Chinese takeout on my way home. It's not a gourmet dinner, but you're welcome to join me if you'd like. My husband's working late again tonight, so I'm on my own."

She hesitated a moment, then a slow smile stretched across her face. "You know what? I'd love that. Thank you."

Ignoring Kristi's cautious expression, I gathered my things to leave.

Kendra waved. "I'll pick you up tomorrow morning, ten-ish. We'll hit the gym first, work on that aggression issue of yours." She gave her usual wicked laugh. "And don't bother getting ready before I get there. I'll bring an outfit for you to wear."

"Sounds perfect. But I'll wait till we get to The Next Level to put it on." No point getting Will upset again about me wearing such a tight outfit around other men. The idea of looking good at the gym appealed to me this time around, which should probably worry me.

HAVING someone to talk to during dinner was nice, even though it was challenging to keep the conversation alive at times. Alexia was very shy, as I'd suspected—aside from that odd moment at Oasis. We talked about work, adjusting to the office, and her father's hopes that he could pass his company on to her when he decided to retire.

By the time we finished eating, it was after eight thirty.

I drank the last of my tea and stood. "Make yourself comfortable. I'm just gonna take a quick minute to clean up."

Alexia roamed through the family room while I worked in the kitchen, clearing our dinner plates and takeout boxes from the breakfast bar that separated the two rooms.

"You have such a beautiful home. I can't wait till all this is mine. Well not *this*"—she made a sweeping gesture with her hand—"but you know, *like* this. A home, a family." She dragged her hand along the edge of the long table behind the couch, studying the collection of framed family photos. "I missed out on a lot, growing up so far away from my father. It was always just Mom and me."

Peter had told me some of his family history, how Alexia's mom had moved to the Midwest with their daughter to intentionally put a great deal of distance between them. Too far for Peter to commute, so he had to choose: family or work. That was back when he was struggling to build his PR business. He figured she'd come to her senses and move back home, but the emotional distance between them soon surpassed the physical. He'd often told me that losing his family was the greatest cost, and biggest mistake, of his career.

She gave a wistful sigh and picked up one of the photos, commenting as she brushed her fingers across the glass. Her soft-spoken words were difficult to hear—something about being a great dad.

"What's that?" I said, moving to stand beside her.

"Hmm? Oh, this picture." She angled it to show me the photo in her hand. "Your son is adorable. And you can easily see the love in your husband's eyes. He must be a great dad."

I touched the frame with one hand, the other sliding to my stomach on instinct as a wave of nausea hit. "That's my husband with our nephew, Caden."

The photo of them playing on the beach last summer was one of my favorites. The warm memory of that day filled the emptiness inside me.

"Will adores him." I turned to her, trying to force a smile. "He would have been a great dad, but we weren't able to have children." My voice faded. "We tried for years."

Alexia placed a hand on my arm, the compassionate look on her face urging me to go on.

I took a deep breath and continued, not understanding why I felt so compelled to tell her something I normally didn't share. "Will said we needed to pick a time to give up, that it wasn't healthy to constantly stress over something that maybe wasn't meant to be." I shrugged. "He picked my fortieth birthday, which was a few weeks ago."

"Oh, Danielle. That's so sad. I just can't imagine it." Still holding the frame, she pulled me in for a hug. "Deep down, every man wants to be a daddy. At least that's the way I see it. And I'm sure you always dreamed about being a mommy too."

The door from the garage opened. Will dropped his keys on the table, tossed his jacket over one of the chairs, and deposited his shoes next to it—his usual routine. When he turned toward the family room, his step faltered. His eyes grew wide.

"What—" He swallowed hard. "Sorry, babe, I didn't realize you had company."

I introduced Alexia, emphasizing that she was my boss's daughter.

"Oh, that's right. Peter mentioned she'd be working with you. I didn't realize you two were—why is she here again?" He drew the words out, sounding confused as he looked between the two of us.

"Her dinner plans got cancelled, so I invited her to join me. That way *neither* of us had to eat alone."

Will didn't respond.

"I was actually about to leave. Danielle was just showing me some of your family photos first." She held up the picture then placed it back on the table. Biting her lip, she gave Will a shy glance. "Sorry for intruding. You were probably looking forward to a little quality time with your wife."

I shot Will a menacing glare, feeling bad for Alexia. She seemed so uncomfortable.

He rubbed the back of his neck and let out a slow breath. "You don't have to leave."

"Oh, I know. But I need to get home, make sure I'm well rested. I have plans for a busy day tomorrow." She smiled sweetly and gave me another long hug. "And so do you. Have fun with your friends."

I walked Alexia to the door, suddenly eager to get rid of her. When I came back inside, Will emerged from the kitchen, carrying a bottle of Becks.

He crossed the room, wrapped me in his arms, and placed a kiss on my forehead. "I don't think I was very polite to your new friend."

"You got that right," I said with a chuckle, settling into his embrace. "She seemed fine when she left though. No harm done . . . as long as Mr. Jamison doesn't call over the weekend to tell me I'm fired."

His body shook with a brief laugh. "I need to relax. You wanna keep me company? Watch a movie?" He kissed my temple. "I'll even let you put on one of those sappy chick flicks, and you can tell me about your evening with the girls."

We curled up together on the couch. True to form, Will was sound asleep and snoring less than five minutes into the movie. Long before I had a chance to tell him about my day or my plans for tomorrow.

CHAPTER 26

TRAPPED IN THE MIDDLE

Kendra's car fishtailed as she turned into the parking lot at Farley's Pub. Snow had been falling for about an hour. While the roads remained clear, a light coating covered everything else. We slid into the space next to Kristi's car.

It had been a long time since I'd spent a day with the girls. Too long. I let out a contented hum. "We need to do this more often."

Kendra laughed. "Sweetie, you're the one who can never come out to play. I'm in. You just tell me when and where."

Kendra and I had hit the gym early this morning and managed to escape without running into Nico. I was relieved, especially after I caught myself looking for him several times. We had, however, crossed paths with Trina, his perky little gym groupie.

Kendra noticed her pretending to stretch while blatantly eavesdropping on our plans for the day. "If you don't start minding your own damn business, I'm going to come over there and show you another use for that mat."

Trina ignored Kendra. She greeted me with a devious smile

then strutted away—boobs pushed out and hips swaying—without saying a single word.

After the gym, Kendra and I had grabbed an early lunch at Pepper's then met up with Kristi at Serenity Spa.

Next stop was Sasha's Closet, where I'd found the perfect little dress for my Valentine's date with Will—red, to match the ruby jewelry he'd be surprising me with. And, of course, sexy new lingerie would be hiding underneath that dress.

The three of us climbed out of our cars and hurried toward the entrance, eager to escape the frigid February weather.

"Hear anything from Will yet?" Kristi said through chattering teeth.

"Nope. I'll have to try again." I'd called him from Sasha's and left a message. Then I'd texted him two times on the ride here. "I'm beginning to think he's ignoring me to get out of coming."

It had taken a lot of pleading this morning before Will agreed to meet us for dinner. He and Kendra had never gotten along very well—tolerated each other, at best—but lately, the animosity between them had reached a whole new level.

A rush of warm air greeted us when we stepped inside the cozy, rustic pub. It was almost as amazing as the smell of Farley's gourmet burgers.

Black iron lights hung from the wood-beamed ceiling, casting an amber glow throughout the space. Large tables that looked like slices of giant tree trunks dotted the room, most unoccupied. But it was still early, not even five thirty.

Flames flickered in the stone fireplace along the back wall. A man sat on a stool next to it, tuning an acoustic guitar, preparing to entertain the dinner crowd.

My phone finally vibrated with a text.

Will: *On my way. Order some wings for me and one of those burgers with the spicy cheese sauce.*

Placing his order in advance was his rude way of reducing the amount of time he'd have to spend with Kendra. I shoved my phone back in my pocket. *Probably should just be happy he's coming at all.*

The host led us to our table. I trailed behind my friends, letting my eyes and thoughts wander. My gaze drifted to a small table in the corner, as if lured by a flashing sign, and settled on the dark-haired man seated there. His head whirled in my direction, and there was no mistaking the moment his eyes found me. The familiar spark only Nico created sent a surge of energy through me, the magnetic connection of our souls.

"Oh, shit." I stumbled into Kendra and grabbed her arm. "We can't stay here. I—damn. I gotta go."

"Christ, Danni." She pried my fingers loose. "What the hell is your prob—oh, shit." Kendra stopped walking and held up her hands in surrender, her wide-eyed gaze bouncing between Nico and me. "I didn't know. I swear, I had nothing to do with this."

"Hey, you guys coming?" Kristi draped her jacket over the back of her chair, settled in, and began tapping away on her phone.

Kendra grabbed my wrist and pulled me toward our table, but I couldn't tear my eyes away from Nico. Or his date. The trashy little blonde practically climbed into his lap, leaning past him to cast a possessive glare in my direction. *Trina.*

I closed my eyes and took a calming breath. *Let it go, Danni. Just friends, remember?*

Trina squeezed Nico's cheeks between her neon-pink talons and dragged his attention back to her, rewarding him with an overzealous kiss. My unexpected outrage at their display faded when he pushed her away to look back at me, but the bliss of my small victory didn't last.

Will is on his way. The reminder played on a continual loop, tightening its grip on my sanity with each repetition. I could hide my feelings from Will when Nico wasn't around, but how on earth would I be able to do that with both of them in the same room? I had to find a way, or all the progress I'd made toward resuscitating our relationship would be destroyed.

Kristi lowered her phone when we joined her. "I can't believe this is the first weekend all year I'm not out with Ben. I really miss him." She let out a wistful sigh. "But at least we can enjoy ourselves today . . . unlike yesterday." She gave an exaggerated shudder.

"Anyway, I'm so excited Will's coming. Probably not as much as you are though. Right? I mean, I can't remember the last time you two were out together . . . well, other than New Year's Eve." She sighed again, shoulders slumping forward. "That's when Ben and I met. I really, really miss him."

"It's only one night. I think you'll survive." I laughed, rubbing Kristi's back.

"And think about how much fun you'll have catching up." Kendra gave a suggestive wink.

The waitress arrived to take our orders, but Kendra jumped from her seat with a giddy shriek and bolted toward the bar.

"Jeeze, Kristi, I think you're rubbing off on her." I turned around just as Kendra threw herself into Logan's outstretched arms.

"You told me you weren't coming down this weekend." She squeezed him then planted a lush kiss on his mouth.

"Last minute change of plans." Logan's face lit up with a genuine smile. "I wanted to surprise you, but you never answered my text to let me know your plans for tonight." He gave Kristi and me a quick nod.

"Damn. I forgot to take my phone off silent when we left the spa. It all worked out anyway. You found me, and you sure as hell surprised me." Kendra grabbed his hands, dragging him toward the other side of our table. "You're planning to join us, right?"

Logan's steps slowed. His expression dropped. "I didn't know you'd be here. I'm—" He looked at me. "I'm meeting Nico."

His unasked question hung in the air. I took a deep breath, thinking about the reaction I'd had to Nico a few minutes earlier. Inviting him to join our group was an insane idea, out of the question.

I looked at Kendra, ready to apologize for spoiling her fun, but I burst into laughter instead. The sight of Kendra with her hands folded beneath her chin, silently begging me to say yes, was priceless. And probably a first. I rolled my eyes at her and nodded.

Kendra practically knocked me from my chair with her enthusiastic hug. "Thanks, sweetie. You're the best." She eased back and grabbed my shoulders. "You can do this."

I didn't have her confidence, but I'd make the best of it. The table was large, and there were four other people in our group —five once Will arrived. As long as Nico sat far enough away from—

"Hello, beautiful." Nico's warm breath caressed the side of my neck as he leaned down to greet me, placing his mug of beer on the table. He grabbed a chair from the empty table behind us and wedged it close to mine as he sat.

Trina tagged along and slumped into the seat next to his, looking less than thrilled with the change in plans.

"Nico, *my friend*. Glad you could join us." I inched my seat away from his. "Need to make sure we save room for my husband. He'll be joining us in a few minutes."

Nico tipped his head side to side, appearing to wage an internal debate. I expected him to make a comment about

Will's history of leaving me sitting, but that was probably just my insecurities running wild.

"Hey, buddy. Everything good over there?" Logan called from the other end of the table. A concerned expression marred his face as he studied Nico.

Nico didn't respond at first—didn't even seem to register the interruption.

I looked at Logan and shrugged.

"Yeah." Nico chugged down half of his drink then rolled his head from side to side. "Yeah, I'm good." He wrapped his hand over Trina's on top of the table and leaned his shoulder against her, his eyes on me the whole time.

The waitress returned with our drinks. After a quick check to see if we needed anything else, she moved on to another table.

"So. Quite a coincidence running into you again," I said. "It's becoming a bit of a habit."

Nico smiled. "Not a bad one. But this was actually Trina's idea tonight. She cornered me at my gym earlier and . . . persuaded me to bring her."

"Hmm . . . imagine that." I leaned across Nico, pretending to check out the drink specials, and glowered at Trina.

Nico tapped my arm. "I'm glad that she did."

She scowled and snuggled in closer to her date, wiggling her half-exposed boobs under his nose. "Nico, baby. I'm chilly. Can you keep me warm?"

He slipped an arm around her, rubbing her shoulder in a brisk manner. "Of course. You want me to grab your sweater from the car?"

"Gee, Trina," Kendra imitated her whiney, sweet voice, "I bet you could go sit by the fire to warm up. I'm sure *Nico baby* wouldn't mind."

"Be nice." Nico gave Kendra an impatient glance and pulled Trina closer.

I turned my back to the two of them before I lost my appetite. Waving my hand in front of Kristi, I tried to draw her attention away from her phone. She'd been glued to that thing since we got here, texting nonstop with Ben.

Kendra and Logan returned to their private conversation, whispering and touching each other. He draped one arm across her back and stroked the side of her neck, his lips pressed to her ear. Kendra's face lit up with a mischievous grin. She bit her lip.

Logan chuckled then slid back his chair. He stood and turned toward me with a playful wink.

"What?" Kendra swatted at him, laughing. She wagged a finger. "I thought you were kidding. You better sit your sexy ass back down."

"Excuse me, ladies. I'll be right back." He leaned down to place a kiss on Kendra's temple, then he was gone. His laughter faded into the conversations around us as he walked toward the restrooms.

Kristi's mouth hung open. She stretched her arms across the table, phone still clutched in one fist, and leaned toward Kendra. "Oh. My. God. Are you supposed to follow him?"

Kendra shook her head. "Nah, he's just teasing." She scrunched her face, pausing, then waved her hands. "At least I think he is . . . either way, I'm not going. My days of restroom hookups are behind me."

"Yeah? Since when?" I laughed and ducked to avoid the napkin ball she tossed at me. "So, Kristi, what were you saying earlier about being able to relax and enjoy ourselves tonight?" I crossed my eyes and tipped my head, trying to point in Nico's direction.

She glanced at her phone before placing it on the table. "Well, I just meant that it would be more relaxing without having to worry about your new pal going all psycho on some-one. You're the only one she's nice to, you know. Probably because she's worried you'll tell Daddy what a total bitch she really is. I mean, you should have heard—"

"You talking about Alexia Jamison?"

Nico's interruption startled me. *Shouldn't he be wrapped around his chilly little bimbo and minding his own business?*

After putting my emotions on lockdown, I angled myself toward him and smiled politely. "We were. Why?"

He took a giant gulp of beer then leaned closer. His voice rose above the outburst of cheers coming from a group at the bar. "She's nice enough. I think she just has a hard time getting along with other women, that's all. You know?"

Kendra studied Nico, a crease forming in her brow. "Really? And how exactly do you know that?"

One corner of Nico's mouth tipped up in a crooked smile, unleashing his single dimple. "We went out once. Well, sort of. She pretty much ignored me the whole night, now that I think about it." He scratched at his stubbled jaw and shrugged.

Logan returned at the end of Nico's comment and patted his back, laughing. "It happens, bro. Not usually to you, but—" He let out a grunt as Nico's elbow jabbed him in the gut.

"Anyway, her date for Logan's party cancelled—'insisted on bringing his wife,' according to Alexia. I filled in, last minute, as a favor to Peter. She ditched me shortly after midnight, claiming to have a migraine, and I haven't heard from her since."

I dropped my arm to the table and pivoted to face Nico full-on, honing in on his eyes. "Wait, that . . . bitch you were dancing with when I first saw you was Alexia? No way. I mean, I keep thinking she looks vaguely familiar; but she's just this plain, timid girl."

Nico laughed. "Maybe so, but when she gets done up for a party, she's smokin' hot."

"Well, if it isn't Wandering Willie. I was beginning to think you'd found something better to do." Kendra's booming announcement was followed by the low rumble of Nico's snickering.

I shot her a look, reminding her to play nice, then turned to greet my husband.

Will's eyes shifted between Nico and me before settling on Nico's hand, wrapped around my forearm.

Shit. How long has that been there? My stomach clenched, even though I hadn't done anything wrong. Nico's fingers flexed, holding me tighter when I tried to wiggle free. I raised my narrowed eyes and gave him a warning glare then managed to retrieve my arm.

With a cheery smile in place, I stood and wrapped my arms around Will, genuinely thrilled—and relieved—to see him. I slid my fingers through his hair and pulled his mouth to mine for a long, slow, inappropriate-for-public-places kiss. A kiss intended to remind both men that I belonged to Will. A kiss that didn't come close to the passionate one I'd shared with —*don't go there, Danni.*

I moved away and stared into Will's eyes, searching for forgiveness. "I missed you."

The tension in his face eased. "I missed you too, babe."

I took his hands and introduced him to Nico and Trina.

Nico stood, rising three inches above Will, and extended his hand.

Will narrowed his eyes. "Yeah, I remember you. You're the guy who was trying to hit on my wife New Year's Eve too."

Nico glanced at me and smiled. "Well, what do you think is gonna happen when you leave someone as beautiful as Danni alone? But, for the record, that night I was checking on her because she appeared to be upset . . . not that I could blame her."

Will crossed his arms over his chest. He scanned Nico, as if sizing up the competition. "I don't owe you any explanations, and I already apologized to Danielle. She knows why I was gone so long."

Nico looked at me, eyebrows raised. "And?"

Logan rubbed the side of his neck. "Come on, Nico. Just let it go." His voice had the same weary tone it did that night at Metro Sky.

"What? I'm curious." Nico continued to stare at me.

"He was stuck in the men's room because of a fight," I said.

Nico held up one hand and struggled to keep a straight face. "Wait, you saying you got into a fight taking a leak?"

"No, I broke up the fight, and security had me wait around to answer a few questions."

A low growl rumbled through me. "Stop it. Just. Stop." I stepped between the two men, poking Nico's solid chest until he finally collapsed into his seat.

He downed the rest of his beer then returned the mug to the table with a heavy thud, ignoring my icy stare.

As much as I wanted to avoid spending more time next to Nico, having Will next to him would be disastrous. *Dammit.* I took Will by the shoulders and guided him to the empty chair on the other side of me. "Sit down. Please. People are staring." I slid my chair close to his and settled in, resting my arm along his thigh.

Nico leaned forward, his elbows propped on the table. He scrubbed his hands down his face then gripped the back of his neck, heaving a heavy sigh. I hadn't seen him this tense since that night on the patio at Metro Sky.

"Christ, Danni, why didn't you tell me the bullshit story he gave you?" He opened his eyes and looked at me, reaching into my soul with a gentle warmth and compassion. "I could have cleared this up for you weeks ago."

Will slapped his palm on the table and leaned over me. "Who the fu—" He paused when I squeezed his leg. "No. I want to know what makes this asshole think my story's bullshit."

Everyone else at the table sat silent, shielding their faces as though that would somehow make the uncomfortable scene in front of them disappear.

Nico took a slow breath, his jaw clenching. "If there had been a fight at Elevations, I would have been one of the first people to know about it." He angled himself toward me, leaning forward as he rested one arm on the table. "You wanna know why?" He inched closer to Will, his voice a low, menacing growl. "Because my family owns Elevations, and I fucking run the place."

His accusation hung in the air as he drilled Will with a challenging stare.

My stomach churned. Nico had to be wrong. Why would Will lie? I turned to my husband, looking for reassurance.

Will's eyes flashed wide, but he quickly masked his stunned expression. Seconds ticked by, filled only by distant chatter and the mellow tune from a guitar.

"Will?" I couldn't bring myself to ask the question.

"Yeah, that's what I thought." Nico let out a quick snort and continued staring through Will. Trina tugged at Nico's arm, but he didn't acknowledge her. He snapped up his empty mug and pushed away from the table, his chair screeching as it slid on the wooden floor. "I need another drink."

"I'll take care of that for you," the waitress said, intercepting Nico before he could escape to the bar. She placed his mug in the center of her large tray filled with our meals. "You sit and enjoy your dinner." She smiled at him. "Besides, then I'll have another excuse to come back over here."

Amazing. Does every woman throw herself at this man?

Trina must have wondered the same thing as she let out a

frustrated groan. She turned away from the waitress, rolling her eyes. I almost felt a little sorry for her. Almost.

I tilted my head enough to catch a glimpse of Nico. He smiled and winked at me, setting off a rush of warmth through my cheeks. With all the other women he could easily have, he always seemed to be focused on me.

The tension between Will and Nico lingered, leaving me trapped in the middle.

Kristi broke the silence. "You know . . . I was thinking it might be fun if we all went out after we're finished eating. Listen to some music. Do some dancing."

I raised my brows to give her an incredulous look.

She shrugged and bit her lip. "Well, it's just that it would only take us forty-five minutes to get to the club Ben's playing at. I thought we could go surprise him."

Kendra and I burst out laughing. Earlier in the day, we'd wondered how long it would take for Kristi to suggest going. When Kristi couldn't stop talking about Ben long enough to get a facial, we'd even joked that we should bet on it.

Kristi pouted but didn't push the subject.

I smiled and silently thanked her for livening things up. Everyone seemed to be relaxed and having fun again . . . except for Will.

He took one bite of his burger then slapped it on the plate and gave it a shove. "Fuck this. I'm not sticking around here and putting up with all this bullshit." He pushed to his feet, crashing his chair into the table behind us. "Let's go, Danielle."

Without a word to anyone else or a glance at me, he was gone, heading toward the exit.

"Sweetie, you can stay if you want." Kendra crossed her arms, her hands balled into tight fists. The strain in her voice told me everything she didn't say.

"I—I'm so sorry." I didn't want to go. I couldn't stay. And I couldn't bear seeing the pity on my friends' faces. "I have to go."

I grabbed my coat and rushed for the doors, keeping my face down. Nico's voice trailed behind me, urging me to wait, but I forced myself to keep moving forward. When I stepped outside, Will pulled up to the curb and impatiently revved the engine. I climbed inside without saying a word, angling myself away from him. Today had been so much fun, and then—how did everything go so wrong?

I glanced over at Farley's and watched Nico fade in the distance, his hands in his hair.

WILL GOT out of the car and stormed into the house. He'd been silent the whole ride home, but his actions screamed—the way he threw the car into gear, the way he smacked the turn signals, and the way he pounded the wheel to the beat of his excessively loud heavy-metal music.

I eased the door from the garage closed behind me and hung my coat on the hook next to it.

"Your new friend is a real arrogant ass. Where the fuck does he get off telling you I lied? He's just worried news of that fight will get out and ruin their precious reputation." He emptied his pockets, slamming their contents on the kitchen counter. "Dammit." He turned to face me, arms crossed. "Do you believe him?"

"Of course not." My voice cracked. I grabbed his arm and tried to slip under it, but he brushed me off. I needed him to hold me, let me know that everything was okay. That *we* were okay. "Please don't push me away. I'm sorry. I'm so sorry." I gasped, trying to control the pounding in my chest. "I didn't know he was going to be there. I barely even know him."

Will let out a bitter laugh. "You two sure looked chummy when I got there."

"Kendra has something going on with his friend Logan, and I couldn't say no when she wanted them to join us." I wiggled my hand into the bend of Will's elbow, clinging to him any way I could.

Will peeled me away. He shrugged out of his jacket and threw it over the back of the chair. "Don't even get me started on my issues with Kendra. Christ, I should've just stayed home tonight like I wanted to." He kicked off his shoes then moved to the stairs.

"You coming back down?" I hated the desperation in my voice, but we needed to fix this mess.

He stopped but didn't turn around. "You sleeping with him?"

The pain in his words cut through me, straight to my heart. "God, Will. No. I love you." I dragged my hand across my face, sniffling as I choked back tears. "I'd—how could you even think that I'd—"

Sure, I found Nico attractive . . . okay, gorgeous . . . sexy. The intense way he looked at me scorched my soul, made me burn. And the way that he treated me—always making me feel special, beautiful. I couldn't deny the struggle it took to resist the strong pull toward him.

Did I want to sleep with him? More than I dared to admit, even to myself, but it would never happen. I'd never cross that line. My heart belonged to Will, and I planned to prove it. I moved behind him, grabbing his arm to push my way past.

His body tensed when I pressed mine against him, rolling my hips but failing to elicit a response. He opened his mouth, as if to protest, but I didn't give him the chance. Pushing my fingers through his soft, golden hair, I pulled him to me and sealed my lips over his.

He resisted, but I continued kissing his limp, motionless lips, refusing to give up—on this moment, on him, on our marriage. The slight movement against my stomach gave me hope, and I sucked in a shuddered breath.

I broke the kiss and looked deep into his eyes. "I love you. I need you. I don't want anyone but you. Now or ever."

I kissed him again with an unrelenting fierceness until his resistance melted. His arms slid around my waist, pulling me tighter. His lips moved against mine with an unfamiliar passion that took my breath away.

I turned to rest my cheek against his chest, squeezing my eyes to clear the image in my mind. "You're my whole life, Will." I took his hands and led him upstairs.

CHAPTER 27

PAINFUL CHOICES

Will and I spent the rest of the weekend in bed, something that hadn't happened since . . . our honeymoon? Not quite that long, however it had been years. Will slept most of the time, but when he was awake—

"Hello, beautiful." A knocking on my desk accompanied Nico's familiar greeting.

I'd been so lost in my reverie that I hadn't noticed he'd come into the office. And after that embarrassing scene at Farley's the other night, I would have preferred to hide from him.

He chuckled. "Look at that smile. I hope you're thinking about me."

Heat rose to my cheeks for all the times my fantasies *had* been about him. I swept my gaze over him, taking in the amazing sight of the man in front of me. Why couldn't he leave me alone?

"What are you doing here? Do you have an appointment with Mr. Jamison that I wasn't aware of?"

He settled onto the corner of my desk. "It's Monday. Time for lunch. I'm here to see you, silly."

His eyes sparkled with the same playful glint I remembered

from that night at Logan's party. I pressed a hand to my chest, memorizing the fluttering beat of my heart that signaled my soul coming to life. It only ever happened in his presence. *This is what I'm going to miss most.*

"I wish you'd have called first. I could have saved you a wasted trip." I signed out of my computer, gathered up a stack of folders to drop at Peter's office on my way to lunch, and stepped away from my desk.

Nico followed closely, bumping into me when I stopped to double-check a file. His warm hands caught my waist, holding me until I regained my balance. It took an enormous amount of restraint, but I resisted the urge to lean into his broad chest.

"Sorry." Nico shrugged one shoulder. "Guess I should have been watching where I was going." He released me and took a step back.

"Did you need something else?" I pulled the stack of folders to my chest as if they would shield my heart.

Nico grinned. "Just thought I'd pop in and say hi to Peter . . . since I'm here."

I'd seen that expression on his face before, the mischievous smile that warned he was up to no good. "You mean manipulate Peter into letting you drag me away from work to keep you company."

"Yeah, that too."

"My schedule for today is really full." I could easily brush him off, tell him to leave. Of course I wouldn't. I sighed, frustrated at my own lack of self-control. "There's a little deli a block away, and I plan to walk there for a quick bite to eat. Nothing fancy, and I definitely don't have time for an extended lunch at Giardano's."

"Not a problem." He pulled his phone from his pocket and pushed a button. "London. Nico here. I'm not going to make it for lunch today. And can you tell my father I'll call him later?

Thanks." Another push of a button, and he slipped the phone back into his pocket. "So, where's this deli? I'm starving."

"Do you even know the word no?" *Do I?*

His face sobered. "I used to. Before I met you."

I raised my brows to stare at the smug bastard. "Fine, but this isn't a date. It's you tagging along to grab a quick bite to eat, and . . . you need to keep your hands to yourself. For real this time." I pinned him with a steely glare, waiting for him to agree.

A gradual smile spread across his face. He clasped his wrist behind his back and leaned toward my ear. "Challenge accepted." A teasing laugh followed his raspy whisper.

It seemed my resolve to resist Nico was being tested at every turn.

After changing into a pair of flats, I led the way out of Jamison and Walters. We were lucky enough to catch the express elevator as the doors began to close. Thirty seconds later, we were on the sidewalk, moving at a brisk pace.

"What's the rush?" Nico reached for my arm, hesitated, then pulled back.

"Thank you." I stifled a grin.

He grumbled something unintelligible then stuffed his hands in his pockets. "Too bad you had to leave so early on Saturday. We wound up at Ben's gig in Hill Valley—had a few drinks, danced. It was a good time."

"Maybe next time." A lie, but he didn't need to know that.

A pink-and-black-striped awning came into view as soon as we turned the corner. The cute little shop reminded me more of a boutique than a deli, but they made delicious wraps. And if Nico felt uncomfortable—well, that might not be a bad thing. He pulled the door open and guided me through, stopping short of placing his hand on the small of my back.

His obvious efforts to make me happy could easily cause my plan for this outing to backfire.

I stopped as I passed him, stretching on tiptoe to reach his ear. "See, you *can* do it if you try." I bit my lip, regretting the words as soon as they were out, but flirting with Nico came naturally. And it made me feel alive. *Might as well enjoy it while I still can.*

"You're lucky I can't smack your cute little butt right now."

My muscles tensed as though he had, and his quiet laughter suggested he knew exactly what effect his skillfully delivered words had on me. How many times had he used them before, and on how many women? Was this just a game to him? Was I just another conquest to be had?

His deep voice interrupted my thoughts. "There's an empty table by the window. Why don't you go grab it, and I'll order for us?"

It was perfect, tucked in a secluded corner but fully visible from the street. I gave Nico my order and went to sit down.

"Nico?" I called after him. "Could you get me a bottle of water too?"

"You got it." He winked then turned toward the counter.

I'd have a few minutes to get my emotions back in check before he joined me. I needed to stay focused and not fall victim to his charm . . . again.

My shields were back in place when he arrived carrying a cafeteria tray.

"Two whole wheat veggie wraps with a spicy chipotle dressing and two bottles of water." He slid one plate in front of me and the other to his spot. "It sounded pretty good. Figured I'd give it a try. I'm a huge fan of spicy food. My mom used to make an amazing fra diavolo sauce. They use her recipe at Lorena's and Giardano's, but no one makes it like she did."

In the time it took him to relay his love of chili peppers, I'd eaten several bites of my wrap. I would have preferred to take my time and enjoy it, but . . .

Nico finally took the first bite of his lunch and hummed his approval, the sensual sound creating a huge distraction. I needed to find the way to end this *friendship*, or whatever we had going on.

"You know"—he grabbed a gulp of water to wash down his food—"I just realized I don't really know anything about you. How come you never talk about your family?"

"There's nothing to tell." I considered the topic closed and took another huge bite of my wrap. The sooner I finished it, the sooner I could move forward in my life. Without Nico.

He watched while I chewed, furrows forming in his brow. "I think there is. You can talk to me." He continued to stare, waiting.

"Fine." I caved to the pressure and gave him the short version of the story about my dad's sudden death.

"Wow . . . Danni, that's horrible. At least you have your mom and sister to lean on."

"So you'd think. Mom blamed me. Every. Single. Day. She even accused me of just standing there, watching him die. Can you believe it?" I swiped my hand through the air, wishing I could erase the memories that easily.

"Then she started drinking . . . a lot. There was never money for food because she'd spend it all on booze. She stopped taking care of Jen and me. She'd go out every night and eventually stopped coming home—days would go by without even a call. She finally packed up and left for good on Jen's eighteenth birthday, and we haven't heard from her since."

Very few people knew that part of my life. It wasn't a topic that popped up, and it was never worth discussing. Jen and I preferred to consider it a life lesson and keep it filed away.

"No one should have to go through all that." He laid his

hand on the table, his fingertips just shy of touching mine. "See, now I wish I hadn't promised to keep my hands to myself."

"Ah, but you did." Part of me wanted to be touched, comforted, especially by Nico.

He hesitated, studying me with a pensive look on his face. His gaze fell to the table, and he pulled back his hand, giving a consolatory nod. "You're right. Sorry."

We sat in silence in the aftermath of my horrid story. At least I was able to finish my lunch without interruptions.

So many emotions stirred inside me. I couldn't do what I needed to do. "I better get back." I pulled on my jacket and gathered my bag. "Thanks for lunch."

"Danni, wait." He jumped from his seat to rush after me, pulling his coat on as he walked. "Why are you running off?" His hand hovered above my shoulder for a moment before he swore and shoved it in his pocket. He fell in step beside me, oblivious to the turmoil tearing me apart. "I'm sorry I didn't react well. I-I didn't know what to say. I want to know more, as much as you're willing to tell me."

"It's not important," I mumbled and kept walking, pushing my pace.

"So, getting back to your story. I understand now why you and Jen are so protective of each other."

I slowed to look at him. "What do you mean?"

He laughed and rubbed his neck. "She really tore into me that night at Metro Sky after we—after you left me on the patio with her. She can be quite intimidating. I don't think I've been put in my place like that since I was seventeen."

An amused expression filled his face. "My mom came home early one day. Caught me . . . making out, rather *enthusiastically*, with Maria DiMarco." Nico chuckled and shook his head. "Guess it was bound to happen sooner or later, but I let Mom believe it was the first time. I learned to be a bit more discreet after that . . . and to double-check her schedule before I brought a girl home."

Nico grabbed my arm and quickly released it. "Sorry." He pointed to the coffee shop on the corner. "We have some time yet."

He walked in without waiting for a response, and I foolishly followed him. Four people were in line ahead of us.

"So what's the deal with you and Will?" His casual question seemed to come from nowhere, but I probably should have expected it.

"We've been married nearly fifteen years. What more do you need to know? We're in love. And we're happy." Maybe he'd get the hint to leave me alone.

"I saw the way you looked at each other Saturday night. More like the way you *didn't* look at each other." He shook his head and watched me. "Other than one limp hug, he didn't even touch you. He doesn't hold your hand, brush your arm, your neck, your lips. And you don't seem to mind."

"That's not true."

The woman in front of us glanced at me.

I turned my back to her and lowered my voice. "You don't know what the hell you're talking about. Where's *your* wife? Where's *your* committed relationship?"

"I know more than you think." He dragged a hand through his hair, giving a muffled groan. "When are you going to tell him?"

I crossed my arms, annoyed with this conversation. With him. "Tell who what, Nico?"

He took a step closer. It was hard to breathe with his face so close to mine. I licked my lips and swallowed hard.

"Your husband." He spit the last word. "Don't you think he deserves to know you aren't in love with him?"

I leaned closer, trying to contain my anger. "I love my husband. And I'm committed to my marriage."

"Even if that means lying to yourself? To him?"

I pulled back. His words stung as if he'd slapped me. My eyes burned from the tears I wouldn't let fall. At least not in front of him.

"I'm tired of you screwing with my head." *And my heart.* "We're done." I shook my head then forced myself to stare into his eyes. "You and I, we can't be *friends*. It's best if—no, I *need* you to stay away from me."

My throat tightened as I said good-bye to him. A clean break was the right choice, but it would take some time to convince my aching heart.

"Sir . . . Sir, can I take your order?" the woman behind the counter said.

Nico reached for my arm. I took another step back, afraid of how I'd react if he touched me. When he turned to the barista, asking her to give him a minute, I slipped away.

EVERYTHING after the moment I walked away from Nico was a blur, but somehow I made it back to the office. By the time I got there, I'd received two e-mails from him. I deleted both without opening them.

My cell phone vibrated, the screen indicating a call from Kendra. My plan was to let it go to voicemail, so I didn't know why I pressed the button to answer.

Her voice boomed through the earpiece. "What the hell is going on? I was in the middle of talking dirty to Logan, but he had hang up to take a frantic call from Nico. Said it had something to do with you?"

I opened my mouth a few times before I could force out the

words. "H-he's gone. Out of my life. I told him he couldn't contact me anymore." The harsh reality of what I'd done hit like a wrecking ball to my chest, crushing my heart.

"Wow. He's apparently a mess over it too. What happened?"

I told her the whole story, surprised that she didn't interrupt.

Kendra hesitated. "Are you sure he isn't right?"

The ominous tone in her voice unsettled me. "I-I don't—no, he can't be."

"Look, sweetie, I'm just saying, fifteen years ago, you and Will needed each other. But that might not be the case anymore. If Will doesn't appreciate you the way you deserve, maybe there's someone out there who will. Someone better for you."

"And by *someone* you mean Nico. Can we talk about this later? I gotta get back to work."

"Fine, but don't think you're gonna to blow me off. You need to talk about this."

I ended the call but couldn't get Kendra's words out of my mind. I stared blankly at my computer and another e-mail from Nico that I would delete without reading.

Joe from security pushed open the office doors. He approached my desk carrying a large vase stuffed with at least three dozen white roses. "Special delivery. The guy downstairs said I should bring these right up to you."

I didn't need to look at the card to know who'd sent them, but I couldn't stop myself.

I'm sorry. Please forgive me. ~Nico

CHAPTER 28

WAITING FOR LOVE

Four days had passed since I'd forced Nico out of my life, and each day my confidence in that decision grew. In no time at all, he'd become a distant memory. At least that was what I kept telling myself. In the meantime, I simply needed to keep up my guard and continue to avoid him.

Easily done tonight, since he would be at Elevations while Will and I would be at Giardano's. Hopefully. The light snow predicted for today had grown into a major winter storm, dumping several inches of snow and ice on the area by mid-afternoon. The worst had already passed, but the remainder of the storm was expected to linger through the evening.

I pulled on my coat and stopped by Mr. Jamison's office on my way out. "Have a good night, and enjoy your weekend."

"Same to you." He looked up from his computer with a warm smile. "Your big date with Will still on?"

"Far as I know. I tried calling to see if he wanted to cancel, but I couldn't reach him. His secretary said he'd been out of the office all afternoon for a meeting." I gave a nonchalant tip of my head. "Knowing Will, he'll probably be pacing inside the restaurant when I get there, complaining that I'm late." And judging by the clock on Peter's wall, I would definitely be late.

"Take your time getting there. I heard the roads are pretty slick. If you'd like me to call for a car—"

"I already did, but thanks. It should be here any minute. Tell Alexia I hope she feels better."

She'd been leaving work early a lot lately, looking tired and run-down. The past two days, she hadn't been in the office at all. No one seemed to know what was wrong, and I didn't want to pry, but I was worried about her.

"Will do. She finally moved into her own place, so this will be my first weekend on my own in months. It'll be nice to just relax." He leaned forward and lowered his voice even though no one else was around to hear. "I love having Alexia here, but she's not the easiest person in the world to live with."

His candor made me laugh, and I had a feeling his sentiment was fairly accurate. "Your secret's safe with me."

THE CAB SLID up to the curb outside of Giardano's. I paid my fare, adding a generous tip and a heartfelt thank you. Driving in snow topped my list of things I hated most about winters in the Northeast, so I avoided it at all costs.

A quick glance at my phone showed I was ten minutes late for our reservation. I pulled open the large wooden door, breathing in the aromas of garlic and rich herbs. I stepped inside, removing my gloves as I walked, and found myself face to somber-looking face with London. Her elbows, propped on the hostess podium, supported her chin as it sank heavily into her palms.

She didn't look up before offering her standard, albeit lifeless, greeting. "Welcome to . . . Giardano's." She lifted her face mid-sentence, eyes growing wide. It was easy to tell the moment she recognized me, but she managed to remain professional. "Are you meeting Nico for dinner?"

She wore a scandalous grin, probably assuming Nico's plans had changed. No doubt she was busy plotting her next move in whatever game the two of them had going on.

"Sorry to disappoint you, but I'm meeting my husband for dinner." I could have told her Nico and I weren't even friends anymore, but I kind of enjoyed letting her suffer.

"Really." She gave a short laugh then spoke softly, almost as if talking to herself. "Well, this could be interesting." Her smile returned and she continued in her perky hostess tone. "Does he know you're coming?"

"Well, he made the reservation. So yeah, I'm pretty sure he knows." I shook my head, chuckling. "It's under Will DeLaney, and he's probably here." I leaned toward the arched opening to the dining room, expecting to see him already seated.

London scanned the screen in front of her, humming a cheery tune. "Nope, not here. He's probably delayed because of the weather. Lots of people are."

A shiver ran through me as the entrance door swung open. I turned, eager to greet Will, and smiled at the young couple laughing and shaking the snow from their hair.

"Mrs. DeLaney," London called, emphasizing the first part, "I'd be happy to show you to the bar if you'd like. You can relax and have a drink while you wait for your husband."

I glanced toward the door again, wondering if it would be a waste of time. "Um, sure. That sounds fine."

She greeted the other couple and excused herself for a minute. London led me through the sparsely filled dining room, following the same path Nico had taken when we had our lunch non-date. She stopped at the small bar I'd noticed from our table that day.

"Here you go. Best seat in the house." London pulled out the stool at the end of the bar and tapped the seat, wearing the same scandalous grin as before. She leaned close and lowered her voice. "I'm sure Nico wouldn't have it any other way."

I leaned past her to brave a glance at that table, taking comfort in knowing it wouldn't be occupied by him. My sharp gasp cut like a knife in my throat, and I finally understood London's odd behavior.

As if I'd called to him, Nico lifted his gaze from the dark-haired woman seated across from him and looked directly at me.

I clutched my chest, wrapping my hand around the gold heart that dangled between my breasts—a silent reminder to my own heart of the choice I'd made.

"Hey, Drew," London called to the man behind the bar.

The sandy-haired bartender disengaged from what appeared to be an intense conversation with two beautiful young blondes. He gave London an annoyed stare.

"Mrs. DeLaney is going to wait here until her husband arrives. Maybe you can pull yourself away from your little love-fest long enough to get her a drink?" London turned to me with a contemptuous glare. "I'm sure you could use one." She walked away, laughing quietly.

"Be right with ya." Drew held up one finger to me while one of the girls wrote something on the palm of his other hand.

I climbed up on the tall bar stool, annoyed at myself for angling it so I could see Nico with just a slight tip of my head. A dreamy sigh escaped me. Who was I kidding? With scenery like that, I'd be a fool to even think about turning away.

His date sat with her back to me, sleek black hair dancing along her shoulders with each movement. Her animated gestures and constant touching of Nico's arm couldn't keep his attention. He seemed to be more focused on me, but I looked away every time our eyes met. The woman occasionally glanced over her shoulder in my direction, usually after waving a hand in front of Nico's distracted stare. Then she'd laugh and give him a playful nudge.

"What can I get ya?" Drew rested his forearms on the bar top.

"I'll have a strawberry marg—you know what, let me change that." I closed my eyes for a moment, trying to remember. "I had a really good red wine the last time I was here—kinda sweet and had a little bit of a nutty taste, but I can't remember what it was called. Something like Modera or Madery."

"You mean Madeira Reserva?"

"Yeah, that's it." I wasn't too far off. "Can I get a glass of that?"

"Coming right up." He hesitated before stepping away. "You realize that's a little pricey, right? About fifty bucks a glass?"

I hadn't considered that, although I probably should have. Nico seemed to have expensive taste. The difference in our social classes was one of the first things I'd noticed when he introduced himself at Logan's party . . . right after how incredibly sexy and charming he was, of course.

I guess it had slipped my mind since he never flaunted his wealth or acted superior. In fact, he always treated me as if *I* were special. This was a perfect example of that. He could have made a big deal about the cost of the wine at lunch last week, but he'd never even mentioned it.

Drew stood watching me, waiting for my approval.

I glanced at Nico, wondering how many other little things I'd overlooked, taken for granted. The throbbing in my fingertip drew my attention to the gold chain wrapped tightly around it. Will's heart. I closed my eyes. None of this stuff about Nico should even matter to me. Why couldn't I stop myself from obsessing over him?

Tonight was a special occasion. The celebration of getting my marriage back on track. True, it still lacked passion, but Will and I could work to find that.

Opening my eyes to look at Drew, I nodded and went ahead with my order. "I'm going to run to the restroom while you get it, so take your time." I wanted to make sure I looked my best before Will arrived.

The ladies' room was located near the far end of the bar, which meant I was able get there without passing by Nico and his date. I stood in front of the bathroom mirror, scowling at my reflection, confused by the rush of irrational animosity that tore through me every time I thought about that woman touching him. I lifted my hair to massage the back of my neck, trying to ease the tension building there.

After repositioning a few wayward curls and reapplying my lip gloss, I pushed open the door to return to the bar. The sight of Nico leaning against the wall, waiting, sent a shot of adrenaline through me.

He stepped forward to meet me, a guarded look on his usually confident face. "Hey, beautiful."

I pressed my palm against his solid chest, forcing him to move back. It took a great deal of restraint to ignore my body's reaction to the brief contact. "What are you doing here, Nico?"

A hint of mischief sparkled in his dark eyes, and he leaned toward my ear. "My father owns this place. Remember?"

His rough jaw brushed against my cheek, making me shiver. He had to know the effect he had on me.

I rubbed my chest, trying to ease the nervous feeling of being alone with him again. "I meant here—outside the ladies' room, here. But why *are* you here at all? Weren't you supposed to be at Elevations tonight?"

He lifted a single shoulder and glanced toward the dining room. "There wasn't a reason for me to be there." He returned his attention to me, desperation in his eyes.

Kristi was right—he wanted to spend tonight with me. That realization pulled at my tattered heart, but I wouldn't give in. Not this time. "You're supposed to be avoiding me. Did you forget?"

Another woman entered the hallway from the dining room, slowing as she approached the ladies' room.

Nico took my wrists and pulled me away from the door while apologizing for being in her way. He led me a few steps to a small alcove at the end of the hall.

"I'm trying." He gripped the back of his neck. "Christ, Danni, I wish I could just walk away from you. But I can't."

"Who's your date, Nico?" The words erupted out of me. "Not that it matters to me who you go out with." I picked at an imaginary piece of lint on my dress and tried to appear disinterested.

A knowing chuckle escaped him as he inched closer to me. His eyes locked on mine like a magnet, pulling me in. "You're so cute when you're jealous. Her name is Raffiella. Her father is the guest chef at Lorena's."

"Your father's friend?" I tried to sound nonchalant, prove him wrong.

He nodded. "She wanted to come with him. See the US. I'm keeping her company since she doesn't know anyone."

I'm sure you are.

Nico lifted his hand, hesitated, then brushed a curl from my face. His fingers skimmed the side of my neck as he lowered his hand to my shoulder. The feather-light stroke of his thumb beneath my jaw soothed me. My eyes fell closed as my head tipped to the side, instinctively opening myself to him. A sweet sigh slid through my parted lips.

"God, Danni, you're so beautiful."

"Don't." My weak command was barely audible. I stepped away from his touch, bumping into the wall behind me. It limited my retreat but offered much-needed support to my trembling legs. I forced my eyes open and looked at his face. "Please stop."

Nico shoved his hands through his hair and took a few deep breaths, his gaze intently focused on me. He pushed his hands into his pockets and seemed to regain his self-control. "I'm sorry. For this and for stepping out of line on Monday. I swear, neither will happen again."

I drew in a slow, shuddered breath. "That's right, because we aren't going to be hanging out together anymore, or putting ourselves in situations like this where things get out of hand so quickly." I motioned between us and struggled to hold myself together. "It's obvious we can't be *just friends*."

There was nothing more to say. My good-bye speech to Nico on Monday had been difficult enough. I didn't have the strength to go through it again, especially not tonight. I needed to focus on Will and me, on making every moment perfect.

"Will should be here by now. I need to go."

I moved to push past Nico, but he blocked my path. "Danni, please don't run off on me again. I keep screwing up. I know that. But dammit, I'm—I'm trying."

The pain in his gentle voice nearly broke my heart. I lowered my head, averted my eyes. "I have to go."

He hesitated then turned sideways, allowing me to leave.

I hurried back to the bar, disappointed that Will wasn't there yet. At least my very expensive glass of Madeira sat waiting for me.

"Thanks, Drew."

He was busy flirting with the girls at the other end of the bar again but waved to acknowledge me. I climbed on my bar stool and gripped the stem of my glass, holding it to my lips. *Why did I order this?* It was a reminder of a perfect moment with Nico, but there wasn't a place in my life for him.

What's keeping Will? I'd sent several text massages throughout the day and left a voicemail on the ride here, but I hadn't heard back from him. I looked at the time on my phone. Our reservation was thirty minutes ago.

The early edition of the news played on the television behind the bar. The sound had been muted, but it didn't take a rocket scientist to figure out what the meteorologist on the screen was talking about. She stood by the weather map, pointing to details about today's big storm, while viewers' snowy pictures flashed in the lower corner.

The news cut to a special report, a live feed of a traffic mess on the freeway. *Wow. Hope those poor suckers don't have dinner reservations.*

The image on the screen changed again, cutting to a closer view of the accident that caused the road to be closed down.

I heard the crash before I realized the glass had slipped from my hand. Wine spilled across the bar like blood as my heart ripped open. A shrill noise filled my ears. I struggled to pull air into my lungs.

My vision blurred, but I could still see the image on the screen. It would be burned into my mind forever. A jackknifed tractor-trailer. The lime green Challenger wedged under the body of it.

Will's car.

Will's car draped in a blue tarp where emergency crews had cut it open. The news station was kind enough to blur out the license plate, but the stripe pattern on Will's car was distinctive, easy to recognize.

God, that noise. Make it stop!

Someone touched me, draped an arm across my back.

"Shh . . . Danni, what's wrong?" Nico's voice. "Hey, look at m—oh, shit. Drew, turn the TV off."

"No problem. Let me finish mixing this dri—"

"Now. Turn the fucking set off now." Nico moved, stretching across the bar. He reached behind it and grabbed a remote.

The screen went blank. The image in my mind remained.

Nico's arms engulfed me. He pulled me to his chest. "Shh . . . I'm here, Danni."

His fingers brushed across my lips, and the raspy noise finally ceased. God, had it been coming from me?

"There you go. That's better."

I sucked in a few ragged breaths, my body trembling. Silence filled the icy room. Lifting my head, I looked past Nico's pale face. All of the restaurant's guests were staring at me. Concern and confusion marked their faces.

"We need to get you out of here." Nico's soothing tone again.

I grabbed his wrists and tried to focus enough to look into his eyes. A gentle nod was the only response I could manage.

CHAPTER 29

REALITY

I groaned, trying to wake up. Trying to think. *Valentine's Day, that's right. Where's Will?*

His strong arms tightened around me, pulled me closer.

"You're here." I smiled, snuggling into his solid chest. "I was worried." I drew in a deep breath. The crisp, fresh scent wasn't Will's usual woodsy cologne. "Hmmm . . . you smell so good." The steady beat of his heart vibrated against my cheek, the soothing rhythm threatening to lull me back to sleep. "I love you."

He tensed but didn't respond.

"What happened?" My voice sounded weak, distant. "Why were you so late?"

"Shh . . ." Warm lips pressed gently against the top of my head.

The soothing tone of Will's muffled voice sounded familiar, but something was off. It was too deep. A faint buzz filled my aching head. Nothing made sense.

"Will?" I took another deep breath and struggled to open my eyes. The blurry room wasn't familiar. It appeared to be an office. "Where—"

The door opened, and a man wearing a black chef's coat walked in. I'd seen him before. Somewhere. He approached cautiously, speaking in a whisper. "She awake?"

"Just. She seems pretty confused." His hands moved along my arms. "They sending someone over?"

A light tap sounded on the doorframe. Kendra's ex-husband entered, dressed in his police uniform. A grim expression replaced his usual bright smile.

"Nate?"

"Hey, sweetie." He crossed the room to squat in front of me. "How you doing?"

Nate looked past me and extended his hand. "Officer Kearsley."

Why is Nate introducing himself to Will?

"Nico Giardano." He removed one of the strong hands from my back, stretching around me to shake Nate's hand. "This is my father, Angelo. He owns Giardano's."

"Nico?" I lifted my head to look behind me at Nico's somber face.

"I'm here." He hugged me tighter and placed a kiss on my temple.

"No. You promised you'd stay away." I squirmed in his lap, struggling to get free. "Why are you here? Why am *I* here?"

"It's okay, Danni. Just relax." Nate took my hand. He flashed a glance at Nico. "Do you remember what happened?"

I shook my head. "Where's Will? I need to get out of here before he—"

"You were sitting at the bar, waiting for him. Do you remember that? And the news was playing on the TV?"

I nodded, pressing a palm to my pulsing temple.

Nate continued asking questions about what I'd seen on the special report. He spoke in a calm voice, but I'd never felt more on edge than I did right now. He explained details about the accident they'd shown on TV—how the storm had created dangerous travel conditions, and some of the roadways had iced up. A tractor-trailer had jackknifed on the freeway, colliding with a car.

"Sweetie, the car involved in the accident was Will's. He was hurt pretty bad, and he's at Memorial Hospital. I'm gonna take you there. Okay?"

My chest heaved with painful sobs as the images from the news returned to me. Will's car, covered with a tarp, wedged under the truck. "H-how bad?"

No one answered.

The pounding in my chest echoed in my ears. I tried to shout. Nothing came out.

The three men talked amongst themselves, discussing my options as though I weren't in the room. Nate planned to take me to the hospital and get me settled in the waiting area. Kendra would meet me there as soon as she could.

"I'm staying with her." Nico tightened his hold on me.

Angelo hesitated, watching us, then moved closer. He rested his hand on Nico's shoulder, studying his face. "I think it's best if you let her go, son."

His tone and expression seemed to imply more than just his words.

Nico's body tensed around me. "But, Papa, she—"

Angelo raised a hand to silence him. "I may be old, but I'm not blind." He took a deep breath, shoving a hand through his graying hair. "Think about what you are doing, Nico. Think about where you have been. I know you want to help, but she has friends and family who will do that. She needs to focus on her husband, and only him." He tipped his hand, motioning between Nico and me. "This is not right, but you already know that."

Nico lowered his head to rest heavily on my shoulder. "I

know." The rapid beat of his heart pulsed through me as I leaned against him. His chest heaved with a shaky breath. "I've tried, but—I know." He released his tight hold and lifted me from his lap, setting me next to him on the leather couch. He brushed my hair from my face, his eyes searching mine. "Nate, I think it's best if you take care of Danni from here."

Angelo's fingers flexed on Nico's shoulder. He gave a slight nod, his expression filled with empathy.

Nico stood to face me. He leaned forward, gripping my arms, his eyes cast downward. "I'm here if you need me, Danni. All you have to do is ask."

He glanced at his father then gave Nate a pat on the back before walking out of the office.

How many times had I asked Nico to leave me alone? I should be relieved to see him go. Instead, the knot in my stomach grew tighter. Wrapped in his arms, I'd felt safe.

Nate led me down a small hallway and past the kitchen. Guests in the main dining room froze, their forks midair, and watched in silence as we walked through.

He drove me to the hospital in his police cruiser then escorted me inside, straight to the surgical intensive care unit on the fifth floor. A short, round woman in purple scrubs greeted us. Her badge identified her as Patrice, RN.

"I'm here to see my husband." My trembling voice broke on the last word.

Nate took control of the conversation, speaking on my behalf. I squeezed his arm to thank him and tried to follow their conversation, but I couldn't stay focused. Besides, blocking everything out meant I could pretend this wasn't real.

"Danni?" Nate placed a hand on my shoulder. "This is Patrice. She's gonna be Will's nurse."

I held my hand out, a robotic reaction. "Where is he? I want to see my husband."

"I'm so sorry about your husband, Mrs. DeLaney." She led Nate and me to a small office behind the nurses' station and tried to make me comfortable. "Your husband was rushed into surgery, but Dr. Asher is coming up from the ER to speak to you. He'll answer all of your questions."

A firm rap on the open door startled me.

A man with gray hair, wearing blue scrubs and a white lab coat, entered the room. He sat on the stool across from me, flipping open the chart he'd carried in. Dr. Asher introduced himself then droned on about Will's injuries—head trauma, ruptured spleen, lacerated liver, obstructed airway—using a long list of medical terms I didn't understand.

"William is with our top trauma surgeons. They're seeing to the most critical of his injuries, but his prognosis is questionable." He placed the chart on his lap. "Do you have any question you'd like to ask me?"

I grabbed the box of tissues Patrice offered and mopped the endless stream of tears from my face. I struggled to breathe through a bout of gasps but finally managed to find my voice. "He's . . . he's going to be okay, though. Right?"

"Ma'am, your husband suffered a lot of injuries. He has multiple fractures in his face, collarbone, arm, and ribs, and he has a lot of bruising. There's some swelling and bleeding in his brain, and we need to remove a piece of his skull to relieve the pressure until that swelling goes down. Dr. Cooper is working on him, doing everything he can to save him. But you have to understand your husband suffered life-threatening injuries, and his condition is critical. It's going to take some time until we can expect any significant improvement."

He paused for a moment then looked at a note on the front of Will's chart. "If you have any other questions, you can let one of the nurses know. They'll get in touch with me or Dr. Cooper, and we'll be glad to sit down with you to go over them."

He wished me well then spoke quietly to Patrice before leaving.

Nate sat on the chair beside me, rubbing my back. "Kendra texted to let me know she can't get the car up the hill by our . . . *her* house, so I'm going to stay here with you."

As much as I wanted someone to lean on, it wasn't right to keep him from his work. "You don't have to do that. I'll be fine till Kendra gets here. I should probably call Jen anyway to let her know what's happening."

Nate rubbed his brow. "Danni, I don't think I should leave you alone."

"I'll take good care of her till her friend gets here." Patrice rolled Dr. Asher's stool toward the corner.

Nate hesitated. He pulled me in for a long hug. "You call if you need me. Okay? And I'll stop back in a little bit to check on you."

Patrice placed her hand on my wrist. "I think we have your husband's room ready for him. Why don't I take you there? You might be more comfortable than in the crowded waiting room."

I pressed my lips together and fought back another round of tears. "Thank you." I struggled, choking out the words.

"Come on." She held my arm with one hand and slipped the other around me, supporting me as she guided me down the hall.

A standard hospital bed filled most of the room. Will's room. It still didn't seem possible. Monitors, gauges, and strange equipment covered the wall behind the bed. A single chair and small table sat next to it. I sank into the chair, pulling my coat down around me.

"This is a lot to take in." Patrice stooped in front of me. "He's in good hands, honey. Dr. Cooper is the best neurosurgeon in the region." Sorrow filled her pale green eyes.

I nodded and looked away, afraid of what she wasn't telling me.

The soles of her shoes squeaked against the linoleum, the sound fading as she left the room.

I let my head fall back against the chair and closed my eyes, waiting to wake up from this nightmare. Minutes passed, marked by the constant beep of monitors from the hall.

"Mrs. DeLaney?" Patrice's compassionate voice pulled me from my trance. She crossed the room, stopping beside me, and rubbed a gentle hand across my back. "How are you doing?" She placed a small bottle of water and a pack of shortbread cookies on the table beside me. "Thought you might need a little snack after your nap."

I tried forcing a smile, but it wouldn't come. My jaw quivered. "Do you know how he is? When I'll be able to see him?"

"I'm sure he'll be a while, but I can try to get a message to one of the technicians. They may be able to ask the doctor a few questions."

"I'd appreciate that."

"It might take a little time though. Why don't you go down to the cafeteria and get something to eat? You need to keep up your strength." She paused, maybe expecting a response. "You have a cell phone?"

I nodded.

She reached into her pocket, pulled out a small tablet and a pen, and handed them to me. "Write down your name and number for me, and I'll call the minute I hear any news about your husband."

The thought of food made my stomach churn. I stared at the curtains on the far wall. "Maybe I will. I just need a few more minutes before I'm ready to be around people." If someone were to ask why I was here, I wouldn't be able to hold myself together.

She stood but didn't move away. "There's a chapel on the main floor of the East wing . . . Never hurts to ask for a healing hand."

By the time I turned around, she was gone. A glass wall separated me from the busy nurses' station. The sheer curtains didn't provide much privacy, but they filtered out most of the harsh fluorescent light.

Waiting, not knowing, was brutal. *I hope she can get an update.* I crossed the room, wishing I had someone to hold me, tell me everything would be fine.

I pulled aside the curtain and stared out the window. White flakes glowed in the night sky, swirling and dancing. They appeared harmless, but I knew the truth. I wrapped my arms across my midsection. Fear burned in my chest—fear that I might lose Will. It hit with a merciless force, making every breath difficult. I trembled, a dry heave rolling through my body.

Nate's voice accompanied a gentle knock on the door. "Any word?" His somber tone was as dreary as the space around us. He waited for me to face him before entering the dimly lit room, carrying a small cardboard box.

"No one's told me anything." My uncontrollable sobbing resumed. "I'm so scared. What if—what if he—"

"Hey. You can't think that way. Will needs you to be strong for him right now." Nate wrapped one arm around me, consoling me until I finally pulled myself together again. He placed the box on the bed, letting his hand glide along the top. "I was able to grab some things from Will's car."

An uncomfortable silence filled the air. He stood watching me, shifting his weight from side to side.

Nate cleared his throat. "I just, um—" He looked at the floor, rubbing a hand down his face. "Kendra isn't sure she can get here, but she's still trying. She talked to Jen, and Jen said she's going to wait for you to call her." He raised his brows, watching me.

I turned away. "Thanks. I couldn't do it earlier. I'm not up to talking right now."

"She said she figured as much." Nate hesitated, rubbing the back of his neck. "It's none of my business, but I just can't figure out why he was on the freeway. Kendra wondered too. That's nowhere near his office, is it?"

I'd been asking myself the same question. The freeway was on the other side of town, a full thirty-minute drive out toward the mountains. Sometimes Will met with local clients, but his current project was in Chicago. I shrugged.

Nate tipped his head toward the door. "Listen, I'm gonna call in to the station. Let 'em know I'll be following up on an earlier case for a while."

"You don't have to do that. I'm sure it's a busy night for you. I'll be fine by myself."

"Nonsense. Chin up, sweetie. It'll all work out." Nate gave me another long hug before leaving.

I drew in a deep breath and gagged, repulsed by the sterile, antiseptic smell of the hospital. The constant beeps and alarms coming from the nurses' station reverberated throughout the unit, ticking off each pulse of life, warning of impending death.

"Code Blue, room 12." The PA system repeated the calm message until it became the only thought registering in my mind.

Men in scrubs rushed by, one pushing a large cart and shouting orders.

The reality of the night, of Will's accident, pressed down on me. I hugged myself, shivering. Images of his car burned bright every time I closed my eyes. I heard his screams as vividly as my own. Did he suffer as much as I was now?

The relief I'd felt at the news he'd survived was short-lived.

Every minute spent in this room ripped at my soul, filled me with doubt. With gut-wrenching fear. I pressed my hands to my ears, trying to block out the words that echoed in my mind. *Life-threatening injuries.* He could die.

Patrice had mentioned a chapel on the main floor. Asking for a little divine intervention couldn't hurt, but I'd wait for Nate to return.

I needed a distraction, something to erase the painful possibility of losing him. My eyes settled on the box. Small pieces of Will that I could cling to.

I turned on a small light then sat on the edge of the bed, pulling the box close. Will's ice blue scarf lay across the top, the exact color of his eyes. I lifted it to my face, breathing in the woodsy scent of his cologne before draping it around my neck. The wool scratched my cheek as I nuzzled against it, reminding me of the rough texture of his stubble at the end of the day.

Sifting through the box's contents, I pushed aside the meaningless things that accumulate in everyone's cars—garage door opener, phone charger, E-Z Pass—and revealed some old CDs. Will's music that I hated so much but couldn't wait to hear him play again. I hugged them to my chest, wishing they were him.

Light reflected off something gold in the bottom of the box. The metallic seal on a manila envelope I hadn't noticed before. Probably papers from Will's meeting this afternoon.

The uneasy feeling I'd had all evening grew stronger as I turned it over. The envelope had Will's name written across the center in bold letters and a label on the corner—The Law Offices of Sherman & Foster. Our attorneys.

My stomach clenched. I hesitated before breaking open the seal to remove the contents. Panic gripped me, tightening like a vise around my heart.

I held the papers as steady as I could with one trembling

hand. The other clawed at my chest, twisting in the chain that held Will's heart. I struggled to keep the words in focus, forcing myself to read on. Each word, every sentence, tearing at my soul. *This must be a mistake.*

Tears fell freely, staining the pages. There was no reason to stop them.

Will had filed for divorce.

It was no mistake. His signature mocked me from the bottom of the page. A yellow flag indicated the place I was to add mine.

How could I have been so blind? So stupid? God, what I fool I'd made of myself trying to improve our relationship, believing that he loved me.

The papers fell to my lap. I pulled my hands to my face, covering my mouth. Muffling my screams. Pain, unlike any I'd ever felt, cut through me like a dozen knives. Every drop of hope drained from the gaping wounds. Gone.

Divorce. How could this happen?

No matter what the outcome of Will's surgery, whether he lived or died, he'd be gone from my life. And I'd be alone. Again.

I slid off the bed, shoving the envelope and papers aside. *I need to get out of here.*

After grabbing my coat, I rushed down the long hallway toward a bank of elevators. I pressed the button at a frantic pace, tapping until one of the cars finally arrived. Once inside, I sank to the floor and clutched my roiling stomach. The motion of the descending elevator magnified my intense urge to vomit.

The elevator doors opened. I looked up at the group of people standing between me and the exit. They rushed toward me, hands extended, asking questions and offering to help. I stumbled to my feet, ignoring them all, and pushed my way through to the doors.

The snow had stopped except for a few lingering flurries.

Within seconds, the frigid air froze the tears clinging to my lashes. It chapped the damp skin on my face. I didn't care. I pressed on, disregarding the sudden stream of calls and worried texts from Nate and Kendra.

I didn't know where I was going. I only knew I couldn't stay there.

The exposed skin on my legs burned. I kept going, running away from the nightmare. The images in my mind flashed between the horrid scene of Will's car under that tractor-trailer and the devastating decree of divorce he'd had with him at the time.

How long had he planned this? Why hadn't he told me?

Violent shivers tore through me, my body shaking from the cold as well as the pain of losing my husband. I wasn't sure how long I'd been walking—fifteen, maybe twenty minutes? I scanned my surroundings, shocked at where I'd gone.

I kept moving, crossing the parking lot at Giardano's. I'd be able to slip inside and warm up, wait for a cab to take me home. That probably would have been the smart thing to do in the first place instead of wandering out on foot.

Tall arched windows lined the front of the restaurant. I glanced through each as I passed by, unable to control my need to search for Nico. The tables all appeared empty.

Three people occupied the lone table by the window closest to the entrance. I ducked into a shadow to peek through the glass. Angelo faced me. Nico sat across from him, next to a woman with wavy black hair. At first, I expected her to be Nico's date from dinner, but this woman looked older, closer to my age.

She rubbed Nico's shoulder while Angelo spoke, animated hand gestures reinforcing his words. Nico didn't look up from his slumped position, his face buried in his hands.

My fists clenched as the woman gave him a hug. He didn't

return it, but the way he leaned into her made it clear they weren't strangers. He nodded, then she pulled away. He turned to look at her as she stood.

Angelo smiled, watching the two of them. The woman grabbed Nico's arms, tugging him from his seat. He didn't seem to resist and fell right into her embrace. She wrapped an arm around him and steered him out of the room, toward the office I'd woken up in earlier.

As they walked away, Nico slipped an arm around the woman. He pulled her close and leaned down to kiss her cheek.

I touched my wet face. Why did I come here? How many times did I need to have my heart broken in one night?

The wind picked up, the cold breeze irritating my tear-streaked face. Going inside now would be too humiliating. I'd call for a cab and wait outside the entrance. My phone buzzed again before I reached into my pocket. This time I didn't recognize the number on the screen.

"Hello?"

"Mrs. DeLaney, this is Patrice at Memorial Hospital. Your husband's nurse?" She paused until I acknowledged recognizing her. "Dr. Cooper asked me to give you a call. He'd like you to come back up to the floor so he can speak with you."

Will. "H-how is he? Is he out of surgery?" Not that it should matter anymore, but it did. My teeth clenched. A wave of anger rolled through me, joining the turmoil of emotions already raging inside.

A long silence followed.

"Dr. Cooper will go over everything when you get here."

"I'm not at the hospital. I-I had to leave. Can't you just tell me how he is?"

Another long pause, then a man's voice took over for Patrice's. "Mrs. DeLaney, this is Dr. Cooper. Is there someone there with you?"

"I'm—there's—no, but what does that matter? Why can't you just tell me what's . . . what's g-going on?"

"Mrs. DeLaney, I'm very sorry—"

The phone slipped from my grasp, crashing against the ice-covered ground.

CHAPTER 30

LETTING GO

Sitting on the edge of my bed, surrounded by darkness, I'd never felt more alone. Empty inside.

I'd been such a fool to think Will cared about our marriage. About us. Did he ever truly love me, or had all those years together been one huge lie?

So many questions flooded my mind. Questions that would never be answered. They could all be summed up with one word. *Why?*

Why had he been on the freeway that day? Why would he pretend everything was fine? Why, after fifteen years of goddamned wedded *bliss*, would he divorce me like that?

There was only one logical answer, and I couldn't bear to think about it.

I ignored the gentle tapping on my door, but it creaked open anyway. Jen's face appeared, wearing the same concerned expression she'd worn for days.

"People are looking for you." She crossed the room, stopping to turn on a small lamp before sitting next to me. She took my hand and leaned into my shoulder.

"I don't want to see anyone."

"I know. They don't expect you to talk much."

"I don't want to talk at all." I pushed to my feet and moved to the window, easing aside the curtain. Dozens of cars lined the street and driveway, friends and coworkers here to pay their respects to the grieving widow. "What is there to say? Am I supposed to lie about how wonderful he was? Such a great husband. Oh, and by the way, did you know the bastard filed for divorce and never even told me?" I choked back bitter tears.

Jen followed, hugging me from behind. "Shhh . . . you have every right to be angry. Just let them offer their condolences, and they'll be on their way."

"They shouldn't have come here in the first place."

I thought I'd made that clear by saying his services would be private. Imagine my surprise at finding a small group of people gathered on my driveway when we returned home afterward. Unwanted guests continued to arrive in a steady stream throughout the afternoon. They all brought covered dishes or bottles of booze, intending to stick around and celebrate the life of their dearly departed friend.

The thought disgusted me.

My bedroom door creaked again as Caden pushed it open the rest of the way. "Aunt Danni? There you are." He bolted toward me, wrapping his arms around my thighs when he crashed into me. His suit coat was missing, his shirttail pulled out, and his loosened tie hung to one side. "I couldn't find where you was hidin'."

I tousled his hair. "You look very handsome today. You know that?"

"Yeah, Mommy says I look all growed up." He yanked at his tie, pulling it away from his neck. "But I don't like wearin' this thing."

I loosened the knot and helped him slip it off.

"Whew, that's better." He rubbed his neck. "I miss Uncle

Will. Mommy said we're never gonna see him again." He looked up at me, tears ready to spill from his innocent eyes. "Is that true?"

I knelt down, pulling him to me. "Yeah, 'fraid so, buddy. But he'll always be with you . . ." I took his little hand and pressed it over his heart. "Right here."

Jen brushed a tear from her cheek and rested her hand on my shoulder. "You ready to do this?"

"Yeah," I said with a sigh. "Let's get it over with."

I held my breath, searching the room as she led me down the stairs. We inched our way through the crowded rooms and mingled among the guests. Jen stayed by my side the whole time, steering conversations away from areas that would upset me.

Two hours later—it felt like an eternity—the mourners were nearly gone.

Only Mr. Jamison remained. He shook his head, twisting his lips in a pained grimace as he reached for my hands. "Another good man taken away from you too soon."

Will didn't deserve to be put into the same category as my father. I nodded, averting my eyes to hide my animosity for my deceased husband.

"Alexia would have been here if she could. She thinks of you as a sister, you know?" He squeezed my hands. "Well, she hasn't been up to talking to anyone, but I'm sure she sends her sympathy. As soon as she's feeling better, I'll have her fill in for you at the office." Peter crushed me in a long embrace that left both of us sobbing. "You take as long as you need, Danni. Your job will be waiting for you when you're ready to come back."

After closing the door behind him, Jen pulled me in for a hug. "You made it. It's all over. And I'm so proud of you for holding your head high the whole time."

"Thank you. I couldn't have done it without you."

We moved to the kitchen to help wrap up the last of the food left behind. Ryan, Kristi, and Kendra had been working furiously, cleaning up the plates and glasses left scattered around. And they'd kept Caden entertained by giving him small tasks to help out.

"You guys are amaz—"

A huge vase filled with white roses sat in the center of the breakfast bar.

My chest grew heavy. I struggled to pull in a steady breath. "How did these get here?"

"They came while you were upstairs. Aren't they just beautiful?" Kristi pulled out the small envelope that was tucked among the blooms and handed it to me.

My hand shook as I opened it, but I didn't need to see the card. I knew who had sent them.

I'm here if you need me. All you have to do is ask. ~Nico

Kendra draped her arm across my back, resting her head against mine. She let out a woeful sigh. "He wanted to be here, sweetie. It tore him apart to stay away, but he thought you needed some space. Time to heal and work things out."

I moved to the window, imagining his blue Ferrari parked by my driveway. The engine roared to life, and the car disappeared down the road.

After all the times I'd told Nico to leave me alone, he chose now to finally listen and stay away. I'd made my choice, for better or worse, and had only myself to blame.

I should have listened to my heart.

BONU SCENE

Get ready for the conclusion of Danni and Nico's story with a
special bonus scene from Nico!

(Book 2 will be told from both of their points of view.)

Don't miss this fun, sexy, and tumultuous conclusion to Danni
and Nico's story!
Our Love Was Meant To Be

BEFORE YOU GO . . .

If you enjoyed *Your Love is All I Need*, please take a moment to leave a brief review on <u>Amazon.</u>

Believe it or not, a book lives or dies based on its reviews. A sentence or two from you can make a difference! Besides, I'd love to hear your thoughts.

And don't forget to recommend *Your Love Is All I Need* to your friends. I always appreciate when a friend saves me from having to search for new book to read and love. Yours will too!

Thanks again for reading! ~CJ

ACKNOWLEDGMENTS

For years I've dreamed of being a published author, worked hard to become one. So I have to admit that sitting here to write this final page of my debut novel is a bit surreal. I've accomplished my initial goal and reached the starting block of a whole new adventure, one that holds new challenges and opportunities that I'm eager to explore.

But I didn't get here alone. Despite all of my hard work, realizing my dream would not have been possible without the help and support of some very special and important people. I cannot begin to thank you all enough, but I will try.

First and foremost, my wonderful husband and love of my life. Barry, the sacrifices and concessions you've made that allow me to focus on writing go well beyond anything I would have ever asked of you. Thank you for your patience, for making me laugh when I want to cry, for reining me in when I push too hard, and for being there to celebrate each small victory along the way. You are my better half, and I love you so much.

Andrew and Jason, your support and encouragement mean more to me than you could ever imagine. You believed in me when I didn't believe in myself. You pushed me to go on when I felt defeated and cheered for me every step of the way. *You* are the reasons I never gave up. I love you both with all of my heart, and I am so deeply touched by how proudly you share my accomplishment.

Thank you to my amazing critique partners, fellow authors Ellie, Hijo, Jenny, and Dan. You have taught me so much, guided me, made me a better writer and a stronger, more confident person. Your relentless nitpicking (which you know I love you for) helped to shape *Your Love Is All I Need* into a story I am proud to share with the world. I truly could not have gotten here without you.

Thank you to my beta readers, Jennifer and Shea. Yours were the first eyes on my finished story, and I greatly appreciate your time and helpful feedback while making sure my baby is ready for its public debut.

Last but not least, thank you to my readers for allowing me to share Danni's story with you. I hope you enjoyed reading it as much as I enjoyed writing it.

Love . . . always. ~CJ

About the Author

Emerging author CJ Andrews writes contemporary romance stories filled with emotion and realistic characters that pull you in and make you feel like you're a part of their lives.

A lifetime fan of romance and rom-com, CJ creates captivating stories that are an entertaining blend of lighthearted humor and real-life drama. She takes her characters on an emotional journey, filled with a whirlwind of unpredictable twists and turns that will melt your heart one moment and break it in another...when you least expect it to happen.

But don't worry, in the world of Romance Books, all stories have a happy ending—or at least the promise of one.

CJ lives in Southeastern Pennsylvania, nestled between the historic city of Philadelphia and the scenic Pocono Mountains, which she uses as inspiration for the fictional towns in her novels.

She is happily married to her high-school sweetheart and is the proud mom of two adult sons. When she isn't glued to her computer or e-reader (which isn't often) you can find her enjoying time with her family, experimenting with new recipes in the kitchen, or dreaming of her next escape to a tropical beach.

CJ loves hearing from her fans. Connect with her on Facebook or at AuthorCJAndrews.com.

9 780997 908732